THE TRAINING GROUNDS

Charlotte had stopped fighting her superiors now; her buttocks were flushed. 'Please – anything,' she whimpered, moving her tied arms and legs the little she could.

'Tell me you deserved that spanking,' said her tormentor, holding his large palm in the air so she could see it.

'I deserved that spanking, sir,' Charlotte said.

'That's better.' The man ran his hands over her posterior for long, tense moments.

'Tell me you deserved to feel my right hand on your arse.'

'I – deserved to feel your right hand on my arse, sir,' mumbled Charlotte, blushing further. She hung her head, and stared at the floor.

'Tell me you've been a naughty girl.'

'I – I've been a naughty girl, sir.'

By the same author:

SERVING TIME
DIFFERENT STROKES
LINGERING LESSONS

Other Nexus Classics:

AGONY AUNT
OBSESSION
THE HANDMAIDENS
HIS MISTRESS'S VOICE
BOUND TO SERVE
BOUND TO SUBMIT
SISTERHOOD OF THE INSTITUTE
THE PLEASURE PRINCIPLE
CONDUCT UNBECOMING
CITADEL OF SERVITUDE
THE DUNGEONS OF LIDIR
SERVING TIME
DIFFERENT STROKES   *September*
LINGERING LESSONS   *October*

A NEXUS CLASSIC

THE TRAINING GROUNDS

Sarah Veitch

This book is a work of fiction.
In real life, make sure you practise safe sex.

First published in 1994 by
Nexus
Thames Wharf Studios
Rainville Road
London W6 9HA

This Nexus Classic edition 2000

Typeset by TW Typesetting, Plymouth, Devon

Printed and bound by Cox & Wyman, Reading, Berks

ISBN 0 352 33526 2

1

A man. A woman. A chair. A moving hand. A whimper. The door to the penthouse slammed shut, blocking out the shadowy view. Charlotte winced at the sudden loss, the feeling of exclusion. Inside there'd been action, energy, abandon, atmosphere. Just for a moment, as the sunlight peaked, she thought she'd seen ... But that was impossible, ridiculous! Couples didn't behave like that nowadays.

At least they didn't at home – but she was far from home now. Just how far? An opportunity to explore new horizons, Vernon had said. She'd asked *which* horizons he referred to, of course, but he'd simply refused to enlighten her. He had gone on instead to arrange this two month sabbatical, promising it would be a complete change of scene.

She sighed. They'd got here last night in the smallest of planes, for Vernon's colleague, Guy, had a pilot's licence. The three of them had flown for days over forests and oceans, touching down every so often to refuel and eat and sleep.

They'd arrived at last. Guy had landed the plane. A luggage boy, a breakfast maid and various other lackeys from the island's hotel had hurried over in total nudity to bow and smile. All small and suntanned, they'd greeted him like a long-lost friend; he'd apparently done some photographic shoots on the island last time. Judging by the way some of the girls kissed their way down his body, that wasn't all he had done ...

Now, leaving the enigmatic penthouse scene behind her, Charlotte hurried along the forest paths after Guy and her live-in lover Vernon.

1

'Wait, you two! Where are we off to now, for God's sake?' she snapped, kicking the tendrils of a pretty vermilion flower out of the way.

Vernon grinned slyly: 'You'll see!'

She'd see about leaving here. She'd see about going someplace where the reception staff wore clothes, where you swam in an indoor pool rather than an outdoor one. She'd . . .

Charlotte stopped short as they reached a thirty-foot clearing. Three naked women stood silently on the plush green lawn, with about a hundred of the island's nude inhabitants gathered round. She blushed as she focused on their taut bottoms and hard-nippled bare breasts. With submissively bowed heads, they seemed to be waiting here expectantly, even eagerly. But for who, Charlotte wondered, and for what?

'What the hell's going on?' she asked Vernon, wishing her own voice sounded less helpless.

'They've failed in their duties,' he murmured, gripping her arm.

'So they're subjected to this public humiliation?'

'They're being given the opportunity to make amends.'

Charlotte looked up at Vernon as he spoke, then stared over at Guy, on his other side, who was ignoring her. Neither were focusing their cameras, but they were staring intently at the three naked girls. As Charlotte followed their gaze, a tall muscular man who was stripped to the waist walked into the clearing. He carried a long, light whip.

When they saw him the waiting girls all dipped their heads still closer to the ground. He motioned to the nearest to approach him and she did so, keeping her eyes downcast.

'Take up your position!' he said, sternly. His words carried round the assembled staff.

Charlotte shifted her sandalled feet uneasily as the girl walked towards a six-foot tall wooden post which was hammered into the ground. It had strong metal rings near the top. Surely he wasn't going to . . .?

As she stared, the girl lifted her slender wrists, and a dark-skinned boy produced a leather thong and bound them to the steadfast metal circles. Now her nudity was even more apparent; each muscle stretching upwards, her buttocks taut and breasts lifted as she stood securely tied.

For a moment the man wielding the whip just stared at her, as if gloating over her helplessness.

'You know not to move your feet,' he said, but the words were an instruction rather than a question, and his tone was firm.

'Yes, Master,' whispered the girl. Because of the way she was secured, her face was turned away from him, away from Charlotte. Everyone looked at the straining globes of her buttocks, at the still idle whip.

As they stared, the Master drew back the implement till its tip went over his shoulder. Then he brought it forward across the girl's backside. Charlotte gasped. She looked round, expecting to see amazement or disbelief on the faces all around her. But no one seemed surprised. Twisting round, she stared at Vernon, but he was still concentrating on the scene unfolding before him. By their side, Guy, whom she'd never liked much, was also looking as if he witnessed such a flogging every day.

The sound of the whip bearing down again made her turn back to the punishment. Was the girl really keeping her position? Given that only her wrists were tied, it would be easy to twist her body round to the other side of the pole. That way the thick hard wood would deflect at least some of the strokes, saving her tender buttocks. She watched carefully as the third whacking whispered through the warm, still air. Again, though the girl flinched, she kept her bare feet firmly in place.

Charlotte looked at the other maids. Presumably this correction awaited them also. It must be terrible seeing one of your companions being chastised. She studied them as they focused obsequiously on the ground, her own heart speeding. Were they dreading their own disciplining, or anxious to have it over and done with, get the chance to lick their wounds? Whatever their emotions, two sets of buttocks twitched in sympathy each time the lash came down on their friend.

3

Three. Four. Five. After the sixth stroke the Master ordered the girl to be untied, and sent her back to kneel beside her companions. Charlotte stared at the pink glow of her small pert derrière, and wondered how she must feel. It must hurt, the relentless sun shining down on your punished bottom. But she had no time to ponder the girl's plight further, for a second girl was taking her place against the post.

'What have they done?' she whispered to Vernon, finding her voice with difficulty.

'They failed to give the Master's guests sufficient pleasure,' he said.

'And who is this "Master"?' She spat the words out sarcastically.

'He owns this island; brought civilisation to it,' Guy murmured, breaking in on their conversation and making Charlotte scowl.

Was Guy going to be with them all the time, then? Charlotte had hoped he'd go off to do some photographic work, leaving her with Vernon all to herself for most of the time. Better still, maybe the two men would go off to do some detailed photo shoots, leaving her to be pampered by the staff, and to think of Jeff . . .

'Stop chattering – just watch what's happening, Charlotte,' said Vernon abruptly. He didn't normally speak to her like this. He was usually respectful; virtually putty in her hands.

'Yes, sir,' she said sardonically.

Another nude boy with a stiff swollen cock led the second girl into place and tethered her. Everyone except herself, Guy, Vernon and the Master seemed to be naked. There were to be no secrets here!

'God – he knows what he's doing!' Charlotte whispered as the Master carefully meted out the controlled arse-whipping.

Guy grinned: 'He's had plenty of practice, believe me!'

'Do all his staff displease him, then?'

'Let's just say it takes them a few months to obey him fully. There's a lot to learn . . .'

4

Charlotte turned her attention back to the action, but Guy seemed anxious to explain the reasoning behind it. 'This is more to teach them humility than anything else,' he offered, obviously enjoying himself. 'These fillies have never been chastened before a crowd of spectators before. Their friends seeing this . . . it's their modesty that's really pained.'

'It must bite, though,' said Charlotte, looking at the second girl's defenceless bottom.

'You ain't seen nothing yet!' Guy said, with a snorting laugh.

Surely the man couldn't get away with this? Surely his staff could report him, could leave his employment?

'This is an island, remember,' said Guy, as if reading her thoughts. 'As the owner, he can make up his own rules.'

'And you really want to photograph this place?' Charlotte asked, looking at Guy's face and then her boyfriend's. Both men nodded, still directing the bulk of their attention to the correction of the third girl which was now taking place before their eyes.

Then the pain ended and the pleasure seemed set to begin. And what pleasure! Two members of staff wheeled a long wide padded trestle – like a satin double bed – into the clearing. The Master commanded the first girl to clamber on to it, then lie flat out on her belly and put her head in her hands.

'Are you sorry you were bad?' he murmured.

'Yes, Master.' The girl's voice was little more than a whisper. The listeners craned their heads.

'*How* sorry?' He slid his palm across the heated flesh as if polishing it. The girl closed her eyes against the sensation.

'Very sorry, sir.'

There followed a long, long pause during which he stroked the recalcitrant rear end that was bared for his attentions. Charlotte knew how wonderful strong male hands could feel when they took the time to pleasure a woman thoroughly, inch by inch. Was the prostrate maid feeling the same sexual excitement? The man fingered on and on and on.

'Sorry enough to want to make amends?'

'Yes, Master.' The reply was low, hesitant. The girl was obviously aroused, but it was as if she didn't really quite repent.

'Ask me nicely to take your mind off your sore bum.'

'Please ...' whimpered the girl, writhing against the plush padded bedding.

'Pretty please,' said the Master, continuing to caress her arse.

A long drawn out sigh escaped the girl, and her shoulders drooped slightly. 'Pretty please,' she whispered, scissoring her legs apart and looking back over her shoulder beseechingly. 'Please take my mind off my having had my bottom thrashed.'

'And how would we manage that?' asked the Master, running his thumb along the line where thigh met buttock.

The girl paused: 'By ... you know! Oh please!'

The man caressed on and on and on. The girl slithered about on the bed and moaned her lust through small clenched teeth and fast-reddening lips. She pushed her arse back against his exploring fingers, crying out for his touch each time he teased his hands away. Watching, Charlotte had the feeling that some strange power struggle was going on; that they'd played out this scene before.

'I need ...' whispered the maid.

'You need what?'

She tried to push her pudenda back against his fingers, but he slapped lightly at her creamy thigh backs and inner surfaces.

'Don't push back or try to wriggle away.' Smiling grimly, he ran a knowing finger down the crack of her rounded arse until she tensed involuntarily against his hand.

'I'm sorry!' she gasped, writhing at each provocative touch. 'I can't help wriggling. I need to come, Master. There – I've said it! It's what I need!'

'But do you *deserve* to come?'

'No, sir. But ... please! Oh, let me!'

'Please what?'

'Pretty please!' the girl all but wept. Her mouth was an

6

open wail against the pent up sexual heat and humiliation. Her tits were swollen with her craving, rubbing lewdly against the bed.

'I'm feeling merciful.' The man crouched at her side to run a thumb from behind her ear, all the way down her naked profile, to her shuddering slender ankles. 'I think that I'll oblige.'

The Master's voice carried over to the impatient watchers. As the girl's bottom relaxed, he added: 'But you mustn't come within the first twenty minutes. You must show control.'

'But you make my clit so hot, Master!' The owner of the scarlet buttocks sounded breathless.

'Exactly,' said her Master, moving away. He turned to the boy who'd originally tied her up: 'Bring the clitoral stimulator from the first hook on the wall of the second Correction Chamber.'

'Christ, how many stimulators has he got?' asked Charlotte, feeling perspiration beginning to trickle between her bulging breasts.

'Hundreds! Have patience – you'll find out later,' Guy said, with an enigmatic grin.

Charlotte looked to Vernon for elucidation, but he was still scrutinising the waiting girl's dripping labia, doubtless wondering how the colours would look on a series of stills or as part of a film. Vernon had made masses of money from his offbeat London photographic exhibitions. Up till now, though, he hadn't specialised in chastened nudes ...

'Here he comes!'

A sigh went up from the crowd as the youth appeared, holding a small vibrating phallus and grinning broadly. Was it a sigh of horror or of pleasure? This was all so new. Charlotte looked at each face, trying to gauge their reactions. She hadn't worked out how she herself felt yet.

'Fasten her down,' added the Master, signalling to the boy as he drew closer. All eyes turned to the straps on either end of the magnificent couch. Whistling, the boy walked over to the randy wench and took hold of first one wrist then the other, gripping her arms as if afraid she

7

might run away. Then he bound her slender ankles which she obediently kept spread far apart.

'Where does this little beauty go?' murmured the Master, sliding his right hand beneath her body and rubbing the little vibrator over her hardened nipples. The girl gasped at the rapture.

'Sir – you know!'

'Yes, I know, but we mustn't be coy. We must say it, mustn't we? You've seen girls go through such sessions before.'

'But everyone can hear . . .' whispered the girl.

'Of course they can hear, that's the whole point! They're all watching you.'

With a choking sob, the girl rubbed her pubis against the couch and pulled against her bonds.

'Raise your arse,' the man added.

Opening eyes that were suddenly hope-filled, the girl arched her bottom in the air. Now her butt was vulnerably spread and high, her clitoris accessible.

'Twenty minutes denial, we agreed?' asked the Master, running the vibrator over her areolae on its lowest speed.

'Yes, Master,' murmured the prisoner, then added, 'if that's what my Master desires.'

Charlotte looked at the man, realising she'd never seen anyone look so humourless, so emotionless; he was not the kind of person you would want to disobey. But now the girl was submitting to his orders – such difficult orders! And she was being pleasured by an instrument of potential ecstasy that hummed her flesh into the horniest heat . . .

What exactly went on in this place? How often did they hold these punishment and pleasure sessions? Why did the boys get so excited as they tied up their particular slave? Yes, that was the first time she'd used the word, but that was what these women were – slaves to pain and pleasure, not workers, not hotel staff; at least not the kind of hotel staff she'd known before.

But it was pointless thinking about her day to day life. She was here for the next eight weeks: she might as well see the sights, no matter how alien and exotic. So far she'd only seen that impressively majestic penthouse and her own less majestic hotel room, with its cane-woven divan and overstuffed chairs.

The hotel was clean and bright, but decidedly basic, and neither it nor the penthouse were large enough to support the crowd of a hundred or so now making up the audience for the punished slaves. Later, she promised herself, she'd explore the island and find out where its other buildings were. So far she'd had no chance, for an hour after she'd unpacked and eaten, Guy had knocked on her and Vernon's door, and brought them here to show them what he'd called 'an amazing sight for sightseers'. She'd thought he was going to show them a volcano or a waterfall! Instead, she was about to witness this lust-crazed female hold her desire in check for twenty minutes or more.

'Ask nicely to feel the stimulator on your clitoris, girl,' the Master said, staring at the globes of quivering scarlet.

'Please, Master, use that wonderful little vibrator on my hungry engorged clit,' the girl said. You could see from her face that she was recounting lines she'd learned, and that she was humiliated. You could also see the eroticised appetite in her eyes.

She groaned and wriggled in her loose restraints as the man played the humming bud over her breasts, and down towards her belly. Her lower lips now gaping visibly, she pushed forward against the descending promise with her thighs.

'Greedy!' said the Master, keeping the stimulus centred on her tummy button, despite her pushing and pulling to receive the pleasure further down, against her *mons veneris*. 'I want some more humility this time.'

'I've been a bad girl ... I don't deserve to come for twenty minutes,' the slave girl gasped, skulking about on her belly and rubbing her mound against the mattress with sex-slicked heat.

'No, you don't, do you?' said the man, and played his pleasure-bringer along her stomach a second time.

The girl was groaning with need now. Her shoulders

9

shaking, her hair falling across her flushed features, her mouth was open in a silent plea that she be allowed sexual release.

'Only nineteen minutes to go,' said the Master, pulling back her hair and looking deep into her eyes for long, long moments. 'I'm told the nineteenth one demands the most control.'

It would, thought Charlotte, quivering. The heat that the earlier whipping had brought to the girl's base must be making her feel doubly desperate, and as soon as you were told not to do something, it became all you wanted to do.

'Teach me self-control, Master,' the slave whimpered, closing her eyes tightly and moving her chastened buttocks. The man ran the stimulator down, down, down.

The girl cried out loudly. A gasp went round the arena on hearing her wail. Would she be punished some more for making a noise without permission? Would she be gagged and given further strokes of the whip? Instead, the man pulled the stimulus ruthlessly away again.

'You don't deserve this much pleasure yet.'

Her labia were dripping freely; liquid excitement ran from both lips onto the couch, where it pooled in glistening abandon. Her sex was vermilion velvet. Her Master squeezed and stroked her toasted hindquarters. He ran his palm round and round, then up and down.

'Shall we start again?'

'Yes, sir!'

'You'll not be wilful?'

'No, sir. I won't come for nineteen minutes, sir.'

'I may make it more.'

The girl sighed and another trickle of lust slid down one thigh. 'I will wait till my Master gives me permission to take my pleasure.'

'Good girl. Let's play with that soft little tummy again.' He pushed the vibrator under her eager torso and positioned it at the very top of her pubic patch. She bit back a wail.

'Steady. Wait your turn. Don't do anything without permission.'

'No, sir. I promise, sir.'

Again the taunting prelude to overwhelming pleasure began.

'Such a soft tummy!'

He played the stimulator across the roughened hair. He played her like an instrument. The girl groaned.

'Do you think your clit needs some attention, girl?'

'Yes, sir! Oh please, sir!'

'And it'll remain obedient?'

'Oh yes!'

'I hope so. For your sake I really hope so.'

He slid the humming implement a centimetre further down. It wasn't enough, or it was too much. The slave pushed forward, pulled up, and whimpered ravenously.

'Easy. We mustn't be impatient. We must wait our turn.'

'Please! I need . . .'

'You *want*. There's a difference.'

'I want it so much, so very much!' the girl said.

'Tell me what you want.'

So the game had begun again. But it didn't feel like a game, thought Charlotte, watching dazedly.

'I want the vibrator just below my clitoris, Master. Want it bad!'

'Not *on* it?'

'No – that's too much!'

'But I could put the stimulus on it directly if I wantd to?'

'You can do anything, Master. You know you can!'

'Only we want to give you pleasure, don't we? Too much stimulus would defeat the point, would fail to excite you.'

The girl looked hopeful: 'Yes, sir.'

'So we'll give you rapture, but in our own good time – we don't want you to get complacent.'

'No, sir. Whatever you say, sir.' The girl's mouth tensed into a frustrated, sex-unsated line.

'Now where were we?'

'You . . . you had the stimulus against my pubes. You said you'd kindly go down a bit, Master.'

'Did I? Did I really say that?'

Looking amused, the man played the vibrator down her labia in an absent-minded way.

'Oh yes! Like that! Oh please, sir.'

'Mmm? What am I doing, giving you this much so soon?'

'I'll be so good sir – I'll do anything, everything!'

'If you'd shown this courtesy to our guests in the first place you wouldn't be here tethered like this at all.'

'Yes, sir. I know, sir. I'll be so good from now on, sir.'

'Well start by controlling your clit, my dear. You've another fifteen minutes of self-denial to go.'

Whimpering some more, the girl slumped against the couch, but she soon started to wriggle again as the man pushed the humming nub between her legs and inserted it high into her vagina. It wasn't a dildo as such, so it couldn't give total satisfaction, but it was enough to make her groan.

'Like that?'

'Yes, Master.'

'Like that for another fifteen minutes?'

'Oh, sir, please no – please touch above my clit. I beg!'

'I like it when you beg,' murmured the man. The crowd seemed to like it too. Their cocks and clits were obviously rampant. Charlotte took a step closer, watching the man's fingers pushing the pleasure-tool further inside the girl's hungry hole.

'I beg to be allowed to come!'

'Fourteen minutes to go. I hope you're not *too* excited?'

'No, sir,' the girl moaned. Sexual frenzy was reflected in her taut spread thighs and her hectic face.

'We may be kind and take the vibrator for a walk,' added her Master, slowly withdrawing the implement from her vagina and rubbing to either side of her trench before centring just below her clitoris.

'Oh, God! Oh, that's heaven!' the girl gasped.

'No, heaven is my cock.'

'I want your cock, Master!'

'But you don't deserve it.'

'Please . . . someway, anyway, just to be allowed to come,' the girl begged.

'Thirteen minutes.'

He kept the vibrator in place, staring down at her closely. She had closed eyes, and an open mouth. Her skin looked flushed and perspiration had made her fringe slightly wet.

'Your clit is almost as red as your arse.'

The slave gasped hard. 'Master, I'm going to . . .'

'I may get bored holding this stimulus here. I may decide just to take it away.'

'Oh no! Oh don't!'

'Perhaps you should beg some more!'

'I . . . oh, Jesus!'

He kept the joy-stick trained on that most sensitive place and she pushed hard against its contours and came and came and came.

'Oh yes, my pretty bitch, let it out. Oh Christ, you needed that!' whispered the man as she contorted with the pulsings of passion.

The mottled sex flush of her orgasm went on and on. She pushed her ecstatic *mons* down as her lower body convulsed with erotic Eden.

'Fuck me!' muttered Guy. 'You don't get many of them to the pound!'

Vernon stared fixedly. Charlotte gulped.

For a while the bound girl continued to tremble, her bottom juddering. Then slowly she started to push herself slightly forward, as if trying to position her pudenda over the vibrator which had fallen under her right thigh and which was buzzing encouragingly on. Murmuring something about her lack of control, the Master continued to caress her heated derrière. Then he stood up and ordered her to be untied.

'Have her brought to my quarters,' he added and the boy responsible for tying her down undid her bonds, and helped her into a sitting position. Two larger men came forward carrying a heavily-cushioned rickshaw. The girl kept her head coyly downcast. Carefully they picked her up, and laid her on her stomach in its cosy confines. Lifting the vehicle gently, they carried her away.

It was obvious that she was going to get a good fucking from her Master later. It was also obvious that she was more than ready to come for a second time! The Master's next words seemed to confirm this, for he turned to the youth, who was looking disconsolately after his prize.

'She can bring you satisfaction tonight, boy, with that hot little pleasure hole,' he said. 'I'll have her sent to your cell at seven.'

Staring through the shimmering heat, Charlotte could see a huge bulge of lust straining upwards at the Master's groin, his large plum-like scrotum evident even through his loose cream silk trousers.

'Now, my disobedient little beauties,' the man said as he turned to the two remaining girls and addressed them, 'You were whipped this afternoon for failing to bring my guests as much pleasure as they desired.'

He paused, and walked over to them both, behind their punished bottoms. For long moments he inspected their flesh with his eyes, and then followed through with a considering, stroking palm. He smiled, obviously enjoying the warmth of their well-chastened hindquarters. 'Before you fail in your duties next time, think of how the whip felt as it came down.'

'What duties?' whispered Charlotte to Guy. He seemed to have all the answers.

'They're about to perform them properly,' he murmured back. 'Just watch.'

Vernon shot his girlfriend a look of mild annoyance. 'I've already told her to do that,' he said.

What was eating him? More importantly, what was that slave now eating? Charlotte looked back into the arena in time to see something large and purplish disappear into a female mouth. Squinting through the heat, she saw that the second girl to feel the lash was now feeding the head of a boy's cock between her eager lips. Looking closer, she recognised the boy as the one who'd tied the same girl to the whipping post with such rock-hard glee an hour earlier.

Ah! That explained why the youths had been so excited!

Their reward for tethering a slave properly was obviously some kind of sex. Had this boy chosen to be kissed down there? Or was that what the Master had decided the youths were to indulge in? She looked at the other girl, amused to see her nervously licking her lips.

As she stared, the maid took half the youth's phallus into her gullet. She started to slide her lips back and forward, round and round. The boy moaned softly, and entwined his fingers through her hair, while his thigh muscles pulled. He closed his eyes as she increased the rhythm of her mouth.

The kneeling girl slid a small sure palm beneath his scrotum and lightly brushed it. Charlotte fancied she could hear her making sucking noises in the breathless quiet that surrounded them on all sides. She glanced round at the watchers, noticing that more and more of the men had hard-ons. Some of the women in the crowd had become flushed, their nipples darkening and growing increasingly erect.

She turned back to the arena. The boy was moving convulsively now. His small firm hips thrust backwards and forwards. The girl sucked and sucked.

Her enslaver came with a drawn out cry, his head pulled back and his mouth opened in a phallus-fed frenzy. His balls jerked, obviously pushing out every last droplet of fevered juice. Looking pleased, his pleasurer sank back onto her haunches, and kissed and licked at his inner thighs. She tasted the saltiness of his sex shaft and licked the rivers of male perspiration away.

'You can go,' said the Master, and the youth bowed lightly before walking through the crowds, looking dazed but happy. 'Go,' said the Master to the girl, and she slowly got up from her haunches, and walked stiff-legged towards the crowd.

They parted to let her through: she didn't look at anyone. Charlotte stared after the slender figure with the pinkened buttocks until she met up with the newly-milked youth. As she watched, the pair embraced and the boy slid his hand between her recently-punished thighs with insinuating promise. The girl's mouth opened in an encouraging gasp, and she cleaved towards him, her soft tits against his hard hirsute chest. As Charlotte looked on, the re-erecting youth scooped his pleasure-seeking partner up and walked with her along the path until they both disappeared from sight.

The Master beckoned to the third girl and the third boy. The girl looked to be about twenty-two. How must she feel to be pleasuring a young male of eighteen whilst an audience looked on? Obediently she sank to her knees before him and, at a sign from her Master, started to lick round the boy's quivering rod.

She licked lightly, on and on. The cock jerked and swelled, but obviously craved further contact. The youth tried to push forward, to get his stiffness inside that warm wet aperture. The girl drew back, muttering something, and the boy looked over uncertainly at the Master. The Master nodded. The boy tried again.

Shaking his head, the Master walked over and touched the slave on the left shoulder. She turned round and, seeing him, instinctively covered her punished bottom with her small hands.

'Silly girl. That's why you're here in the first place,' said the Master in a coolly conversational tone. 'I don't want to have to chastise you for failing to please all over again.'

'No . . . please. I haven't done this before!'

'Use your palms, then, girl. Please in any way you can – but give pleasure. Otherwise . . .'

'Master. I'll do anything, I'll . . .'

'Just fondle him properly,' he said, warningly stroking her roasted rear end.

Starting at the root, the novice nibbled her way up to the helmet. She flicked her tongue over the hole at the top, then licked slowly down. Smiling, she put a forefinger and thumb at either side of the boy's balls and squeezed them gently. Then she ran her teeth up and down one side of his ever-thickening shaft.

The youth's hard-on was massive now, and her mouth

trembled as she prepared to take him on board again. Cautiously she opened her lips, and took the first half inch in. She sucked lightly, and mouthed a little further down his rampant rod.

The slave stayed like that for a while, tonguing him gently; her glowing bottom quivering, her tits bouncing up and down on either side of his dick. Next, she moved her lips from his cock and used them to kiss his shaft's hard ridge. At the same time she sent her other hand running lightly over his balls, and skimmed one middle finger round to rim the fragile opening to his arse.

The boy pressed forward and grimaced with approaching bliss, his leg muscles clenching. He groaned deep in his throat, then jerked several times and came over her lightly-tanned shoulders and breasts.

'The boys go to the girls' quarters now and pleasure them for hours,' Guy said enviously. 'Seemingly, these wenches come two or three times after they've been whipped!'

It was over. As if by some pre-arranged signal, the crowd gave the Master deep bows of appreciation and respect, and started to move away silently. Most went in the opposite direction to the hotel where Charlotte and the other two were staying. Only the luggage boy and breakfast maid turned to go her way.

'Where are they off to?' she asked Vernon.

'To the Master's quarters,' Guy answered. 'We're to go there to take photographs tonight.'

'I don't know if I want to . . .' started Charlotte, then thought better of it. She might as well tag along with the men. After all, the alternatives were limited. She didn't want to be left in that boring sparse hotel room all alone!

Also, the entertainment Guy was promising might be quite spectacular. It had been rather exciting watching a woman go down on a man. It was thrilling too, in a strange way, to see these large native eyes widen at the threat of a whipping; fascinating to watch those little bottoms go a comely pink. She shivered, wondering what it would feel like to be corrected. She was glad that she'd never have to find out.

2

'What's this place called anyway?' asked Charlotte an hour later, as she sipped a sweet native drink on the verandah outside her hotel room.

'The island?' asked Guy. 'The Training Grounds is what the Master calls it. Obviously it doesn't have a name – it's unknown to all but a few people outside.'

'How do you know this ... "Master"?'

Guy smiled mysteriously. 'Let's just say that in England we have discreet mutual acquaintances that like the same things.'

Like seeing disobedient tarts being chastised? Unsure of what to say next, Charlotte returned her gaze to her glass and its contents. Whatever she was drinking, it wasn't alcoholic. She'd asked the drinks boy for something intoxicating but he'd said the Master wanted everyone fully aware at all times of what was going on.

I'll bet he does, thought Charlotte, glowering. He'd looked hugely excited as he toyed with those girls before treating them to the sting of the lash, his tormenting fondling fingers. As for the things he'd said ... Still – assuming they were to meet him this evening – he should be in a good mood. By then he'd have exploded the contents of his balls into that sex-mad young maid.

'Don't suppose there's a shower in this dump?' she asked Vernon.

He was staring into the distance and smiling slightly to himself. After she spoke, there was a silence. It seemed to take him a moment to collect his thoughts.

'Not in the hotel, no,' he said, frowning at her slightly,

'but you only have to walk for five minutes to reach a little stream where the natives bathe.'

'Wash with a bunch of foreigners' exclaimed Charlotte, haughtily.

'They were all British originally,' chipped in Guy. 'They've become darker over the past decade or so – the Master has been here for fifteen years.'

Charlotte shivered. In that case, the man must have come here when he was about twenty. She could imagine being in awe of him even then! The strong sure torso was part of it, but it was the impassive gaze and unsmiling set of his mouth that really captivated her. She shivered further, and picked up her glass again. Captivated was too apt a word for a place like this!

Remember you're your own person, she reminded herself sharply, let them live by their rules, and you can abide by your own desires!

'If this Master is so rich and influential,' she said curiously, 'how come the only hotel on the island is as basic as this?'

This time Vernon answered. She hadn't realised he knew so much about it all.

'The hotel's just a building to leave your clothes in and have a siesta and a snack when you first arrive,' he said. 'Once newcomers are rested, they go on to the Master's quarters as his staff or his guests.'

'Don't tell me – I'll have a guest bedroom with en suite bathroom,' Charlotte mocked lightly.

Guy and Vernon grinned at each other, then Guy nodded his assent. 'This place isn't without its luxuries. You'll find the Master's estate is much larger and more opulent than you think.'

Vernon's girlfriend paused.

'Why do you both call him the Master?'

'It's his name,' said Vernon.

'Because he runs this place like a military academy, and deserves our respect,' Guy replied. He looked steadily at her: 'I've been here twice before, and they've treated me brilliantly. You can have a good time here, Charlotte, if you follow the rules.'

She could be having a good time at a nightclub in London! Could be exploring Paris; could be on a plane bound for Amsterdam.

'I suppose the climate's good here,' she said grudgingly.

'Hot enough for you?' Guy said, and smiled twistedly again.

Nasty little man! She wished he and Vernon weren't so friendly. Vernon hadn't been nice to her since they boarded the plane. Or was she just imagining it because she was missing the gorgeous Jeffrey? He'd hopefully be missing *her* by now.

'Time to go,' said Guy, looking at his watch. 'It would never do to be late.'

'Yeah? What would they do – tan our hides?' muttered Charlotte. Then she touched her shoulder bag which contained her passport. It made her feel safe.

For half an hour they trekked through the jungle. Sometimes large butterflies startled her, and strange birds flew over her shoulders whilst trees waved their pink-blossomed branches over her head. This had better be worth waiting for, she thought as her safari dress dampened with perspiration and clung to her breasts.

'Can I carry your bag, Miss?' asked one of the guides, a slim naked youth of eighteen or nineteen.

'No, I can manage,' Charlotte said. She wished she'd left her bra and pants in her hotel room. Undergarments dug into you in this ongoing heat. Maybe the natives were right to go nude!

She looked at her guide more closely, wondering if he was one of the boys who'd received a good sucking this afternoon. The boy stared back at her questioningly, and she blushed.

'Almost there,' murmured the girl who had been clearing the path of flower-rich creepers before them. She too was naked, and faint bruises on the back of her thighs showed she'd recently felt the cane.

'Who did this to you?' asked Charlotte, suddenly curious.

The girl turned round surprised, then shook her head silently. Irritated, Charlotte caught her wrist.

21

'Answer me.'

She shook the girl lightly, and noted the pretty blush that covered her face and bosom, and doubtless spread to her lower cheeks.

'In class I failed some tests – I didn't study hard enough. My teacher was angry. The Master gave me to him to correct.'

'I see.'

Charlotte let go of the girl, who immediately turned away and began pulling back further intrusive creepers. 'She seems too old to be in class,' she said, and Guy grinned.

'The Master believes that education is for life, that we can always be taught new tricks, Charlotte.'

Try stepping in front of a bus, Guy, Charlotte thought, continuing to plod through the trees.

She sighed as a thorn scratched at her ankle, and immediately the girl was on her knees sucking the blood away. 'Please don't tell the Master,' she whimpered. 'I'll kiss it better, Miss.'

Ashamed at the sudden rush of heat to her groin, Charlotte pushed the girl's warm lips away. 'Just see that it doesn't happen again,' she said shortly. 'Don't know what I'd do if I got injured in this Godforsaken place.' She looked at the assorted guides. 'Judging by what I saw today, your Master has a huge staff who are well trained. Why on earth doesn't he get you to clear a proper path between the hotel and his estate?'

The servants looked at Guy, obviously uncomfortable.

'They're scared they'll get into trouble if they tell you things, Charlotte,' he explained. 'Just direct your questions to me,' he winked. 'They're not the only experts! I know quite a lot about this place.'

'Why doesn't . . .?' she started to repeat again waspishly.

'Because only the staff and guests know about this sacred isle. Even if some outsider was to fly over, they'd only see forest. You can't spot the hotel or the Training Grounds from the air.'

'Why the Training Grounds?' asked Charlotte, slowly.

'Why not?' Guy murmured, with a wink.

So the thrashings were a regular thing then, presumably. She swallowed hard: 'How can one man have so much power?'

'Money. Intellect. Connections,' Vernon chipped in. Feeling unusually small and insignificant, Charlotte took his hand.

He let it stay there, but gave back no answering pressure. Once he'd have entwined her fingers in his, kissed her palm, and turned to take her in his arms.

'But there must have been a hundred people at the whipping area today. If they wanted to, they could overwhelm him, could . . .?'

'Many are his sex slaves; they are all very loyal,' Guy said evenly. 'Plus he has friends working as tutors, gym teachers, overseers. The new girls cannot be sure who's friend or foe . . .'

He looked straight ahead as he walked, obviously familiar with the journey.

'The Master started with just five devoted servants, women he was sleeping with – and spanking, of course! They appreciated his skills in . . . re-education, and agreed to explore the world with him to find an untainted place.' He circled his hand around him with a flourish. 'They travelled for many months, and finally discovered this uninhabited land and started their own community.'

'A community of correction,' Charlotte said.

'Only for those who need correcting,' Guy said softly, staring at the slightly bruised thighs bounding ahead of him. He continued with his explanation, ignoring Charlotte's sigh. 'Over time the Master went back to the mainland and recruited another two or three young women – women who would ultimately be given duties to perform here on the estate.'

'More fool them!' muttered Charlotte.

Guy glared, and shook his head.

'As time went by he had too many staff that were going idle. That wasn't a good thing, so he got in touch with colleagues of like mind,' Guy smiled. 'They started to recuit suitable guests to enjoy the girls. It keeps these wilful little maids out of mischief – and keeps their sex parts sated and well warmed up for future sessions, of course!' He shrugged. 'And if the guests fail to find satisfaction with their chosen female, the Master takes the lazy girl in hand.'

And didn't she know it! She felt her own bottom twitch at the memory, and the caned slave girl's derrière seemed to tremble as she hurried ahead of them.

'Almost there,' she murmured, turning back to them shyly.

Charlotte was aware of Vernon's hand gripping her more tightly as he increased his step.

Suddenly they stepped out of the woods into a massive playing field. The girl started to walk through it, and the three newcomers followed with the luggage boy in tow. Deep in thought, they walked past a row of wooden stakes, spaced about five feet apart from each other. Were they whipping posts, Charlotte wondered? Just how disobedient could the Master's slaves be?

Averting her eyes, she looked to one side of the huge grassy area and noticed several long low buildings. These has been recently whitewashed: large drums of paint were stocked neatly at one side. Each building boasted a heavy door which had two large bolts.

'Don't ask!' said Guy, following her gaze. 'I'm sure we'll all find out in good time.'

'They weren't here on your last visit, then?' Charlotte asked curiously.

'Hard to say, with the place being so vast. But I suspect not. The Master's never satisfied. He adds new . . . refinements all the time.'

As if to confirm his words a low wail echoed out from the nearest chamber.

'Please have mercy . . . please!' implored a throaty female voice.

'That's our new cook. She dropped the yams on the floor,' their naked guide murmured. Though her voice was low, her eyes sparkled and a strange flush came to her cheeks.

'I think she has a love-hate relationship with this place,' Vernon said to the others.

'Yeah – loves it when the pain stops, hates the thrashings!' Guy said, and grinned.

Wincing, Charlotte continued to walk along, feeling her palm grow damp in Vernon's. She wished that he'd smile at her rather than continually stare at the punished contours of their little native friend.

'Can't you cover yourself up?' she snapped, stopping to take off her underskirt and hand it to the girl.

'Our Master says we are to serve our guests naked,' the girl replied. 'Only the most dutiful slaves have their clothes returned to them.'

'Surely it's not that difficult to go along with the bastard for a few weeks?' Charlotte asked. 'You know, just humour him to get what you want!'

Vernon glared at her, and increased his pressure unpleasantly on her fingers till she winced. 'That's Charlotte's recipe for living,' he said to no one in particular. 'Well, it has been so far, at least ...'

'When you're nervous ... you can drop something,' said the girl, looking down at the ground again. 'Or you're told to be silent for a week, but you forget and speak to someone for a second or two.' She touched the back of her thighs as if remembering. 'I swear to my Master each time that I'll be better, but it's really hard never to make mistakes.'

It sounded it! Charlotte told herself jokingly that tonight she'd better be on her best behaviour. Don't be silly, she chided herself, you're one of his precious guests.

'That's the gymnasium,' Guy pointed out as they skirted the edge of a domed high building. 'And over there you'll find the dance hall. The girls do a version of the Can-Can you'll never forget.'

The light beginning to fade at last, he hurried them on till they came to a large dirt pathway. Looking way ahead, Charlotte could see the most beautiful stucco mansion, extending over acres of land.

'The Master's Palace,' Guy said with reverence, 'containing the most stringent correction academy in the world.'

'Can't hear the screams,' quipped Charlotte, feeling secretly overwhelmed at the lavishness of the structure they were approaching.

'Many of the punishment chambers are soundproofed,' Guy explained. He chuckled: 'You'll see and hear the pleading soon enough, I promise. The Master insists his guests have the grand tour of at least a few of the rooms.'

She'd seen her first whipping now, Charlotte told herself as they neared the enormous arched front door. She must act cool – the man probably liked people to feel embarrassed or in awe of his punishing power. He wasn't going to make her fidget, though: already she was getting used to the naked people around her. It wasn't such a big deal, youthful nudity. She could cope.

The door was opened before they reached it by a boy who bowed low and long, then gestured for them to walk inside. Charlotte was disconcerted to see the Master standing there in the vast polished hall. His impervious dark eyes looked her up and down for a long, tense moment, then he gave the flicker of a smile.

'Welcome,' he said to all three of them. Vernon and Guy gravely inclined their heads. Charlotte mustered up a haughty half grin, then turned her back to look at the paintings on the walls.

'You have eaten?'

'Yes. Your hospitality is much appreciated,' said Guy softly.

Looking over, Charlotte raised her eyes heavenwards to indicate that she thought he was a creep.

'Then let me entertain you!' said the Master. 'I've asked some of my prettiest girls to dance. They do so exquisitely.'

'Does that mean we have to go all the way back to the dance hall?' Charlotte groaned to Vernon, pulling a face.

The Master frowned: he had obviously overheard. 'No, I'm training a few select beauties in the Scarlet Room. You'll be there in seconds if you just step this way.'

As Vernon shook his head at Charlotte's rudeness, the three of them traipsed through one of the many doors leading from the hall, and walked along a slim shadowy corridor. Reaching a heavy door, the Master inserted a key from the impossibly heavy bunch that was clipped to the belt round his waist.

'Just in case they try to dance away into the night,' he said coolly. 'Though I don't think they'd like the consequences if they did.'

They'd receive another whipping no doubt, thought Charlotte, yawning. She followed the man into the room, and stopped. No wonder it was called the Scarlet Room! The walls, ceiling and floor were made of a rich red cushioned upholstery, which gave the place a luxurious glow. Four girls of around eighteen were lying on their stomachs on a king-sized red bed. Looking closer, Charlotte could see that two of their bottoms had been reddened too.

'A failure to concentrate on the dance steps,' said the Master, shaking his head. 'They paid attention after I set my hand to work on their posteriors!'

'Bare bum spanking?' Guy asked, with obvious interest.

'Mostly. Sometimes we wet their buttocks so that it stings much more.'

Walking over to a scarlet-painted cupboard, he brought out a leather glove and put it on.

'Amelia. Bend over and grip your ankles. Hurry now!'

'Yes, Master.'

As the girl got into position he turned to the others: 'I was in the middle of correcting her when a maid came and told me our guests had reached the grounds.'

He stepped back, contemplating the already pinkened globes before him.

'Oh do stop whimpering, Amelia, or I'll have to start all over again!' He paused: 'I promised you ten spanks and you've had . . .'

'Six.'

'Six, sir,' corrected the man. 'They obviously didn't make much of an impression.'

'They did! Honest!'

She wriggled provocatively, though she stayed bent over grasping her ankles, her arse temptingly bare.

'Spank seven coming up,' added her Master. 'Try to

learn from it.' He pulled his arm back, and brought his gloved hand slapping into her waiting cheeks.

Immediately the girl let go of her ankles and jumped up, wailing.

'You get an extra one for that,' her Master said.

'But I couldn't bear . . .'

'You must learn to bear it.' He snorted grimly. 'Remember that if you have to be tied down it'll end up hurting all the more.'

Swallowing, Charlotte stared at the warmed arse before her. She looked at the men and saw that they were all staring at the disciplined derrière too. Again the girl bent, and again the Master spanked her soundly. Unlike the scourge of the whip, his leathered palm made the whole bottom a hot blushing pink.

'Not long now. You know how you love it when I stop,' he whispered, and the girl cast a libidinous glance between her spread thighs at the other females who seemed equally pleased.

What did that look mean, Charlotte wondered, wincing in sympathy as the next slap hit the tender crease at the top of the eighteen-year-old's thighs.

Whimpering, the girl jumped from her position and rushed to the door, scrabbling half-heartedly at the handle.

'She plays those little games when she's on heat,' whispered the Master. 'She gets twice the spanking, but she also gets to come at least twice.'

He jerked his head at the other three dancers, who leapt from the bed and pulled her back roughly.

'She'll have to go over the stool now,' the Master said evenly, 'and she does hate it so.'

'No – anything! Have mercy! Not the stool!'

The others ignored the punished slave girl's cries and held her firmly. Without further prompting one of them got a heavy red stool from the corner of the room and brought it into the centre of the floor. She stood back, smiling lasciviously, waiting for her colleague's chastisement to go on.

'Four extra hard spanks for you, for disobedience,' said

the Master, running his gloved palm along her arse which was twitching at the prospect. Still held by the arms by her companions, the girl stared at the floor. 'And if you don't go over the stool without help I'll triple it,' the man continued. He nodded and the other girls released their grip.

For a moment the hot-cheeked girl just stood there, then she took a step towards the stool, and looked at her Master uncertainly.

'Get that arse up high in the air, bitch,' he said. Licking her lips, she took another step nearer her prison, and another. Finally, standing on tiptoe, she bent her body until her belly was touching the wood.

'Fasten her in place, girls,' said the man, nodding approvingly as one of them brought strong silk scarves from the cupboard. Kneeling, they tied her wrists and ankles to the bars towards the foot of the stool.

'Bind her hard,' the Master added. 'This glove doesn't half make her wriggle. I want her to feel every stroke and know she can't escape.'

As if the pummelling had already started, the girl wriggled her backside as best she could.

She couldn't do much more: there was nowhere to go this time – just a bottom served up for punishment, and a hand that came down hard. As the guests watched open-mouthed, the man started in on the wicked little rump again, teaching it to do exactly as it was told next time. 'Count the strokes out loud,' he instructed.

The helpless girl did so. Her bottom tensed before every spank, and when it came she jerked her body forward the little she could, and howled.

'Please . . . no . . . don't!'

A torrent of words and gasps and cries poured out between each pounding. She looked as if she was hurting – but her labial lips were feverish and thick and wet.

'What have we here?' the Master murmured when he'd finished spanking her. He used one leather clad finger to spread apart the girl's sexual petals, exposing the flushed inner canal. 'Sophie – show your little colleague how to dance without moving her feet,' he said with a knowing smile.

Amelia groaned, and tried to look up imploringly but the way she'd been bound made it difficult for her to raise her head. Grinning, Sophie slithered down from the bed and approached her dance mate's open quim.

'These little bitches tease each other all the time,' the Master said. He stared at the girls. 'What shall it be?' he mused aloud. 'The strap-on dildo or a good finger fucking?'

'The dildo,' whispered Amelia.

'Finger fucking it is, then,' the Master said. He turned to the watching guests. 'She has to learn to control her desires, to unleash them when I tell her too. The pleasure is all the sweeter in the end.'

Sophie looked over at the man and curtseyed with her naked body.

'Permission to penetrate the slave girl, sir.'

'Permission granted. Stand to one side so that our guests can see your fingers going in – and coming out, of course, if she isn't sufficiently obedient.'

Amelia exhaled heavily: 'I'll be obedient, sir!'

'Don't speak without permission,' warned the man. He looked over at one of the other dancers: 'Write her infringement in the punishment book for later. Next time I thrash her I may have to employ a gag.'

Amelia shuddered over the stool. Her breasts were hanging towards the floor, but her nipples were hard with wanting. Her belly pressed down as if she were already fucking someone or something. Sophie moved towards her, then stood as directed to one side.

'Tell her what you're going to do to her, then do it,' said the Master to the eager Sophie. 'She's allowed to move as much as she wants, but if she makes the slightest noise you're to stop.'

'Yes, sir,' Sophie murmured. 'I'll finger fuck her good, sir. She knows better than to make a noise when I'm around!'

The Master looked from Charlotte to Guy to Vernon. 'I sometimes think they gang up on the more recalcitrant girls when I'm not around, and give them a hard thrashing.

Leastways I sometimes see a reddened arse that has nothing to do with my tutors or me. They're not allowed to mete out discipline without permission of course, and if I caught one of them . . .' He touched his belt.

'I'm a good girl, sir. I aim to please, sir,' whispered Sophie, her eyes opening wider.

'Then get your experienced little fingers up your little friend,' the Master said.

Sophie flexed the middle finger of her right hand, then positioned it between Amelia's spread legs and ran it down each leaf of her inner labia. Amelia moaned loudly.

'Stop!' the Master said.

Sophie stopped, looking frustrated. Amelia looked ready to bite her own tongue out.

'What did I tell you, Amelia?'

'Not to make a sound, sir.'

'And what do we do to naughty girls who make sounds without permission?'

A drawn out sigh: 'We spank their wicked bottoms, sir.'

The Master turned to Guy.

'Glove or palm?'

'Palm' said Guy. He looked lovingly at the girl's spread arse. He looked as if he'd been given a present. 'Can I really . . .?'

'Be my guest.'

Putting one hand on her back, Guy drew the other back to spank the helpless little buttocks. This time Amelia obviously knew better than to groan.

'Sophie – give her a hand job she'll never forget.'

Guy stepped out of the way, and again the second naked girl got in place and played with her colleague's soft wet places. This time Amelia kept her eyes and mouth shut tight.

'Rim round her hole,' said the Master as he turned to Guy and winked. 'That drives them crazy. They come for ages at the end. If your finger or cock is still inside they grip it like a hot wet fist.'

A sadistic grin on her youthful features, Sophie rimmed round and round and round.

31

'I think her little hole is hungry. Amelia – ask nicely for one of Sophie's fingers.'

'Please, Sophie, put a finger up me!' Amelia begged.

Sophie looked at the Master for elucidation.

He nodded: 'But just give her half a finger for starters. She's been very truculent today.'

Licking her lips, Sophie again parted Amelia's sex and slid the top half of her middle finger into the obviously soaking aperture.

'Remember – silence,' said the Master quietly. Amelia obediently repressed her moans.

'Trace her sugar walls really lightly. That's it. Pretend your fingertip is as soft and gentle as a feather.'

Amelia's eyelids flickered and she jerked in her bonds as Sophie followed the Master's knowing words.

God, she looked hot as hell – no, hotter! Charlotte wiped a drop of perspiration from her own cleavage as she stared at the unfolding scene. What must it be like to be strapped down like this, quim bared for the world to see, sex mound dripping? What must it be like to be teased by a girl who was taking her instructions from a more powerful man?

'Round and round the mulberry bush,' whispered the Master mockingly as Sophie continued to taunt the other dancer's excited vulva. 'Now give her a full finger as a reward for keeping quiet,' he said.

Amelia pushed back on the disappearing finger and it disappeared even further up inside her.

'Don't go up and down yet – she's too expanded to feel it. Just stir your finger round as if it were a spoon in a bowl,' the Master said.

Sophie obeyed. Amelia trembled with desire. Charlotte felt her own vulval rim ache in sympathy. She refused to look at the men in the room. It was too humiliating. She wished it was one of them tethered there.

'Now *two* fingers,' said the man. Amelia seemed to sigh. Sophie stayed her hand and looked at the Master questioningly. He smiled: 'Continue.'

Everyone else in the room sighed with relief.

Two fingers. You could see Amelia's already taut thighs

straining further as she tried to push back and enjoy more of the teasing digits. But she wasn't going anywhere, and Sophie seemed to enjoy keeping her in her place.

'Push them up to the hilt,' said the man. 'That's it, so she feels them against the top of her cervix. Now pull out a little bit.'

Amelia's whole body was moaning silently for relief, her eyelids fluttering frantically. Despite the bindings, her feet drummed against the stool, and her wrists jerked in their bonds.

'Now slide your free hand under her tummy. That's it, so that she can rub her clit against your fingers. Don't help her though. Just keep your thumb there and let her do all the work.'

Amelia was working overtime, rubbing forward against the promising hand then pushing back against the penetrating fingers.

'Such a vulgar maid. Such a greedy, horny little wench,' the Master said.

He pulled back Amelia's hair and stared into her eyes. She opened them reluctantly. 'Tell our guests how disgusting you are.'

'I'm a dirty little girl who needs to come,' Amelia half-sobbed.

'A girl who likes to get finger fucked?'

'Yes, sir,' Amelia sighed, opening up her body for the ongoing fucking.

'A girl who's so lewd she wants the fingers of another girl?'

'Yes! Yes!'

'What else do you want?'

'I want a cock up my crevice, want a man in my mouth, want . . .' she moaned loudly.

'Want three men? Four men? Five men?'

'Yes! Yes! Yes!'

Sophie drove three digits inside her and seemed to push her other hand more firmly against the other girl's clit, giving pleasure from all quarters. Amelia howled with delight and her face creased into the wild, not-quite-human mask of orgasm as she drove her torso down.

'Oh yes, yes, yes! Aaah! Aaaah! Aaaaaaaaaaaaaah!'

Eventually her dancing stopped and Sophie withdrew her hands.

Amelia gulped: 'Please forgive me for shrieking without permission, Master.'

'We'll add a flogging to your punishment book for next week and leave it at that.'

Amelia relaxed in her bonds, and stayed there, for the Master didn't give anyone the order to untie her. Didn't she feel humiliated, her raised red arse on show like this? Was she not shamed that complete strangers had seen her come; seen her beg for it? Charlotte tried to keep her cool. She saw the Master walk over to the chastened slave girl, and saw him reach out to stroke her fevered flesh.

'You get horny again so quickly, don't you, Amelia?' he whispered, as she wriggled her hot globes and tried to direct her lovehole in his direction. 'All tied up like this . . . just waiting for me . . . just begging for my cock.'

'Yes sir.'

Amelia sighed the word; her large eyes closed in near bliss; her full lips parting slightly. The other girls looked left out, abandoned, and sad.

Damn him, thought Charlotte, would he really do this in front of her, in front of the others? They weren't extras in his film set – they were supposed to be his guests!

'I've been ignoring your tits, and I shouldn't have done that, Amelia. I know how much pleasure these hard little nipples can bear.'

So saying, he pushed his trousered groin against the back of her quim and against her arse cheeks. He leaned forward slightly and slid his arms to the front so that his palms cupped her hanging breasts. Leaving her bound over the stool, he played his fingers lightly across her turned-on mammaries until the watchers could see them swelling and darkening in his hands.

'Sophie – suck her nipples. I'm sure she'll return the sensation later.'

The hapless Sophie did as he asked. Amelia sighed as he took his own fingers away.

'Not a word, now,' he warned her. 'Silent excitement.'

She nodded, and trembled as he rubbed his clothed thick cock down her open pussy slit.

He looked huge, Charlotte admitted to herself – did he feel this big to Amelia? Was she wondering what he'd be like when he entered her or had she had him before?

'Happy tits, a wet mound. What else do we pleasure?' whispered the Master. 'How about these delicious little thighs?'

He put his well-versed fingers and thumbs on the back of her legs at the top and stroked along the crease where her bottom ended. He repeated the sensuous movement again and again and again. Amelia shuddered, but obeyed the dictate not to moan. Her face was flushed and damp again. Charlotte wondered if she herself looked flushed too.

This was awkward; hateful. She glared at Guy and Vernon but they were focusing in on the action; on the man still palming the backs of the girl's bound legs. She was wriggling, dripping, and breathing hard – as were the other dancers.

'I think you quite like that, little Amelia,' the Master whispered. Then he turned his attention to her inner thighs.

Amelia went crazy then; bucking so hard she almost rocked the stool over.

'Easy. Control,' said her Master.

Amelia lay prone across the stool with difficulty.

'Every limb seems to be happy,' added the man, smiling mockingly, 'except . . .'

A cunt wasn't a limb, thought Charlotte savagely. She wanted to look away as the man unzipped himself, but somehow she wasn't quite able to. He seemed oblivious to her anyway, his entire being focused on the excitement of this ardent cock-hungry wench.

'I've bought you a present, little slave.' He took his straining manhood out and positioned it at her hugely-aroused entrance. Amelia's mouth tautened in near-rapture. She looked like she'd be begging, if it were allowed. 'Permission given to ask nicely for it, slave.'

'Please, Master, it's more than I deserve, but put your beautiful big cock up me.'

'Up your arse, Amelia? In your mouth?'

'In my quim, sir. It's so wet and hot and ready for you!'

Even the most casual onlooker could see that it was.

'Is it? I may test the waters.'

He slid into her as if she were a tube of warmed oil, and fucked her slowly for long long moments.

'Mmm, not bad. Though we may have you doing vaginal press-ups to keep you nice and tight inside.'

'Yes, sir. And next time, if I'm untied, I'll close my thighs together really firm and grip your cock!'

'Who says I'll want to shaft you again, Amelia? That I'll find you worthy?'

Amelia groaned.

The Master speeded up his thrusts. He'd kept his loose cream trousers on and just unzipped them himself. Charlotte found herself wondering exactly what his bum looked like. Judging by the way he was thrusting, it would be firm and hard-muscled, with . . .

She bit back the thought. Just concentrate on getting through this next few moments; concentrate on not looking overwhelmed by it all.

'Uh,' Amelia was muttering. 'Uh, uh, uh!'

'No noise, remember, my dear, or I'll have to correct you.' He thrust harder, faster.

'Uh,' groaned Amelia. 'Uh, uh, uh.'

'I really should pull out,' said the man, 'and let Sophie discipline you. Maybe I should leave my belt here when I go, and mention to the other dancers that you've been consistently bad . . .'

He kept his voice steady as he spoke. Only the slight tensing-in of his hands on the girl's naked back showed the watchers that he was close to nirvana. But Amelia was closer. As he said the word *bad* she let out a low groan that swiftly turned to an on-and-on-and-on type keening wail.

'Wicked!' muttered her shafter, straining forward. 'Such insubordination hasn't gone unnoticed,' he added, pulling back. He reached for her hot tits and held them like reins as he pushed into her for a final friction. He closed his eyes and leaned forward for a moment of obvious erogenous rapture, and then pulled out.

'She's still noisy when she comes but I'm making allowances,' he said to Charlotte conversationally, zipping himself up. 'She's new.' He paused, before adding, 'Later they learn not to cry out without permission. Though sometimes they need more lessons than you'd believe.'

3

There were lessons galore going on in this place! Ten minutes after he'd finished fucking the ecstatic Amelia, the man continued their grand tour of the Palace.

'Our gym is really exceptional ...' he started as they walked down a corridor lined with differently coloured doors.

Guy paused outside a brown wooden door, as if listening. A long drawn out apology for a wrong answer came from within.

'Could we ...?' he asked, apologetically. 'I remember this room from last year.'

'Be my guest,' said the Master. 'There's an evening class in session, as you can hear.' He indicated a panel in the wall. 'Do you want to watch through the one-way mirror, or go for a more ... hands on approach?'

'Hands on, please,' said Guy, quickly, his fingers already reaching for the handle of the door.

'One moment. I'll summon a guide.' So saying, the Master pressed a button outside the classroom. A moment later a naked youth came hurrying along.

'Show them to the best seats,' said the Master mildly.

The boy bowed, and bid the three guests follow him into the class.

Ten female pupils sat there: all looked to be in their late teens. Dressed in school uniform, they were grouped in two rows of five. Automatically, Charlotte started to walk towards the third empty row behind them, intending to take a seat.

'No,' said the guide, putting a restraining hand on her

38

arm. 'Pupils are punished facing side on to the teacher's table.'

'So?' Charlotte shrugged, not fully understanding.

'So you'll have a better view of their bottoms if you sit along this wall beside the door.'

Vernon was already making for the ringside seats at Guy's prompting. Silently she followed. When she sat down she realised the teacher was staring at her. Despite herself, she blushed.

'If you are comfortable, I'll continue with the lesson,' he said smoothly. Charlotte looked round, but the Master had slipped away.

'The teacher has permission to keep basic discipline in the classroom,' Guy said softly. 'But if he wants to use more severe chastisement, he must check with the Master first.'

Looking at the split infinitives chalked up on the board, Charlotte shivered. Her own grammar teacher had been a heavy-handed man . . .

'We've been doing some complex grammar. Now we're going to show off our spelling,' the teacher continued. A small blonde girl in the front row bit her lip.

'Sandra,' the teacher pointed to her, and she quivered, 'you didn't do too well last week. I hope the extra tuition I gave your bad little body has produced results?'

'Yes, sir.' The girl looked up, flushing, then immediately bowed her head again, 'I've worked really hard.'

'Spell floccinaucinihilipilification,' said the man, with a knowing smile.

Charlotte gasped. 'Is there such a word?' she asked Vernon, doubtfully.

Guy nodded. 'I saw him ask a pupil this one last year, so I looked it up in the dictionary afterwards.' He studied the girl and grinned: 'Bet she gets it wrong.'

The pupil was staring straight ahead, mouth pursed in obvious concentration. 'F-l-o-c-c-i-n-o-c . . .' she began.

'Sorry. It's *nauc* not *no*,' the teacher told her. He shook his head regretfully. 'You must try harder, my child.'

He picked up a polished cane from the desk and played

it through his fingers. He stared at her impassively, and ran it through his hands again. 'Maybe I should ask the Master to make an example of you,' he said thoughtfully.

'Please, sir. No, sir. Just give me the cane.'

'But I caned you on your lazy little backside last week. And here you are, failing in your school work yet again.'

'Please, sir, I did try. I spent hours studying my dictionary. But there are so many words, and I didn't know which ones you'd ask me about.'

'Then you must learn all of them, mustn't you?' said the man quietly. 'How can you help write tomorrow's Rule Books if you don't know how to spell?'

Swallowing hard, the girl hung her head, and wrung her hands together.

'Come out to the front, please, Sandra,' the teacher added, stepping back.

The three guests and the other pupils stared as the small girl got up, pushed her desk forward, and walked towards the teacher's desk. There she stood, staring at the floor.

For the first time, Charlotte could fully inspect the pupil's uniform. Her white blouse was tucked into a short grey pleated skirt. On her feet she wore black patent shoes with a strap and white ankle socks. As everyone examined her she began fidgeting with her tie.

'Hands in front. Over the stool, Sandra.'

As the teacher spoke, he set his stool in front of the blackboard and pointed to the seat. With a whimper, the girl bent over it, trailing her fingertips to the ground. The guests were now facing her backside, still clad in its short grey skirt.

'You know you don't get to keep your skirt over your posterior.' The teacher sounded regretful. 'It wouldn't hurt enough, would it?'

'No, sir,' the girl replied.

'Then pull it up slowly. Show our friends what a bad girl's pants look like.'

Breathing hard, the girl put her hands back and slowly edged up her skirt.

'That's better.'

The man went over and pulled her panties more closely against her waiting buttocks. She had a small bottom, but a perfectly rounded one. 'I think four strokes of the cane are called for,' he said thoughtfully, 'given that this is a repeat offence.'

Charlotte gasped, and the teacher turned to her and smiled enigmatically. Then he fixed his arm, ready to use the stick.

The first stroke went parallel across the cheeks, driving the pantie-clad buttocks inwards. The adult schoolgirl moaned and bucked her rear.

'Less movement, if you please,' said the man calmly. He swung the implement a second time.

The pupil cried out. The sound echoed round the room. The Master looked pleased with himself. The girl's panties seemed to becoming damp with perspiration, for they increasingly showed off the contours of her bottom cheeks.

As the cane made contact with her backside a third time, she reared up from the floor, as if making to rise. Within seconds she realised her mistake, and repositioned herself across the stool.

'Oh dear, we've had chats about this before, you disobedient young whipper-snapper. When receiving a caning, you must keep your fingertips on the floor at all times.'

The girl twisted her tear-stained face to the side to look up at the man.

'I know, sir. I only lapsed for a second. It hurt . . .'

'It's supposed to,' the teacher said. He looked down at her, then tapped the cane against her pants. 'You know the score, Sandra. Failure to keep your fingertips on the floor means you take the rest of the punishment on your bare bum.' He smiled mirthlessly. 'The main thing to be pained will be your pride, dear. Lucky for you that you've only one stroke left to go.'

Guy and Vernon were straining forward now to see the girl's unveiling. Despite herself, Charlotte did likewise: she suspected the girl would have a very pretty little rear.

After looking at the three of them, the pupil flushed, and turned her head away. She brought her hands back, and arched her hips in order to peel off her pants. Slowly she edged the white cotton down over lightly browned skin, revealing a pert young derrière with three parallel marks.

'Edge them down to your knees,' the teacher ordered. He smiled at the guests. 'Leaving some clothes on makes a bothersome little slave girl feel the vulnerability of her naked, punishable quarters even more.'

He took up position again, and played the rod teasingly across her fast-reddening little rump. The girl whimpered, but kept her fingertips in contact with the ground. Her crevice was saturated; sex-scented. You could see and smell her need.

For a second the teacher stood back to admire his handiwork, then he laid on the last measured stroke.

'Sometimes,' he addressed the guests, 'I ask a bad girl to spell a word while I'm punishing her.' He smiled at Charlotte, 'Luckily for Sandra I'm in a good mood tonight.'

'Remind me never to come to one of his spelling lessons,' Charlotte whispered to Vernon, touching his arm gently. She watched, fascinated, as the errant pupil was teased and taunted with the caressing curse of the corrective wand.

'Now stand in the corner for the remainder of the lesson,' said the teacher, sliding his palm across her seat. 'No, keep your pants round your knees, and your skirts hitched up to show you've been a misbehaving girl.'

'Sir, my clit needs . . .'

'Later, when you've earned it. You know the score.'

Squirming with frustration, the girl went to stand in the corner behind the desk, affording the other pupils a perfect view of her chastened rump cheeks.

'We should move on,' said the guide, looking at Guy as if for confirmation. 'The Master wants you to see some of the newer girls put through their exercise class.'

Guy grinned to Vernon: 'You'll love this!'

'For men only, is it?' asked Charlotte sourly as they ignored her again.

· 'No, I'd like you there with me,' Vernon said.

At least he was being civil to her again: that was something! For a moment she feared he'd found out about Jeff . . .

Sensing that they were about to leave, the teacher turned to them. 'Perhaps you'd like to give Sandra something to remember you by before you go?'

Charlotte's eyes widened, and Vernon sucked his breath in.

'Sandra, come over here and lie over my lap,' Guy said.

Still standing motionless, the girl looked over at the teacher, who nodded. Instinctively she reached down to pull up her pants.

'I don't think there's much point,' the man said knowingly.

Reddening, the girl shuffled over; her knickers falling round her ankles like a small loose bond. Her skirt was still tucked up inside the tied waistband of her blouse, revealing her small hot cheeks.

Reaching Guy, she hesitated for a second. He pushed his chair forward so that there was free space at both sides. Staring up at her he patted his trousered lap.

'Hurry up, girl,' he said. 'Don't be shy.'

Behind her, the teacher struck his cane down lightly on the desk top. Hearing the noise, the girl stretched out so that her soft belly was across Guy's thighs. Her head hung down towards the ground, and her hair covered her features. Her legs were taut as she took her weight on her fingertips and straining toes.

'Oh, you have been naughty, haven't you?' Guy said quietly. 'You've been very bad to earn yourself such a hot, sore bum.'

'Yes, sir,' whispered the girl, cringing closer to the ground with embarrassment. Identifying with her confusion, Charlotte looked away.

'It's not nice being spanked by a stranger, is it?' Guy continued.

Despite herself, Charlotte looked back, watching the man's large pale hand meandering over the girl's scarlet seat skin.

'No, sir,' the girl whimpered, writhing a little.

'But then you're not supposed to enjoy it, are you?' Guy grinned.

43

'Please don't hurt me any more, sir – I'll do anything!'

'Will you now?' said Guy, unzipping himself. He pushed her upwards, and she scrambled off his lap, and got down on her knees, putting her trembling full mouth to his protruding phallus.

'That's not what I want. I was just getting him out,' Guy said.

He stood up in front of the girl and she stayed on her knees, looking up at him uncertainly.

'Stretch out over these chairs again,' he said. 'Vernon – hold her wrists.'

Getting up, the girl lay across two chairs, belly downwards. Then Guy pushed her calves towards the ground. By elongating her limbs as much as she was able, her straining toes just reached the floor giving a perfect back view of her quim and her dripping pussy lips. Charlotte stared at Vernon in confusion. Was he going to help Guy? Even as she wondered he took hold of the girl's tensing wrists.

As she watched, swallowing loudly, Guy positioned himself in between the backs of the girl's thighs, his cock against the entrance of her love canal.

'Ask me nicely to fuck you,' he said, rimming round her warm wet hole.

'Please, sir, I want you to stick your cock in me,' whispered the girl, blushing, her hips begging for it.

Pushing in a half-inch, Guy struck her, palms down, on her naked bum.

'I want you to give it to me hard. I want to feel your balls touch my bottom!' the girl gasped, pushing her arse back towards him with even greater enthusiasm.

'Say pretty please,' murmured Guy, circling his hips so that his shaft stirred round and round.

'Pretty please. Pretty please, sir!'

She tugged at the wrists Vernon held as if wishing she could free herself. Presumably she'd then guide Guy's prick right up her, and he'd forget about spanking her hard.

'I don't think you really mean it,' said Guy, sadly, pulling out of her. Rubbing his erection against her nearest thigh, he warned her of all the things he'd do to her bottom if she wasn't good.

'Right, let's try again,' he said. 'This time with feeling.'

'Give me a proper fucking, sir,' begged the girl breathlessly, pushing her rear towards him. 'Stick it right up me and fuck me so hard it feels like your cock is in my throat.'

'That's better,' said Guy, positioning himself at her sex and driving himself in to the upmost. 'God, you're wet,' he said. 'You must have wanted this all along.'

He thrust forward, seemingly oblivious of the teacher, pupils and his two colleagues watching. Charlotte sat there, staring at his muscled thrusting bum.

Now she'd seen it all! It seemed that anything could happen on this island. Who ever would have thought she'd watch her boyfriend's co-worker shoving his cock up some over-age schoolgirl with a well walloped arse? She looked at Vernon's face, but his eyes were focused on the spread legs. He was avidly watching as Guy's shaft thrust in and out.

They both jumped as the girl started to shudder convulsively. Seconds later, a long low wail of euphoria escaped her and echoed round the class. All thoughts of the lesson forgotten, everyone was watching her intently. Charlotte noticed that the teacher seemed to have a hard rod in the area of his crotch as well as in his hands. The pupil's cries obviously finishing him off, Guy came too, moaning his pleasure as his teeth nibbled her smooth young shoulders.

'She'll be a tired little girl. We'll let her go back to her cell now,' the teacher said, and then shaking his head at Vernon: 'Don't let go of her just yet, though.'

He turned to Charlotte: 'Would you like to kiss her bottom better, my dear?'

'No, I would not!'

Charlotte shrank back in her seat, appalled at the suggestion.

'Maybe later ...' the man said with a regretful shrug, and ran his cane through his hands; something he seemed to do habitually. 'In that case, hold her wrists so that your friend here can take his leave of her,' he said.

It sounded like a command rather than a question,

Charlotte thought, moving to take Vernon's place at the girl's head. Anyway, holding her wrists wasn't the same as kissing her arse!

The girl looked up as she imprisoned her wrists, her face tear-streaked and tired.

'Please, don't punish me any more,' she whimpered.

Her words were directed at Charlotte, but it was Vernon who answered.

'I'd rather punish you from the start, and turn your white little bum to scarlet,' he said.

Charlotte looked at him in surprise, but he was concentrating on palming the girl's buttocks.

'I'm going to come back here next week after I've devised a little test for you,' he murmured in her ear. He stared into her eyes for a long silent moment. 'This Inspector gets very angry when a pupil doesn't please him. I hope you don't fail.'

'Sir, please ... can you tell me what it'll be about? I'll study ever so hard.'

'General knowledge,' said Vernon, winking at Guy.

He spent a few more moments stroking her arse, whilst she writhed and whimpered. 'Sweet dreams,' he said, standing up to go.

Charlotte stared at the small camera hanging limply round his neck: so much for the photo sessions! She glanced down at his nether regions, realising they were far from limp ...

So, seeing a disobedient damsel being thrashed obviously did something for him! Judging by the swell of his crotch, the spectacle had affected him in a big way. He'd always loved being sucked and having his balls guzzled; she hadn't realised watching a caning turned him on too.

As they moved on through the Master's Palace, she considered exactly what this could mean to their relationship. Vernon seemed to be going off her, yet she didn't want their liaison to end; she wanted to continue living in his luxurious flat. Okay, she didn't love him – she loved Jeff – but she did like him. And she liked their lifestyle. And she liked the fact that they could afford to travel like this.

Charlotte mused over the situation as they walked on through the Master's Palace. If only she could use Vernon's new sexual inclinations to her own advantage without, of course, suffering the lash herself.

4

Vernon reached for the top button of Charlotte's dress and feverishly pushed it through the buttonhole. His cock had been throbbing for hours, since they'd first been shown into the Scarlet Room. Then when he'd touched the haunches of that punished over-age schoolgirl he'd thought his balls would explode with wanting. Such tender curves!

Now, an hour later, the Master had shown himself and Charlotte into a guest bedroom with a king size four-poster. They were to be left alone here for the remainder of the night . . .

He reached for Charlotte's second button and she smiled at him lazily. Not for the first time, he wished she'd move her arse and undress him too.

'Want to be fucked?' he whispered, rubbing his erection against her inner thighs.

'Mmm. Might do.'

She had that come-get-me look in her eyes.

She was horny all right – but lethargic with it. She would lie back and let him have her; she would come, and would quickly go to sleep. What he really wanted was a woman who'd go down on him occasionally, or just slide her tongue into his mouth, and make promising thrusting movements. He wanted a woman who'd make an effort, pushing her tits together to provide a hollow in which he could shoot his load . . .

He had her safari dress peeled down to the waist now, and he reached breathlessly behind her to undo the flesh-coloured bra which pushed up her cleavage. Her breasts sprung free; the nipples red, swollen and hard; hard and lengthening. He licked them in turn, feeling them expand and quiver inside his lips.

'Tell me you want it, baby.'

He wanted her to talk dirty. He wanted her to say what the other girls this evening had said: please and pretty please and fuck me deep.

'I want it,' Charlotte murmured, reaching out for him. Still, he couldn't help feeling she was thinking of someone else.

'Where do you want it?' he muttered, unzipping himself and starting to lick at her neck, and nibble at her shoulders.

'Use your imagination,' said Charlotte. He put his cock against her crevice and plunged right in. He saw her look of surprise: normally he pleasured her tits and arse for ages till she squealed. But he was desperate and she was very wet, and soon they were bucking feverishly away.

Thrusting forward into the velvet underground, he wondered who Guy was enjoying right now. This place was Paradise for the single man; girls ripe for the plucking, for words which rhymed with the same; girls who walked around showing off their shaven pubes and tits of various sizes; girls whose hands and mouths had been exquisitely trained to please.

His cock jerked at the memory, and Charlotte inhaled sharply. He could see her growing agitation in the way her fingers were tightening in his hair. He pulled back a little, just to tease her, and grinned as she grabbed his arse and pulled him back in.

'I think you like seeing other women. I think you get off on it,' he gasped raggedly. 'I think you enjoy seeing their small pale bums turn salmon pink.'

'I . . .' Charlotte closed her eyes, seemingly unsure how best to answer. Vernon increased his speed, delighted when she gasped.

He put a heavy palm on each full tit and closed his fingers around the swell, palpating them gently. He felt the nipples push eagerly against his hands.

'Imagine being tied down like that in the clearing, Charlotte.'

Her heated nipples hardened.

'Picture all these lewd spectators gathered round.'

'Yeah, sure!' she muttered, but her voice was thick with excitement.

'I wonder if you'd have rubbed against the vibrator?'

Another moan.

'Or shoved your slit down hard against young Sophie's hand and begged her to finger fuck you more?'

'Fuck you, Vernon!'

He thrust in more fully, wishing she'd do some of the work. He transferred his palms to her bottom and pulled her roughly against him till it seemed like his very belly was joined to hers.

'I could forbid you to come.'

She whimpered, and wound her arms round his neck.

'I could keep you on the edge, just hovering.'

She was going over the top now – he could feel it. Her thighs were trembling, and clamping closer together; her firm arse was lifting off the bed.

'Just stick it up me hard!' she whimpered, flushing all over. She opened her mouth in a silent wail – and came.

Mouth against her shoulder, hands sliding the journey to her breasts to knead and tease them, Vernon felt his own triumph beginning to build. He stared at her face: the mouth open in a pout, the fevered cheeks. He saw her gasp, inhale; her eyelids flickering as she felt the incredible pulsing down below.

'Jesus!' He strained more fully into her, feeling the ecstatic gush leave his body. His balls emptied and emptied. He groaned his lust. 'Charlotte . . . baby,' he said, feeling a rush of love for her.

Moments later, he withdrew and took her in his arms, only to find she was asleep.

'Let's explore the woods,' he said the following morning.

'Count me out,' said Charlotte, concentrating on her breakfast of pancakes with pineapple and cream.

'Want seconds!' He held a particularly tempting piece of fruit to her lips, but she ignored him.

'You and that creep Guy can do what you like. I'll stay here and read my book.'

So he'd gone alone, feeling an increasing anger and rage towards her. Guy had been busy with some cock-craving maid, so he'd spent a solitary two hours in the bush, and had come back to find Charlotte flirting with the teaboy. She'd been wearing her skimpiest denim shorts; the legs newly frayed so that they just covered her pubic area and a tiny portion of thigh.

When he'd walked in she'd been bending over the mattress, pretending to smooth the mosquito net. The boy was staring, as he was meant to, at her delectable little rear. Both had the grace to blush when he entered, and the boy covered his erection. Charlotte had several of her buttons undone, revealing her throat and her shoulders and the flesh that followed down. She must have been flashing her tits almost to the nipple, showing the lad the shadowy promise between her breasts . . .

Once, they'd have laughed about this; rolled about on the bed together. Her flirting with another man would merely have been a prelude to an incredible session with Vernon himself. Now he wasn't so sure she wouldn't go further than flirting; that she would have taken that youth's jerking hard rod and fed it between her receptive legs.

For months now he'd felt she'd needed warming up a little. He'd said so half-jokingly to Guy at work, and Guy had said he knew just the place. The man had gone on about knowing the right people, and the need for discretion. He'd thought he'd been exaggerating at the time.

But it was all true – and more! Much more! He'd told himself that if the constant naked flesh and fornication didn't get Charlotte going, nothing would. Yet when he'd made love to her last night she hadn't tried too hard; she'd soon turned away from him and fallen asleep. And since they'd arrived here, she'd continued to be unfriendly, even rude.

He sighed. Guy had been urging him to do this from the start, but he'd hoped it wouldn't be necessary. Yet drastic measures were obviously called for now.

'Charlotte,' sending the tea boy away, he addressed her.

'We've had another message from the Master. He's putting on a special floorshow for the two of us tonight.'

'Is he now?'

Despite her casual tone, her eyes widened and her skin glowed: he could tell she was elated. He wondered how she'd feel when she got there and saw the show. What with paying the outlay for the plane and fuel bills, this trip was costing him a lot of money. It had better be good . . .

It was. Arriving at the Palace that evening, they were met by a young female servant.

'Boy this way,' she said, handing Vernon over to another guide. 'Girl comes with me.'

Shrugging, Charlotte followed her along the corridor. Vernon stared after her, mentally saying goodbye.

Seconds later, the Master appeared by his side. 'Come into the lounge for drinks,' he said quietly, touching Vernon's arm.

'What'll you do to . . .?'

'She'll be taken away and stripped. She'll doubtless be a little frisky, so the boys will fit a mild restraint. Then we'll bring her into the Inauguration Hall.'

Vernon nodded and gratefully accepted a whisky – alcohol being reserved strictly for the guests – from a curtseying maid servant.

'You'll be seated behind one of our special mirrors,' added the man. 'Charlotte won't know that you're there.'

'And you'll . . . start her off gently?'

'She's your property. You can decide how far we go.'

Another naked girl came into the lounge and nodded. 'She's ready. She struck out at her enslaver, so we had to tie her wrists.'

'The enslaver can be the one who punishes her tonight then,' said the Master, smiling gently. 'I'm sure he wants a little revenge on her more tender parts.'

He turned to Vernon.

'That is, assuming she needs punishing. You've given us a list of her faults, but if she repents . . .' He signalled to the girl to pour Vernon another whisky. 'Anyway, come see for yourself. The one way mirror's over here.'

Picking up his glass, Vernon followed him to what looked like a five-foot square window. It had a two-seater velvet settee behind it, on which he was invited to sit. To his surprise the girl who brought him his whisky curled up beside him.

'This is Suki,' the Master said. 'She'll do whatever you want whilst you're our guest.' He took a seat far in the background. 'We've arranged for Suki to have a little room just off from your suite. Enjoy.'

Vernon smiled down at the girl, who returned the gesture. She was about five foot two, with coffee coloured skin that looked soft and invited your fingers to lightly touch. Heavy-looking breasts were topped with juicy dark nipples. Her tummy was slightly rounded, her thighs firm.

Sensing his curiosity, she stood up and turned round slowly. The movement showed him her curvy bottom, and the fact that her raven-black straight hair reached halfway down her back. The hair on her pubes was similarly untrimmed, a bushy black haven. He wondered how her sex lips would look . . .

'Let the inauguration begin,' said the Master quietly. Vernon looked through the one way mirror to see Charlotte being led into the hall. She was naked, save for leather thongs binding her wrists together in front of her. A collar round her neck was attached to a long leash, with which her enslaver was pulling her into the room.

'You'll not get away with this! I'll tell Vernon!' Her words carried to him easily. They must have a loudspeaker system, for it sounded as though she was speaking into his ear. He felt momentarily guilty, and wondered if he should ask for her to be liberated.

'Remember, you gave her several chances,' the Master said.

As if in agreement, Suki nuzzled against his arm and looked up at him endearingly. Vernon felt his balls twitch and his cock start to rise. Fighting back desire, he stared right in front of him. He couldn't be unfaithful to Charlotte this soon . . .

'Kneel,' said the enslaver now, jerking at Charlotte's

lead a little. When she ignored him he took her shoulders and forced her onto her knees.

'Bastard!' she said. 'I'll get you! I'll report you!' She pushed her tethered arms forward the little she could, obviously wishing they held a gun.

Seconds later she tried to get up again, and the enslaver ordered that her feet be tied. One of the several boys who were watching the spectacle obliged. Vernon wondered if this main enslaver was some kind of second-in-command. He was older than the other youths, in his mid-thirties, strong and tall.

'You've been wicked,' he said now. 'You've displeased your partner.'

'Go fuck yourself,' said Charlotte. Her eyes flashed fire.

'I'm giving you a chance to repent, to become a better person,' the man continued, sounding almost ministerial.

'Gee, thanks!' Charlotte mocked, spitting in the direction of his face.

The spittle fell far short of him, but his features darkened.

'Take her over to the chair,' he said. The boy holding her lead started to pull on it mightily. Charlotte resisted for a few seconds, making slight gagging sounds as the collar tightened round her neck. When the lead was taut between them and the boy kept pulling, she was forced to move her feet.

Slowly the boy dragged her over to a large well-upholstered armless chair with a high broad back. As Vernon watched, the second-in-command enslaver strolled over to it and got himself seated comfortably in place.

'I'm waiting,' he murmured, patting at his lap and gazing up at Charlotte. Despite her stalling, she was pulled nearer and nearer her fate.

When the boy had drawn her to the side of the chair, he looked at the man for confirmation.

'Over my knee like a bad little girl,' the man said. Grinning, the boy used one hand to draw the leash down, and pressed the other firmly on her shoulders. After a few seconds of resistance, Charlotte was stretched over the waiting knee.

As Vernon watched, the boy played out the leash, still attached to Charlotte's collar, till it reached a metal ring in the floor some distance from the special chair. Carefully he fed it through and tied it. Charlotte was now tethered in place. With her hands and ankles also bound, she was a helpless victim. Obviously enjoying this, the man began to run his right palm over her unmarked bum.

'It's a nice little arse. A disobedient arse,' he said quietly. 'And disobedient arses have to learn how to behave.' Vernon saw Charlotte tense her bottom and close her eyes tightly. She opened them wide again as the first slap came stinging down.

'Aaah! Aaah!'

She cried out as each subsequent slap warmed her posterior.

'It really hurts, your first spanking,' Suki whispered. 'The flesh is so unused . . .'

Vernon stared at the man's large hands ricocheting off Charlotte's rounded bottom. She was certainly wriggling like crazy in her bonds!

'The first spanking lasts a long time,' added Suki, her eyes dreamy. As if in confirmation, the hand beat down and down. Both buttocks were growing pinker by the second. When an eager maid came along to suck the man to orgasm, he called to one of the larger boys to take his place.

Hard-on jerking, the boy supported Charlotte by the belly whilst her tormentor slid out from under her. Then he slipped into the chair and started to arouse her with youthful zeal.

'Please don't tease!' moaned Charlotte, as he flicked his fingers over her nipples till they stood to attention.

'You should have thought of the consequences before you were rude,' said the spanker, playing his thumbs around her ardent nipples.

Finally, when her tits were swollen with wanting, he stopped and nodded to the older, now well-milked enslaver. 'Sir, I think she's seen the error of her ways, and will obey.' Grimacing to show he wasn't convinced, the older man approached with a measured tread.

'She's been very insubordinate so far,' he said, squatting beside her haunches and fingering them. 'I think a longer lesson may be required.'

'No! I'll do what you want. Please don't spank or tease me any more,' whimpered Charlotte, trying to rise from her well-leashed position.

'We only chastise you if you fail us,' the man explained. 'Tell me you've deserved this little spanking,' he added lightly, still stroking her bum.

Charlotte blushed with the humiliation of it all, and earned herself an extra hard spank.

'She's wasting her time making a noise,' the Master cut in quietly. 'Her trainer will stop when she truly repents of her wicked ways.' He paused. 'What a fuss the girl's making! It's hard to believe we're breaking her in slowly. Why, some of the girl's have an inauguration that's much more demanding than this!'

Suki nodded.

'After my first spanking, I was strapped onto the Punishment Bench and received the knout across my bottom. It was on fire!'

'Ah, but you didn't have a boyfriend who wanted us to be gentle with you,' said the Master with slight amusement. 'Your little rump was all mine to do as I pleased with from the start.'

'Yes, Master. Thank you, Master,' Suki whispered. She rubbed her quim against Vernon's right thigh as he stared at the show.

Charlotte had stopped fighting her superiors now; her buttocks were flushed and frantic.

'Please . . . anything,' she whimpered, moving her tied arms and legs the little she could.

'Tell me you deserved that spanking,' said her tormentor, holding his large palm in the air so she could see it.

'I deserved that spanking, sir,' Charlotte said.

'That's better.'

The man ran his hands over her posterior for long, tense moments.

'Tell me you deserved to feel my right hand on your arse.'

'I . . . deserved to feel your right hand on my arse, sir,' mumbled Charlotte, blushing further. She hung her head, and stared at the floor.

'Tell me you've been a naughty girl.'

'I . . . I've been a naughty girl, sir.'

Vernon listened unbelievingly: it was amazing, his haughty Charlotte saying all this!

'How naughty?' asked the man, playing his fingers over her buttocks again.

'Naughty enough to receive a sound spanking,' Charlotte croaked.

'There, but it's all over now, providing you're good,' explained the man, looking covetously at the twitching buttocks.

'Thank you, sir,' said Charlotte, uncertainly, still wriggling whenever she was touched.

'We'll just do one last little test to show you've learned humility,' her tormentor added easily. 'Say thank you, sir.'

'Thank you, sir,' said Charlotte, with obvious difficulty. Her eyes were closed tight again, as if saying such demeaning words actually hurt. Vernon stared at her hanging breasts, at her raised red bottom. It was incredible to see her like this!

As he watched, the second-in-command ordered the other slaves in the room to form a line facing the disciplined new slave girl. Then he instructed that her leash be left attached to her collar, but freed from the metal ring. Slowly, making allowances for the restrictions of her closely-tied wrists and ankles, he helped her to her feet.

'Give your new friends a kiss of welcome,' he said, pointing to the lascivious line-up.

Colouring more deeply than her bottom, Charlotte started to obey. It took her a long time to cross the few yards, her walk an uncertain bound shuffle. Reaching the first slave girl, she kissed her lightly on both cheeks, and looked back to her tormentor for approval. Tapping his right hand against his thigh, he shook his head.

Grimacing, Charlotte inhaled deeply, then kissed the girl full on the lips: trembling punished mouth, to smiling assured mouth. Again she looked back and again the man showed by his gestures that she'd got it wrong.

'Mouth to their *more sensitive* lips, my dear – after all, we're all adults,' he said encouragingly. 'Plant a kiss on that horny little rose-bud between her legs.'

Quivering, Charlotte sank to her knees before the girl and inclined her head towards the rough patch of hair. Half-heartedly she licked in the general direction, and shuffled along on her knees to the boy who was next. Her eyes widening at his hard vastness, she took his tip in her mouth and started sucking.

'Slaves who pleasure the boys more than the girls can earn themselves extra correction,' the enslaver said.

Charlotte moved on to the next quim and began to kiss it with flickering-tongued enthusiasm. In turn, the younger girl groaned and clutched her pleasure-giver's head.

'Now the next boy,' said the man. 'Give his balls a sucking.'

Charlotte did.

The watchers grew hard.

'Return the favour, boy – but keep these lips teasing a little,' said the man directing the action. Charlotte lay down without further prompting and spread her legs apart. She tilted her hips up with enthusiasm as the boy's head trailed down, down, down.

'Oh, yes!' she whispered, as his tongue found her thrill-bound tip, and his insistent licking forced the little hood back. 'Oh, God, that feels brilliant. Please keep licking just there!'

The boy did. Charlotte pushed her body closer to his mouth; her sore bum obviously forgotten. Or was the feel of its chastened curves just adding to her excitement as she rubbed against the rug?

'Down a bit, please,' she whimpered, as her rhythm quickened.

'No, up a bit,' said the enslaver. 'That's right, boy. Keep her there for a while, tease her famished little cunt.'

As Vernon stared at the labial licking taking place before him, Suki cuddled up at his side, her full lips gently nuzzling his arm. Slowly she worked her way to the flat planes of his belly, just waiting for him to give the word before her mouth slid further down. It was difficult, he admitted to himself, to discern which he was enjoying most – her caresses or Charlotte's frustrated pleas.

5

The cell had gold and white embossed wallpaper, a rich bronze carpet, and a golden chaise longue. Nevertheless, its small contours, plus the bars which formed the door and one tiny window, defined it as a cell rather than a proper room.

Lying on her belly on the chaise, Charlotte stared round with eyes that were still tear-filled from her inauguration moments before. Two of the guides had carried her back and left her here. One of them had smiled: 'For the next two months this is to be your home.'

She sat up slightly, turning on her side to protect her throbbing buttocks. Her gaze took in several empty book-shelves built into the wall beside the door. A large painting – of a girl kneeling beneath the sun – dominated the wall opposite the window. A thickly upholstered saffron col-oured armchair and matching footstool were the only other items of furniture in the room.

She looked more closely, seeking a wardrobe or a cabi-net. Where was she to store her clothes when they returned her personal things? Goddamnit, they hadn't even given her a blanket to cover her nakedness; to cover her sore red flesh . . .

She stared towards the door, towards the window. No one was watching. They all seemed to have slipped off to their own quarters or wherever it was they went. Satisfied that she was truly alone, she raised herself up on her arms and looked back at her bottom. Despite the differing sever-ity of the hand slaps they'd dealt her, both rounded cheeks were a uniform red.

How dare they! How dare *he*! If it had even been the Master himself who'd punished her, it wouldn't have been so bad. She bit back the thought: it was ridiculous. No man had the right to pull her over his lap!

She winced, remembering the humiliation. Not to mention the shock of the pain. Somehow she'd thought of a spanking as something trivial and child-like. But a man's hand coming down hard on your bare posterior hurt like hell.

Strangely curious, she laid one of her own palms against her punished contours. The area felt hot, like holding a roasted pumpkin in her hand. She could imagine what it must have looked like, jerking and wriggling. Such an ordeal to endure by a stranger's hand.

She shut her eyes at the memory. Could Vernon really have ordered this; her easy-going Vern? He'd always done everything she wanted, and been so malleable. Okay, so they hadn't been getting on these past few months, but even so . . .

She hadn't been suspicious when the guide took her away from him earlier that evening. She'd assumed she was to watch a different show. Her tummy had been fluttering with anticipation as she'd imagined some naked girl being sternly corrected. She'd found it hard to breathe.

Even when the guide had led her into a room containing two boys and a girl, she hadn't been alarmed. One had been clutching a collar and leash, the other some leather restraints. Charlotte had smiled at them both and looked round for a place to sit, to watch the action. She'd assumed the bondage gear was for the pretty young guide . . .

But the men had stepped forward and grabbed her by the shoulders. As they held her the girl had torn her safari dress down the front. She'd kicked and screamed as they slid it from her arms, telling her that she was to be prepared for chastisement. Her struggles had increased till the girl rushed back to help, holding her ankles together in a surprisingly strong grip.

'Submit. Accept your nature,' the girl had said. 'You are one of us. You simply haven't recognised it yet.'

Whilst the first man continued to grip her arms the other had gone to the wall cupboard and brought out some large scissors. Charlotte glimpsed several riding crops, a paddle and a studded belt. Dispassionately the female cut her bra and briefs from her body, exposing her creamy contours. Then she pulled her sandals off, leaving her without a covering stitch.

Then – oh disgrace! oh mercy! – they'd wound the collar round her neck and buckled it there, its thick presence somehow reinforcing her naked shame. They had fastened on a long leash with a loop for the owner to put his hand through, as if she was some untrained little pup.

'*Walkies!*' the largest man had said, exerting a cruel pull on her thorax. 'Good bitch,' he'd laughed, patting her head.

She'd struck out then: she'd hit some part of someone, and heard them cry out. Then her wrists had been grabbed again by one of the men, who smirked at her pains. She'd cursed him as her arms were pulled forward, and heavy leather thongs were looped round her wrists and tied firmly in place. The girl had let go of her ankles, leaving her shuffling on the spot.

The feeling of helplessness got worse after that. It was awful to have her arms bound before her, as if in prayer. She remembered how poor Sandra's hindquarters had suffered in the school room, and her own haunches had felt hugely vulnerable and exposed. Any second now the Master might come and use his belt on her and she wouldn't be able to protect her posterior to a single degree . . .

She trembled, and her inner thighs tightened. Her sex felt strangely moist: she must be perspiring between her legs. It was no wonder, with teenage girls and youths staring at her breasts and bottom; staring and commanding and tugging on her leash to take her to God knows where . . .

. . . To what they called the Inauguration Hall. That's when the man had corrected her. Her bum had hurt so much after the spanking, she'd have said whatever he wanted her to say. She'd only hesitated a moment after his instructions, galled at the humiliation of repeating such embarrassing words.

I deserved that spanking. Any woman would have faltered before saying it. She'd never said anything like that to the people closest to her. Not even to the priest as a child at confession. Not even, as an adult, to Vernon or Jeff!

Jeff. She must have been missing him all day, subconsciously. That explained the wet strands glistening between her restless legs. She'd met him when she had her first riding lesson. Since then he'd been her very favourite ride . . .

Now, reminiscing on her chaise longue in the cell, she touched herself lightly, spreading apart her labia. At their first meeting there'd been lots of ten-year-olds queueing up for pony rides.

'Who's running this place?' she'd asked a teenage girl carrying a bucket.

'Over there. That's the Stables' owner, Mr Wilde.'

Charlotte had walked towards the tall dark figure, knowing she looked good in the sunlight. As she got closer, she smiled widely. He nodded, but didn't smile back. Most men grinned at her approvingly, showing their appreciation of her beauty, if only with their eyes.

'Mr Wilde?'

'Jeff.'

'I'm a beginner.'

'I'd never have guessed,' he said, with a lazy grin.

Slightly disconcerted, Charlotte had looked away, her eyes taking in the hurrying adolescents in their hard hats, and the kiddies with their tiny riding crops and leather boots.

'Got a horse strong enough for us bigger girls?' she had asked, lightly.

She had wondered if she sounded as nervous as she felt. In truth, she was fighting shy of the horses. A pal had talked her into this for a dare.

'You're not *that* big. Bet you don't weigh more than eight and a half stone.'

Jeff had looked her up and down keenly. His eyes

63

measured her arse in the hired jodhpurs, weighed the firm but large breasts beneath the crisp white blouse.

'Nine stone, actually,' she grinned. 'But most of it's muscle.'

'I can believe it.'

He looked like he had muscles of his own.

'This is my first time,' she added, aware of the *double entendre*.

'Then we must break you in gently.'

His voice held a less teasing tone.

One hand on the small of her back, he guided her to the third stable in the row, where a black beauty snorted and stared. 'Satan doesn't often get ridden. He's not for the tiny tots.'

'Adults only?' Charlotte joked, hugely aware of the man's scent, and presence. She stood well clear of the massive horse.

'We'll soon get you mounted.'

'Lucky me!'

Her words sounded breathless. Jess called a shy-faced adolescent over, and she quickly put the required tack on the impressive beast.

Unsure what to do with her hands, Charlotte clasped them behind her back as she followed Jeff and the girl into the indoor arena where the lesson was to be conducted. For a few seconds they faced each other, standing at the head of the horse.

'Allow me,' Jeff murmured, putting both hands beneath one of Charlotte's uncertain thighs and pushing upwards. Effortlessly, he lifted her into the cool hard saddle. As she sat there she could still feel the pressure of his fingers. Horse muscle rippled underneath her seat.

'I don't want a crop,' she said thoughtlessly, wanting to keep the conversation going.

He raised his eyes and looked at her appraisingly.

'Are you sure?'

Charlotte blushed and looked away. When she looked back he was still staring at her. She watched children drift in, and saw them allocated ponies and smaller horses by the mainly youthful staff.

Jeff started the lesson, issuing clear instructions to the riders: 'Bring your horses into a wide circle near the fence, and start walking around.'

Obediently most of the steeds got into position without prompting. Jeff led Charlotte's horse himself, whilst continuing to give instructions to the group.

Walk. Trot. Take your feet out of the stirrups. Place them back in. Straighten your back. Tighten your legs at the sides.

'The horse'll sense if you're not in command,' he warned her as she hunched forward a little, holding on to the reins much too tightly.

'I'm not!' she grinned, knowing her limitations.

But *he* obviously was . . .

When it was time to trot he stood back and let her get on with it. Satan took off, galloping at twice the rate of the other mounts.

'Whoa! Good boy!'

Charlotte leaned forward and hung on, her mouth grimacing in terror. Pale faces blurred into one another as she galloped past. Could she hold on much longer? Her knees were gripping the horseflesh. But they were beginning to weaken. Soon she'd fall . . .

She didn't. As if bored with the game, the horse slowed again. Jeff caught up with her.

'He's hot to trot!' he said.

His look said more. Much more. Charlotte felt her crotch turn to liquid heat.

'A ride worth waiting for?' he asked as the hour ended. She nodded, not trusting herself to speak.

'I'll book another lesson. See you next week,' she started, awkwardly.

'Come for a drink in my office and see me now!'

They both knew there was the possibility of more than coffee beans on the menu. Still they kept up the pretence, waving as the other equine enthusiasts drifted away. Long moments later they climbed the rickety stairs to the loft where he did his paperwork, her side brushing intermittently against his.

'We grown up riders must stick together,' he murmured, opening the door for her then closing it behind them with deliberate slowness. 'Makes a change to escape from the Kiddie Club out there!'

'I suppose the job has its advantages?'

'I'm hoping so.'

Suddenly nervous, she looked past him, her eyes seeking a kettle. 'How about that coffee?'

'If that's what you want.'

He was an attractive man – unnerving. She exhaled as quietly as she could as he turned away and switched a coffee-maker on.

'Why do a job when you can get someone or something else to do it for you?' he said, coolly.

'Why indeed?'

Her shoulders felt stiff as she shrugged. A silence descended.

'So, am I your oldest ever rider?' she blurted, anxious to break the quiet.

'No, but you're the most interesting.'

'Oh?'

Usually she was fairly confident and verbal. Her voice caught on the single soft-spoken note. She leaned forward to tug off her constricting riding boots.

'Riveting,' Jeff continued, staring at the dark hollow between her heaving breasts.

'Then I must rivet you further – come back for future lessons . . .'

'I think you need a lot.'

He started to walk towards her. She trembled. Was he going to make a move? Maybe once he'd touched her she could relax and be herself again.

'I'll just find out if you're saddle sore,' he said, reaching her and walking round to the back of her chair. She held her breath.

'Inspection time.'

He tapped his fingers impatiently on her chairback.

Flushing, she stood up. He put his strong hands on her bottom, then squeezed. 'I'd better just check your flanks out properly,' he said.

She breathed faster and faster. What did that mean? Actions spoke louder than words as he slid his fingers into her waistband, teasing round the edge of her micro-pants.

'What if someone comes in?' she whispered, feeling the hot need slake through her system.

'They'll get an extra bit of tutoring,' he said.

He reached for the button on her jodhpurs, and undid it. He pulled the zip down, easing the rich material over the swell of her butt.

'Nice,' he murmured, moving to untie the silken tassels at the side of her panties. 'Very nice,' he added, running his palms up and down her bum as if examining a horse.

'Want to see my teeth?' she said, half-sarcastically.

'Only if they're nibbling my cock,' Jeff answered, entwining his fingers none too gently in her hair. Guiding her down to her knees, he pulled his jodhpurs and jockstrap down. His saltily-scented scrotum was inches from her face.

'Hot to trot?' he whispered throatily.

She tongued his hardness.

'God! I need a proper ride!' he said.

Putting his hands beneath her armpits he pulled her up, only to guide her to the desk and push her over it.

'Doggy style. The way the animals do it,' he instructed, fingers tracing her spine. She felt his cock nudge at her entrance, pushed back towards it. 'Easy. Easy. A ride lasts an hour,' he said.

Whimpering, she felt his palms cup her breasts; his thumbs rimming round the nipples. Round and round and round and round and round.

Her areolae were on fire. She couldn't bear it! As the exquisite heat swelled through her flesh she raised her arse and pushed back again.

'Please . . . I need . . .'

'Say it,' he murmured.

She shook her head, and put her hand back to try and guide him in.

'Ask for my cock inside you.'

He was calm but insistent. And God, these calm insistent

67

thumbs, turning her tits to fleshy flames, making her desperate!

'You know I want it.'

It was hard to get the words out. Wetness was running down her legs, and had somehow smeared over her lower belly and soaked her tummy button. Her thighs were slick with increasing need.

'Ask for my cock inside you.'

He was like a broken record. Same voice, same movements, doing incredible things to her swelling clitoris.

'Please. I want . . .'

She could feel him positioned just at her entrance. Her passage felt cavernous and urgently needed filling.

He stayed there, tantalising her with his manhood. She tried to wriggle him in unawares, but he held her firmly against the desk. Gently his left hand stroked down to her tummy, and then moved down further still, brushing for an exquisite second at her horny hole, making her beg.

'Oh God! Take me! Fuck me!'

'Tell me you want my cock inside you,' Jeff said.

'I want your cock inside me – right up me! I want you to thrust right up my greedy little quim!'

For a second she thought he was still holding back, and her mind groped for more words of persuasion. Then he rammed into her, turning the aching throb into the promise of a come.

'How hard do you want it?' he muttered, his teeth raking her earlobe.

'Hard. Very hard! Ram it into me, please!'

She felt filled with him. Her thighs were taut with need for him. He gripped her shoulders, and moved on to rub at her tits. Then he reared back a little, keeping his cock half in as he kneaded the perfect globes of her arse.

'You like being ridden?' he hissed through clenched teeth.

'I love it.' She was shameless now, arching back.

'What do you love?'

'Your cock inside me.'

'Because it's a new cock?'

'Because you use it so well.'

She could feel his hot breath on her neck, though his voice remained cool and efficient.

'Tell me what it does for you.'

'It makes me so wantful, so wet . . .'

'It makes you feel squirmy.' He circled his hips round so that his cock stirred her quim, and she did indeed wriggle and arch further.

'Yes . . . please . . .' She couldn't see. Couldn't breathe. Couldn't think.

'Your arse keeps wriggling when I thrust into you. Is it sore from being in the saddle?'

'I don't know . . . maybe a little . . .' All she could think about was the pleasurable pain between her legs.

'How does this bit feel?'

Jeff's hand came round and brushed at her clit with butterfly soft caresses. He drove forward at the same time, then pulled back, and removed his hand. He pushed forward and cradled the swollen rosebud once again. She moaned.

'I asked you a question.'

He sounded like he did when giving the riding lesson.

'It feels . . . It makes me want to come,' she gasped.

'Does it now?'

He thrust and stroked and momentarily withheld her pleasure.

'Please . . . I *need*. Put your hand back,' she begged.

'You *want*,' he corrected, keeping his fingers distant. 'I'll decide what you need when you're over my desk like this.'

'I want. Jeff – please. I want! I want!'

She heard his snorting laugh as he teased his hand back in place, increased the rhythm of his shaft, and maintained the steady friction near the clit.

'Aaah . . . aaah!'

Almost instantly she felt herself peaking. She shrieked moments later as the waves went from *mons* to belly, and she tightened her thighs into a cock-squeezing grip.

'Oh God! Oh God!'

She collapsed over the desk; her face in her folded arms;

her mouth gaping open. Jeff kept driving into her, forcing the last of the sweetness out through her now relaxing limbs.

'I loved that,' she murmured, staring at the desk top, her *mons* still pulsing. And he came, pushing forward as though the flesh on his belly could fuse with the soft strength of her back and arse.

Afterwards they lay curled on his office floor, her legs entwined with his.

'Let's go and shower back at my place,' he said. 'Then have dinner, an early night.'

Regretfully, Charlotte shook her head and kissed him on the lips to show how much she liked him.

'There's someone else . . .'

She saw the sharpness of his look, the momentary anger. 'Oh, not a husband. Just Vernon. We've lived together for eight months or so.' She shrugged. 'I'm not working at the moment, so he pays the bills and things. He's a photographer. I did a bit of modelling for him, and we sort of clicked.'

She didn't say much more: didn't feel she had to. Jeff was a brilliant lay, and they'd both enjoyed it. Why should she apologise for her faithless streak?

'Wicked,' he murmured, his tone half of approval, half of condemnation. He touched her arse. 'The poor man thinks this lovely derrière is all his.'

'It's all mine,' Charlotte said sharply, pulling away from him. She felt strangely irritated yet inflamed.

'I could make it mine,' Jeff said, starting to stroke her languorously again, God, he could! He could! Charlotte shuddered, remembering the past few months. He'd made her come at least once every time they met, sometimes three times. He'd brought her to squeals with his fingers, his tongue, and his ever-ready shaft. His hands seemed made to lift and palm her bottom. Just the sound of his strangely impassive voice could make her wet.

She was wet now. Very wet. There was still no one in the vicinity of her Training Grounds cell. Dare she . . .? Tentatively Charlotte put her right hand between her legs, and stroked her middle finger over the warm mound.

'Jeff,' she whispered, reliving another session they'd had at the stables some weeks before. With grooms working just yards away he'd fucked her from behind as she faced the stable door.

Charlotte slipped two fingers inside her leaking lips, and moved them up to her throbbing rosebud. Both their heads and shoulders had been visible at the open top half of the stable; their trousers were round their ankles as they bucked away.

'The riders'll be back at any second,' she'd muttered, grinding her hips back, trying to make his pleasure explode more quickly.

'They'll see more than the mare getting its oats then,' he'd answered, thrusting oh-so-slowly into her aching quim.

He'd made her moan like a bitch on heat; made her cry out for him. Remembering, Charlotte started the exquisite round touches that would ensure her ultimate release.

'Do it to me,' she whispered, closing her eyes and licking her lips till they glistened. In her mind, she could see Jeff's tongue on her pulsing clit.

God, it was incredible, the feeling of mouth flesh against clit flesh; the feeling of male wet upon female wet, that light constant touch. Her fingers slid up and down her inner lips, increasing the slipperiness. They moved back to the centre of her pleasure and teased the tip.

Jeff could hold her like this for ages – her legs tensed hard, her bottom raised in silent pleading. Soon her mouth would ask him – beg him – to let her come.

'Has Vernon made you come this week? Have you been soiled?'

The bastard always had the ability to make her feel small.

There was nothing small about her breasts now – they swelled and surged with pleasure. She shifted her position on the chaise, edging her body to its open end so that she could scissor her legs more widely apart. She could feel the material growing damp and sticky beneath her; she imagined her fluids coating Jeff's hardened flesh.

71

'I've been dirty,' she whispered into the silence. 'I'm *being* dirty.'

The words made her belly contract and her *mons* pulsate. Jeff always wanted to be the one to pleasure her, she acknowledged, running her fingers tantalisingly down the hot wet slit.

But Jeff wasn't here – and she needed to come urgently! Her practised fingers would ably do. Inhaling and tensing, she teased her middle fingers round the beating bud. Round and round and round.

Images flashed through her mind: of herself on her hands and knees; of her lover entering her; of him licking between her legs; of her feverishly tonguing his heavy balls, licking his inner thighs and kissing his arse, and ... The frenzied pleasure coursed through her and she clamped her still-moving hand in place and groaned out loud.

For a few moments she lay there, her eyes tightly closed, her legs immobile through rigor mortis. Her entire universe felt centred on the molten passion that had raced through her private walls. Gradually the fierce heat dulled to a fluttering warmth and she looked dazedly around her. She let her hand slide from her labia and rest on one slick-smeared thigh.

God, she was wet! She touched herself more fully, and looked at her fingers and the lengthening threads of lust that hung from each. Her mound felt like a swamp. Her legs stuck together. She looked round her cell, realising that it didn't contain a wash hand basin, far less a bath or shower. How long did they intend to leave her like this, like a savage? How long would it be until Vernon saw the error of his ways and had her released?

Exhausted, she slept. When she woke up there was a tray of food in the cell, laid on a little golden four-wheeled trolley. Someone must have pushed it in silently as she slept. She sat up, then jumped as a woman's face appeared at the doorway; well, the prison bars which passed for a door, at any rate.

'Ah, you're awake. I came earlier.'

This woman must have brought the food. She must have

studied her nakedness, and watched her troubled dreams. Awkwardly, Charlotte put both hands over her pubes, wishing she could cover her nipples.

'I wouldn't bother to hide anything. I've seen it all before.'

So saying, the woman unlocked the door and strode in to sit on the armchair. She patted her hand between her outstretched legs: 'Come here, girl. Now.'

She was wearing a black leather dress, but Charlotte could see from where she was sitting that there were no panties underneath. Strong black pubic hair matched the long raven tresses that framed her shoulders and much of her lightly-tanned upper tits.

'No,' said Charlotte, scrabbling back and pushing her knees more tightly together. If she stood up the woman would see her soaking labia, and know she'd been playing with herself!

'So. You defy me?'

'I defy you.'

This woman had brought the food, so was presumably just like Sophie the dancer: some jumped-up maid.

'I'm Karo. It is a tradition of the Training Grounds that the new slaves please me.'

'I'm not your slave.'

'You are, deep inside.'

This was getting them nowhere! Charlotte tore her gaze away, and let it flicker round the cell in search of diversions. Still there was something compelling about the woman; something . . . demanding. You couldn't just pretend she wasn't there; not when she sat four feet away, displaying her exotic dark crotch, looking at your secret parts.

'New slaves should show their humility by licking Karo.'

'Karo can go to hell!' Charlotte said.

The woman's eyes narrowed almost imperceptibly.

'Hell's for bad girls. I'm sure they reserve it for slaves.'

She smiled a cold smile: 'You do realise you're being bad, don't you Charlotte? You'll remember your disobedience when . . .' She broke off. 'But you'll find out soon enough – probably tomorrow.' She slapped her hands together. 'You'll learn a lot of painful lessons then.'

She stood up to go, and Charlotte's eyes moved longingly to the food tray. She could see slices of ham and crusty bread and salad, and a crystal glass which looked like it contained the native drink. Would the maid take her food away again as a punishment? Would they let her go hungry on her very first night as a slave?

As if reading her thoughts, the woman picked up the tray and brought it over to Charlotte, resting its strength on the girls trembling nude belly; cold metal against hot flesh. For a second her fingers curled in the younger girl's pubic hair, and tugged down.

'Eat. Rest,' she said, staring at the wanton wetness. She slid one sure finger inside Charlotte till she cried out. Smiling, Karo withdrew the soaking digit. 'You'll need your strength for the training which awaits.'

6

Charlotte turned dreamily on her side, murmuring endearments. She was with Jeff for the morning, Vernon having left for work. Jeff never came to the flat – he said that was Vernon's domain. She always had to go to him at the stables like some hired help.

Still, when she did turn up, it was worth it! The stables held numerous avenues for adulterous sex. She smiled as Jeff approached and inserted his hard cock in the ravine of her cleavage, and grimaced as she realised she needed it in her throbbing canal instead.

It was unusually warm in the stables today. She smelt perfume, then opened her eyes to find she'd been dreaming; that she was still in her Training Grounds cell. A girl – the girl wearing the perfume – was smiling down at her. She was small and pale. As she bent forward her pert breasts stayed upright rather than becoming pendulous as larger appendages did.

'The Master says to enjoy your breakfast.'

She set a loaded tray on the trolley, then knelt at the foot of the chaise. Charlotte's mouth watered at the scent of coffee, at the sight of some dish golden with eggs. Eagerly, she reached for it and ate it, tasting unfamiliar roast meat and succulent vegetables. The girl watched through long dark eyelashes, looking pleased.

When she'd finished eating, Charlotte poured herself a second coffee. That maid last night had said that she would need her strength. She looked at the naked girl still awaiting instructions.

'Have you eaten?'

The girl nodded: 'The Master likes us to have an enjoyable start to the day.'

'Uh huh!' Reluctantly, Charlotte drained the last of the beverage. Fear and excitement vied for supremacy in her stomach. Excitement won. 'So – what happens now? Where are you taking me?'

'To the Artist's Studio. That is, after you've bathed.'

'There are showers nearby?'

The intimate juice had dried overnight on her labia, leaving them feeling faintly itchy. She smelt of sex.

In answer, the girl walked to the large painting. She pressed at a tiny golden flower towards the foot of the frame, and the picture slid back.

Even from the chaise, Charlotte could see a bath, a shower and a toilet.

'And there are saunas and steam baths and jacuzzis just down the corridor,' the girl said.

'Can I . . . can anyone use them?'

'Anyone that's been good,' the girl replied.

Charlotte looked away, refusing to pursue that line of enquiry.

'I'll wait for you,' the girl added, beckoning for her to go and have her bath. Shyly, Charlotte stood up and walked towards the six foot gap in the wall, aware of the girl's gaze on her bottom. She stepped through it, and looked round, realising she didn't know how to close the gap again.

'How do I get some privacy around here?' she muttered.

'There are no secrets from the Master, or from his friends.'

'Maybe it's time someone changed that!'

The guide didn't respond.

Shrugging, Charlotte dipped a toe in the luxurious bubble bath which had mysteriously already been prepared for her. The water was just right – hot, but not uncomfortably so. She stepped in and sank down, feeling it take the last of the stiffness from her hips.

Was it only yesterday that this poor bottom had wriggled and squirmed beneath a male palm? The flesh felt cool now, and didn't hurt at all. Reaching for the scented soap, Charlotte rubbed it over her hair and body, and used the shower spray provided to direct a warm rinse over her head.

This was more like it! No bath at home had ever been so exquisite! For a half hour she lay there, occasionally adding hot water to the long deep tub. Finally she heard a buzzer sound, and heard her little slave guide answer. The girl appeared next to the bath and smiled: 'Can you please finish your ablutions? The Master would like you to be at your work place in half an hour.'

She wasn't going to argue – she didn't want to receive another spanking! Hadn't she heard him say that correction hurt even more if your bottom was wet? Charlotte got slowly out of the water and wrapped herself in a large fluffy towel. Her hair, she noted, was already drying in the strong heat of the island sun. At home she'd have needed fifteen minutes with the hairdryer. It had its advantages, being here . . .

'Lead the way!' she smiled, continuing to hold the towel over her nakedness. Firmly the girl took it from her, leaving her naked yet again, then indicated a line along the wall. She pressed the line and a small chute appeared – a laundry chute. The girl pushed the towel down the chute and it disappeared.

'You will do that daily after you bathe,' she explained mildly. 'It is an offence to keep a towel or any clothing in your cell.'

Madness! Charlotte shrugged and stalked out of the bathroom. The girl followed and did something to cause the gap to shut.

'Now we go to the Artist's Studio,' she said happily.

'I'm to have painting lessons?'

'No. You're to decorate the outside.'

She was to be a glorified whitewasher! Charlotte's heart shrank as she was led towards a building. As she neared it she could see that only the top foot and a half of brickwork was covered with a cream undercoat. Three other naked girls were balanced on ladders, adding to the cream covering. Their fleshy promise was visible for all to see. They turned and glanced at Charlotte for scarcely a second before exuberantly turning back to their tasks.

'You are to work here.'

The girl pointed to a bare piece of wall near the roof and indicated a spare ladder. Feeling her bottom jiggling slightly, Charlotte took the proffered brush and paint tin, and climbed. Setting her tin on an upper rung, she turned back to her retreating friend and called: 'What's your name?'

'My name isn't important. The well-being of the Grounds is what counts.'

These girls were ridiculous! Still smarting at their strange philosophy, Charlotte started to paint the smooth new brick.

After a few moments she stopped to study the girl nearest her. Her short blonde hair was raggedly cut to frame her small timid face.

'Have you been doing this long?' Charlotte asked, indicating the brush and undercoat. The girl stared.

'Four days.'

It seemed an eternity before she answered. The other girl was also staring at Charlotte now. Both looked guilty and confused.

'It's all right,' said the third girl to the second. 'Talking's not forbidden today.'

Talking's not forbidden!

'Lucky us!' said Charlotte, with a sarcastic sneer.

The girl next to her rushed to explain.

'Sometimes if the work's not going quickly enough we're forbidden to waste time in chatter. If you forget ...' She rubbed one hand over her naked backside. Leaning ever so slightly back from the ladder, Charlotte could see that the bottom being consoled was a dull pink colour. Obviously it had been touched by more than a hand in the last two days ...

'What happened?'

'What happened to me isn't important. It's the well-being of ...'

'... Yeah, I know, the Training Grounds,' Charlotte

said, dipping her brush more savagely in the paint. For a few moments she worked in silence. Questions swirled through her head.

'Why are we painting this anyway?'

'To please the Master. To make it look pretty.'

'Why does he need an Artist's Studio?'

'To fulfil the creative needs of some of his guests.'

'And if the guests aren't interested the place just remains empty?'

'No, there are girls being trained in the fine arts even as we speak.'

Were there now! Charlotte promised herself she'd check this out later. She'd seen a door that was bolted from the outside as she was led round by the guide. For now though she'd go along with this painting lark. After being largely cooped up in that plane for days on end, she could use some exercise.

Later the guide reappeared carrying a lunch tray. Was it midday? 1 p.m.? Charlotte cursed the fact that the Master had taken her watch along with her clothes. It felt strange having no control over basic things like when you ate or worked or slept. Wearily she sprawled on the grass with the other two decorators. 'Don't you hate this?'

'We love it here.'

'Even being naked in front of the men?'

'It brings pleasure to the guests at the Training Grounds,' said the shyest girl, blushing slightly.

The bolder one answered that she liked the feel of the sun on her buttocks and breasts.

'Thank God the only guests here at the moment are my boyfriend and his colleague!' Charlotte added. At the thought of total strangers from the outside world coming to examine her, her lower belly fluttered and her *mons* felt strange.

'We're getting this ready for the next guests who're due in six and a half weeks,' the bolder girl said. 'We must serve them well.'

My God – she'd still have a few days left here, assuming Vernon didn't have her released till they were due to leave the island. He wouldn't! He couldn't! She couldn't bear it: unknown men gloating over her exposed flesh, perhaps watching her being prepared for the cane. She could imagine being held down and stretched out; made to say things; made to beg; made to come . . .

'Back to work,' said both girls as some beautiful flute music floated over the island. 'That's the signal for mealtimes starting and ending,' the nearest one explained. Grabbing a last slice of a sweet golden fruit she walked towards her ladder with it clutched in both hands.

Sated, Charlotte walked slowly towards her own ladder and ascended. As the sun intensified, a boy came over with a hose and sprayed them with a scented lotion to protect their skin.

'They think of everything here,' said the shy girl, gratefully.

Tell me about it, thought Charlotte, remembering how they'd made the little dancer in the Scarlet Room grip the stool and count out her punishment all over again.

As she worked, her arms began to feel stiff, her shoulders rebelling at the constant stretching.

'I'm stopping for a breather,' she said.

Both girls looked appalled: 'You can't! Not without permission.'

'Wanna bet?' Charlotte said, checking surreptitiously that there were no overseers around. A vast expanse of green grounds and coloured buildings were all that was visible for as far as she could see. She and her two co-workers were the only people in sight.

Paint was dripping down between her breasts and smeared over her belly. No one could expect her to keep going in this kind of a state!

'You can work through the tiredness – you can rest when the music comes,' said the quietest girl gently.

'That bastard won't tell me what I can and cannot do!'

'Who . . .?'

Both girls stared at her as she descended the ladder.

'Your Master of course. He's a bastard! He's had me treated like shit!'

'He's wonderful.'

80

The bolder girl glared at Charlotte.

'I hate him,' Charlotte said.

'We love him. Take that back,' whispered the small shy girl, clenching her fists.

'Go paint yourself into a corner!' sneered Charlotte, turning to walk away.

The brush struck her towards the centre of her back. She looked round quickly. The small girl was staring at her, now brushless. After a moment's hesitation, Charlotte walked away round the building, out of sight. Her back ached where the brush had hit it, but she refused to give either girl any satisfaction by turning to examine the spot.

When she reached the door she'd noticed earlier, she paused and checked that she was still on her own; that no one was watching. The bolts on the outside were now bolted in place. Softly she seized one and pulled it slowly back. Stretching up on tiptoe and ignoring the tightness in her shoulders, she undid the top bolt. She swung the door cautiously inwards, and looked around.

She was facing a flight of stone stairs which twisted downwards. Carerfully, Charlotte closed the door behind her and began the slow descent. After a few moments she reached another door and peered through its spy-hole. It led into what looked like a lounge bar. No one lounged.

Again she entered, drawing back as she saw the huge window into the Artist's Studio. Three girls sat at easels holding charcoal sticks. Each wore a painting smock which barely covered her pudenda. The smocks had holes cut out round the areolae, showing their thick pink nipples to full effect.

Like triplets, the girls shifted in time on their stools, obviously ill at ease or in discomfort. A man was walking round and round, inspecting them. He carried a thick brown strap. Its two thongs looked deliberately stiffened. Charlotte recognised it from the history books as a tawse.

The tutor turned suddenly towards the window and she closed her eyes and pitied her bottom. He must have seen her – he must have! But he looked blankly through her and started to pace again.

Was he blind? Waiting until his back was turned, Charlotte gestured towards one of the artistic girls. Again the girl looked her way but didn't focus or otherwise register her illicit presence at all. Gradually Charlotte realised that she was looking in a one way mirror – they couldn't see her! Giggling, she curled up on the love-seat before it and relaxed.

But there was no relaxation for the artists.

'Babs, that line is far too smudged,' said the tutor reproachfully. He rested his right hand on the girl's ample backside. He struck the tawse lightly against his own leg, once, twice, three times. 'You really are much too careless. You know that I won't stand for shoddiness of any kind.'

'Sorry, sir,' the girl whispered, shifting on her stool with increasing agitation. She licked lips that had obviously gone dry.

'Sorry isn't enough to excuse low standards though, is it, Barbara?'

'No, sir.' The girl blushed and hung her head.

'What do we do to big girls who've been disobedient?'

'We punish them, sir.'

'And where do we punish them?'

The girl inhaled and hesitated: 'On their lazy backsides.'

'That's right.' The tutor ran the tawse over the visible portion of her still-seated bottom. 'And what position does the bad girl get into?'

'She touches her toes.'

'She touches her toes,' the man repeated with some satisfaction. 'Don't you think you should be touching your toes, then, Babs?'

'Yes, sir.'

Without further prompting, the girl got to her feet and slowly edged her smock up until it displayed her fleshy haunches. Holding her rolled garment under her armpits, she bent as far as she could go.

'How many strokes should a girl get for not trying hard in the Art Class?'

'Three strokes, sir. Please, sir.'

'Only three?'

'Five, then.'

The girl wriggled awkwardly.

'Ten, if you don't keep that pretty arse still.'

'Yes, sir. Thank you, sir.'

Charlotte felt her tummy quiver. How could they say such things before they'd even felt a single lash? It was different for her: she'd only broken down after being disciplined. Had these girls no shame?

As she stared, the tutor stepped back and sized up the considerable expanse of buttock meat before him. When he struck, the leather went over both cheeks creating a crimson crease. The girl winced as he struck again, more quickly.

'We must pay more attention. We must do better in class,' he said, putting tawse to tender flesh.

The other girls worked on, though they wriggled even more than they had previously. One girl's smock rode up slightly, revealing reddened flesh. So she too had bared her bottom earlier in the lesson. Had she also wet herself? Her smock was looking increasingly damp . . .

Charlotte shifted on the love seat, which suddenly felt too small for her.

'Five,' said the man with some satisfaction and let the hand holding the tawse fall to his side. The bottom was now glowing, and looked even larger.

'Maintain the position for ten minutes,' said the tutor, 'whilst you reflect on the importance of being a good little girl.'

'Yes, sir. Thank you sir.'

Presumably there'd be nothing happening now for some moments. Reminding herself that this was what she often did when she was bored, Charlotte let her hand rest between her legs. The tension of being watched in the bath and of being stretched naked upon a ladder must have built up and up in her . . . Staring at the failed artist's blushing rear and fondling her swollen sex lips, she quickly came.

Babs continued to stand in place, her taut thighs leading up to chastened globes that looked quite delectable. Charlotte stared at the unbroken skin. The tutor was staring too, approaching, and speaking.

'Let's see how creative you can be with my cock.'

'Yes, sir!'

The girl backed over to a desk, her features lighting up fast. She lowered herself down so that her back was upon it and the soles of her feet were flat on the floor.

'Put your paint brush up me, sir,' she murmured, reaching for his trouser zip, her sex lips opening greedily to receive his satiation-bringing shaft.

Charlotte felt fervent again, then flinched – someone was coming! Voices and footsteps were approaching the lounge where she sat! Jumping up, she looked wildly round the room for a hiding place, then hurried to the space behind the bar and crouched down.

'. . . wasn't built when you came here last,' she heard the Master's voice saying.

'Always something new to look forward to,' came the gloating reply. She recognised the second speaker as Guy, and trembled at the prospect of him seeing her unclothed like this. As they walked into the room, she froze into position, muttering a silent prayer. If they looked sideways now they would see her. If they walked on she'd be hidden by the front of the bar and could relax.

They walked on. Something which felt oddly like disappointment plummeted in her stomach. She really must be bored if she was spoiling for a fight!

'Drink?' she heard the Master ask. Her nipples tightened.

'No, your guide poured me one in the lounge off the Dance Hall,' said Guy. 'And a second in the Synchronised Swimming Lounge.'

'That's another of our newer delights,' confirmed the Master. 'These silly girls will keep getting the movements out of order . . .'

'I saw one of them whipped through her wet white costume,' confirmed Guy gleefully. 'Despite the material, you could still see her arse going pink.'

Worse and worse! Charlotte held her breath and held her

stomach in. Her knees felt shaky. Her breasts felt heavy on this, their second day without a bra.

'This tutor keeps a specially big ruler in his desk,' the Master was saying. 'Sometimes he uses it to warm up the girls before they receive the tawse.'

'Do you think it's best to heat the skin first then, or just go for the more severe punishment?' Guy asked conversationally. Having had enough, Charlotte crept towards the door. Even if they did see her it wouldn't be so bad as listening to this self-satisfied conversation. Anyway, if Guy was around she might be able to find Vernon, and persuade him to take her away from this impossible place . . .

She crept forward, close to the ground, scarcely breathing. Surely they'd see her? She crept a few paces more. And more. And more. They'd left the door ajar, but she had to edge it open by another few feet to make her exit. Surely they'd feel the slight draught and sense the movement as she made her escape?

They didn't. She crept up the stairs, and reached the top landing. She tried the outer door nervously, fearful that they'd locked it from the inside and removed the key. They hadn't. She edged the door open. A few seconds later she was safely back in the outside world.

Correction, in the strange sinister world of the island. Not that the Master was as in control as he seemed to think! Why, today she'd left her painting post – and nothing had happened. She'd spied on the girls and wanked herself off, and hadn't been punished at all! Now as she wandered around the Artist's Studio, she heard flute music playing. Girls and youths started to walk from all directions towards the huge building that contained her own cell.

It was painted golden on the outside, just like the inside. Determined not to do what she was told, Charlotte sat down on the grass. Naked figures stared at her for a second before hurrying on to their quarters. In a few moments, they'd all disappeared inside.

For a while Charlotte sat there, then she walked on again, past an orange building, and then a red building. None of them had names. Most were bolted from the outside. All seemed empty. She didn't have the energy left to find out for sure.

Her stomach rumbled. It seemed ages since she'd eaten that delicious fruit at lunchtime. A girl walked past her in school uniform heading towards the Classroom. Her short skirt billowed out in the breeze, showing her pants. Her head bowed, her eyes gazing downwards, she was obviously concentrating on holding her folder and four heavy-looking books.

'Hey, how do I get some food around here?' shouted Charlotte.

The girl winced and kept walking, answering softly as she continued her pace: 'Your evening meal will have been left in your cell. As a co-worker will have told you, it's served when the flute music's played.'

Feeling silly, Charlotte made her way back to the golden building. As she entered she asked herself how she was supposed to find her cell again. She walked down the huge passageway realising that all the cells were absolutely identical. She passed thirty or so, each containing a naked slave-girl or boy.

There were yards of empty corridor between each cell, she realised, quickening her pace, wanting to be enclosed in known surroundings. The bars prevented them from being soundproof but the distance ensured no one else would hear the instructions you were issued with. Or hear your screams . . .

After hurrying the length of the building, she returned to the one vacant cell in the golden block. Without clothes or possessions, you presumably just settle anywhere, she thought.

Uncertainly she pushed the bars open and watched them swing closed and lock behind her. Four slices of white meat, a yam and some salted greens lay on a plate on the golden trolley by the chaise. She tasted the food. It was cold now. So was the herbal tea. Charlotte ate and drank them anyway, then lifted the lid off a small dessert plate. She enjoyed the four dates inside, tasting their spicy-sweet stuffing of cinnamon and sultanas on her tongue.

Five minutes after she'd finished, a boy appeared.

'The Master will see you now.'

'Will he, indeed?' Charlotte stretched out on the chaise, 'And if I don't go?'

Staring at her unsmilingly, the guide undid the leash and collar tied round his waist.

'All right! All right!'

She could at least walk there with some dignity. Swallowing hard, Charlotte followed the youth down the corridor and out of doors. 'Where are we going anyway?'

'To the Medical Centre,' the youth said.

Maybe they were just going to give her a check up. She swallowed harder.

'Why . . .?'

'The Master will explain.'

Charlotte didn't doubt it. Someone here was always explaining something. She only hoped he wasn't going to explain with his hands or his belt!

They walked on in silence. Her legs felt tremulous. They reached a tall blue building and walked in. Her bare feet sank into thick carpets. The cool evening air had been warmed by coal-effect fires. Guy had explained days ago that they had their own electricity generator here.

Vast amounts of money obviously went into this place. And power. Charlotte felt the man's power as she was led into a small white room in which the Master sat. The room held the chair he was sitting in, a wall-mounted cabinet and a long low massage couch with straps. Seeing the couch, its punishing potential, Charlotte got ready to bolt.

But the youth was barring the door, looking at her nude body appraisingly.

'Sit down,' said the Master, indicating the couch.

Uncertainly Charlotte sat, just resting her bottom against the edge of the thing. When they relaxed their attention she would make her move.

The Master stared at her.

'You remember yesterday's somewhat painful inauguration?'

'Yes, sir.'

'And what were you told after it?'

She thought back, choosing her words carefully: 'That I should stay in my cell for the remainder of the night.'

'More specifically?'

'That I should never enter a building without permission.'

'So what were you doing eavesdropping in the Artist's Studio today?'

So they *had* seen her – or someone had! At a loss for words, Charlotte stared nervously at the ground.

'You admit you've been disobedient, girl?' the Master said softly.

'Y . . . yes.'

'And what happens to slaves who are disobedient?'

'They . . .'

She couldn't say it! She couldn't! With a half-sob, Charlotte dashed towards the door.

She managed six wild steps before the Master's hand grabbed for her and gripped her shoulders.

'Who did this to you?' she heard him ask, his fingers prodding at her back.

'What? Oh . . .' She remembered the incident with the paintbrush, 'One of the girls I was painting with. I said something which offended her. It doesn't hurt.'

The Master nodded towards the guide, and he slipped out of the room. Charlotte felt too weak to resist as the Master pushed her back against the couch. She whimpered slightly as he turned her over onto her belly. She knew what was coming next.

'What do you think we should do to someone who spies on others?'

'Spank them,' she whispered, and felt the heavy leather straps being fastened over her ankles and wrists.

'How hard should we spank them, Charlotte?'

'Till they promise they won't do it again.'

She was, she told herself, just asking for a spanking to avoid a whipping. Babs in the Artist's Studio had asked for three strokes and had ultimately received five. If you didn't ask for something they simply disciplined you more soundly. She was beginning to learn . . .

With exquisite slowness, the Master palmed her buttocks. He felt the crease at the top of her thighs, and moved endlessly up to cup the swell of her helpless rear.

'To think we trusted you to be obedient,' he said regretfully. 'To think I'm having to chastise you further on your second day.'

'Please. I won't do it again,' Charlotte whispered.

'I'm going to have to teach your bottom a lesson so that it doesn't,' the Master said.

He lifted his hand up and brought it down with a moderate slap against the swell of her rear end. Charlotte tensed, then relaxed: this wasn't so bad! For a while he punished her at this level; the strokes firm but bearable. She could feel her buttocks heating up; she was hugely aware of each separate cheek; of the dividing cleft; of the swelling leaves of her quim . . .

Suddenly the Master stopped and palmed her arse some more. 'Now we've prepared this wicked little posterior for punishment,' he murmured, 'how many blows do you think your proper spanking should contain?'

Opening her eyes, Charlotte stared at the white sheet which covered the massage couch. She might have known he'd find a way to prolong her humiliation and make her suffer anew.

'Ten,' she said, glad that she wasn't Babs, receiving the tawse on her upturned rear end.

'Ten seems fair,' said the Master, raising his hand again. He brought it down with all the force he could muster, and she screamed and kicked her legs.

Or tried to, for the strong restraints held them. As she moaned and writhed the Master planted three more full-force slaps on her smarting rear. Charlotte cried out and wriggled; her eyes watering. An inarticulate stream of words and sounds issued from her lips.

'The ten whacks aren't negotiable,' the man said, teasing the tormented flesh, 'so save your promises.'

He continued to toast his heavy palm against her throbbing rear. Charlotte sobbed as he quietly counted each correction. Five. Six. Seven. Eight. Nine. Ten.

As the sound of the tenth slap echoed round the room, she twisted her head to one side and cried: 'I hate you!'

'I think not,' said the Master amicably, putting his middle finger in her clamping buttock cleft. He ran his finger slowly down till she tightened further, then moved it round to rest between her soft fleshy lips.

'You're a wet little girl.'

She closed her eyes again. This couldn't be happening!

'An excited little girl. A girl who played with herself earlier today.'

Charlotte gritted her teeth; she tried to imagine herself somewhere else, and couldn't. Someone had seen her bringing herself off. No one had ever seen such things except him . . .

'What were you thinking about when you came, Charlotte – about Babs's poor bottom? Did you imagine it was *your* bottom, Charlotte? Did it make you hot like it's making you hot now?'

'No,' she said. 'No! You're mistaken . . .'

'If you say so,' said the man, taking his hand away.

Damn him, his hand had got her started – she needed to come desperately! She couldn't do anything with her hands and legs tied like this.

'Untie me,' she muttered, trying to push her swollen mound against the couch top. She could go back to her cell and bring herself some urgent release.

'Not yet,' said the Master slowly, returning his attentions to her bottom. He stroked it thoughtfully.

'Did you enjoy your breakfast this morning, my dear?'

'Yes, Mas . . .' She choked back the word. God it must be catching, living in this place. 'Yes!' she snapped, writhing as he continued to touch her, both hands lightly massaging her burning bum.

'And lunch and dinner were equally satisfactory?'

'Uh huh.'

'And you enjoyed a refreshing bath, and a good night's sleep?'

'Yes. Thank you.'

She couldn't fault these aspects of his hospitality.

'And yet you repay me by abandoning your work.'

Again Charlotte felt caught out, helpless.

'I . . . I'm sorry.'

'We're going to have to make you sorry,' said the man.

Charlotte felt the almost familiar lurch in her lower belly. Her groin felt hot and large, and was throbbing needily.

'You've failed at the first task we set you,' continued the Master, running his flattened hand thoughtfully over her punished globes until they tingled further. 'Do you know what happens to workers who fail at their allocated tasks?'

'Don't tell me – you spank them!' muttered Charlotte, awkwardly.

'No, they become pleasure slaves. Though, of course, the guests like punishing them with more than spanks . . .'

He paused.

'I think, in a round about way, you'll enjoy it, Charlotte. You can learn a lot about yourself as a pleasure slave. Of course, most slaves have at least a year to learn the job's . . . er . . . refinements. You'll have to learn within six weeks.'

Charlotte moaned.

'But I'll only be here for eight weeks – it isn't worth it!' She wished the man would stop doing such exquisite things to her arse.

'I'm sure the men who push their cocks between your lips will think it's worth it, Charlotte. I'm sure there'll be no complaints from whoever receives this virgin prize.'

So saying, he touched the entrance to her bottom very gently. She wriggled further. She couldn't take much more! As if reading her thoughts he murmured: 'You'll have to take all I can give you, Charlotte.'

She twisted her head round to see him dipping his middle finger in the contents of a pottery jar.

Oil – it was obviously oil! He put his finger against her anus, confirming this. His finger felt warm and gelatinous. As she whimpered he slid it in a quarter of an inch.

'You've never had a finger in there before, have you Charlotte?'

'No, sir.'

The sentence was out before she had time to bite back the 'sir'.

'Nor anything larger, like a man's cock?'

'No.'

'Such a waste. We must teach you to ask for one nicely,' murmured the man. His finger invaded further. Charlotte groaned softly. This was terrible, yet wonderful. Sensation was building like a pressure cooker between her legs.

'Please. I can't bear it,' she whispered pitifully.

'I've bared it for you, you bad girl,' the Master said.

He slid in a little further, and put his free hand on her pudenda. She pushed against it. And pushed and pushed. He finger-fucked her base as she rubbed herself against his fingers. She came and came; the pleasure starting at her quim, spreading out across her belly and coursing through to her newly invaded arse.

The Master went on teasing her after her orgasm had ended.

'Too much!' she gasped, but he continued to finger the over-sensitive bud's outer contours with feather light strokes.

'That's for me to decide, my dear,' he said, conversationally. 'If I want to play with you for another hour, I will.'

'No! Stop!' Despite her pleas, he continued to torment her. She knew some more humble response was needed, 'Yes, sir. You must finger me for as long as you see fit, sir,' she gasped and he moved his cruel hand away.

'There, that wasn't so difficult, was it?' he asked, calmly.

She shook her head. He squeezed her buttocks hard.

'No, sir. Thank you sir.'

She panted out the words as his fingers threatened to stimulate her throbbing sex lips again.

'You're too tight, though. That's unfortunate.'

Her tummy churned further.

'I'm sorry.'

'Don't be sorry, Charlotte. Just help us make it right.'

Walking over to the cupboard he extracted something, brought it over and held it in front of her.

'An anal plug,' he murmured. 'The smallest size.'

He walked towards her feet, and she felt him undo the ankle straps.

'Spread your legs wide.'

She spread them, feeling wetness pool between her thighs.

'Good girl.'

She felt more oil being poured in the cleft between her buttocks. She felt his fingers probing and opened her legs wider still.

'Good. Good.'

She sensed he'd placed something at the entrance to her anus, and tensed automatically. He slapped both her buttocks hard. The oil seemed to intensify the pain, and add to the ongoing throbbing. She yelped and jerked, then used all her will-power to keep her bottom relaxed.

'That's better. We can do it when we try, can't we, Charlotte?'

'Yes, sir.'

She heard the smile in his voice.

'You'll call me Master one of these days, my dear.'

'Never!'

'Taste my whip on your arse before you say never, my pretty bitch.'

How could he talk down to her like this? How could he!

Her lower belly felt strangely excited again. The plug was now against her arsehole and being pushed forward. She cried out as he slid it in place; not that it stretched her much – it didn't. It was just so alien, so strange.

'I'm being gentle with you, Charlotte.'

She shuddered: 'Thank you, sir.'

'I could have had you fitted with a much thicker plug than this.'

At the prospect she closed her eyes, feeling both horrified and breathless. The Master rotated the plug till she squirmed. 'You won't let me down?'

'No, sir.'

'Silly girl – you don't even know what you're agreeing to!'

He stroked her firmly, reminding her of how sore her bottom was.

'Don't fail me this time. Only take this plug out to answer a call of nature. Then wash it yourself and put it straight back.' She sensed him smile. 'Think of me as you're pushing it back into that cute little rump, Charlotte. And think of the men to come.'

Leaving her still tethered by her wrists, he pressed a button on the wall and the guide who had brought her to the Medical Centre reappeared again.

'Our failed little painter has repented of her ways,' the Master said.

Charlotte closed her eyes, ashamed that the youth was staring at her scolded flesh, her invaded bottom.

'Shall I take her back to her cell, Master?' he said.

'Yes. Her bath has been run. A light supper awaits her.' He spoke as if Charlotte was no longer there.

'And can I . . .?' asked the youth, stroking his erection before laying his cool hand on her hot little derrière.

'No,' said the Master. 'She is reserved for the guests.'

But not for him? Biting back the thought, Charlotte lay quietly as the boy untied her ankles. She got up stiffly, without looking at either of the men. As she moved towards the door, she found the presence of the plug meant she had to keep her thighs slightly further apart than usual. She was sure her walk must look ungainly and strange.

'Sweet dreams, Charlotte,' said the Master, as she walked from the Medical Centre. 'You'll probably want to sleep on your tummy tonight.'

7

Charlotte had orgasmed mainly from having her bottom spanked! Vernon stretched out in his armchair recalling last night's session, feeling himself grow hard. He'd sat behind the one-way mirror at the Medical Centre with Suki; a welcome, purring burden in his lap. He'd seen Charlotte stretched out, tied, her buttocks warmed, and her arse invaded with the little plug. He'd wanted to fuck her there and then whilst she was still hot and wet. He had started to signal to a guide . . .

'Wait a few hours,' Suki had whispered, obviously reluctant to let go of him. 'She'll be wider by then. The plug will have begun its work.'

'And will you watch behind the mirror, my sweet, as I fuck the belligerence from my horny little girlfriend?'

'If you desire it, sir,' murmured Suki. Blushing, she hid her head in his armpit, and wriggled against the arm of the chair.

He'd stroked her hair, then guided her head down to his surging hardness. She'd sucked him off a few times now, her sure lips siphoning off his juice. He came all the more, imagining it trickling down her throat and into her belly. He'd come between her buoyantly bouncing breasts, and he'd exploded whilst rubbing himself in the tight hot cleft of her bottom. He was still being faithful to Charlotte in not going all the way.

Not that he wasn't tempted! Gorgeous as the feel of her velvet tongue was, he couldn't help but be drawn to her other fleshy attractions. He had found himself staring with increasing lust at that coffee coloured Mount of Venus, and that tempting rear. Suki didn't help his self-control; continually rubbing her pubic bone against the bulge in his trousers; bending over to straighten the mattress so that he was treated to the sight of those luscious dusky folds . . .

Now, as he reminisced, she returned from her bath and knelt at the foot of the bed. She smiled gently, and kissed his feet.

'Sir, what are we going to do today?'

'We're going to see Charlotte, my little beauty. The Master has promised we can check on her progress for ourselves.'

'And will you . . .' Suki trailed off, obviously realising she mustn't ask personal questions. 'She will want you back,' she said sadly. 'She will plead for you to take her away to the outside world.'

'That's where you're wrong.'

With some regret, Vernon pushed her head away as it planted little kisses up his calves, his thighs, his stirring scrotum.

'She's to be blindfolded. I'm to wear some of your island essence. She won't know who's pleasuring her unless I speak.' He watched as the native girl relaxed a little. 'Come and watch,' he said, staring into her face, noting how she flinched at the humiliating prospect.

'Yes, sir. Whatever you say, sir.'

'I'll be ramming my cock right up her,' he said with deliberate cruelty. 'She's been missing it a lot.'

He showered and breakfasted, then a guide came and took him and Suki to one of the lounges behind the Pleasure Suite. 'Enjoy,' he said, handing Vernon his favourite drink.

Enjoying himself already, Vernon settled himself on a low couch behind the one way mirror, with Suki by his side. They could see through the glass into the suite; the Master was visible, already seated in one of its many chairs. After a few seconds Charlotte walked in behind a guide, her eyes downcast. Hesitantly she walked up to the Master and stood facing him.

'You have bathed, Charlotte?'

She nodded.

'Your body is ready to receive a man?'

'I . . .?' She shrugged, her mouth twisting helplessly. An excited gleam had come into her eyes.

'He may want to touch all your private places.'

Charlotte swallowed hard.

Vernon watched as the man's hand moved to her arsehole, pushing gently at the obstruction then turning it. Charlotte was just standing before him, like a well-trained dog.

There was a pause. Vernon saw Charlotte shudder slightly. What was she up to?

'I hope you've been keeping your anal plug in place, Charlotte?' the Master said.

'I . . . yes.'

'Because it's time to have an inspection.'

'Oh.' Charlotte looked awkwardly at the floor, and studied her feet.

'Bend over that settee, Charlotte. That's right – legs wide open.'

Vernon pushed Suki away from him so he could get a better view. The man was sliding his hand up Charlotte's inner thighs, making her wriggle. 'Steady,' he kept saying. 'Dear me, we're going to have to teach you some control, girl. You're like a bitch on heat.'

He concentrated on caressing her thighs for long moments. 'Now push your arse out towards me. Right out. Push your legs apart as far as they'll go.'

She did so, and he put his fingers against the divide between her spread cheeks. He palpated the plug, and pushed it in slightly further. Charlotte flinched away.

'Bad girl. Stay still!'

The man struck her twice on her posterior. She flinched again, then kept her bottom in its hugely exposed state. Again the Master played with the plug, pulling it half out, then twisting it round. Charlotte whimpered.

'Are you sure you kept that plug in all night?'

'Yes!'

Her voice was a half sigh. She stared at the settee cover.

The man pushed the plug back in fully and turned her round. 'Come and watch a film, Charlotte, a very special film. Perhaps it'll take your mind off how stretched your poor bottom feels.'

The viewers saw her body relax and watched her cross to the settee and begin to lower herself onto it.

'No. Lie over my knees,' the Master said, sitting down on one of the armless chairs and invitingly patting his lap.

'I won't – you can't make me!'

Charlotte turned and sprinted across the enormous hall. Seeking an exit, her gaze darted about wildly. Shaking his head slightly, the Master signalled to the guide. The boy raced after her and caught her, and sadistically took his time in bringing her back.

'Such impetuousness,' the Master murmured, smiling as the guide tied her wrists together before her. The boy then fastened a leather collar round her neck, added a lead to it, and tied the lead to a ring in the ground. Charlotte thrashed around on the floor as he did so. Only her feebly kicking legs were left free.

Vernon gulped and Suki sighed softly as the boy held her, and stretched her over the Master's lap. Now her pale heaving bottom lay helplessly beneath his roving hands.

'This is nice, now, isn't it?' he murmured, teasingly. There was no answer from his blushing lap girl, though the writhing of her buttocks showed how humiliated she was. As the viewers watched, the Master pressed a button for the film to begin.

Charlotte looked at the video before her, obviously trying to take her mind off the ignominy of her position. As Vernon stared at the screen he saw it was of Charlotte entering a lounge; of Charlotte wanking herself, her fingers moving like crazy; of Charlotte coming, her mouth opened in a drawn out cry.

Charlotte blushed even more hotly as she saw the film. She wriggled on the man's knee, then wriggled further. The screen showed her being led into a golden cell. She was walking with her thighs spread apart, her buttocks pink and glowing.

'Sleep well,' said the guide on the film, closing and locking the bars which made up the door.

The screen Charlotte made a face at his retreating back, then lay down on the chaise and stared at her chastened globes. Lightly, she touched the plug that protruded an inch from her ass. After a moment she shifted position, and grimaced. She moved some more, then reached a hand back and removed the plug. For a second she studied it; studied her liberated anus. Then she threw the plug childishly on the floor.

She slept then, a smile playing about her face intermittently. A clock in the corner of the screen helped the watchers keep time. They saw the film fast-forwarded on to 8 a.m., where she wakened and returned the plug to her arsehole. Seconds later a guide with a trolley appeared.

'So you heard the girl coming and pretended you'd done what you were told,' the Master whispered, stroking Charlotte's recalcitrant bottom. 'Why are you so relentlessly bad?'

'It felt strange! I didn't like it!'

'You didn't give yourself time to like it. You didn't like being naked at first.'

Silence. Charlotte's eyes were closed, her mouth open. Her backside was moving convulsively, her nude stomach rubbing against his trousered lap.

'Such a simple request – and you fail me! I'll have to punish this stubborn young derrière,' the Master said.

'Please, no! It was only punished yesterday!'

'You merely received a spanking,' murmured the man. 'It obviously wasn't enough.'

He moved his thighs so that her bottom was raised further; an inviting target.

'What are you going to do to me?' whispered Charlotte, trying to push her posterior back down.

'What do you think I should do?' the Master replied, coolly.

'Belt her,' said Vernon, softly. Suki shuddered and licked his arm. The guide in the lounge looked over at him.

'Sir, should I tell the Master that?'

'Yes. Ask him to take a light belt across her disobedient little bum.'

Suki took the zip of his trousers between her teeth and pulled it down.

'Sir. I can bring you much more pleasure than the Charlotte woman can,' she said, closing her mouth round his flesh.

The way he was feeling now, he could come with both women! Vernon sat back and enjoyed Suki's tongue on him; enjoyed the scene taking place in the Pleasure Suite. He stared as a whimpering Charlotte was pushed down onto her hands and knees by the Master, and made to walk around like a dog led by her collar and lead.

He saw the guide enter and say something to the Master, who then indicated one of the many cupboards lining the walls. Smiling, the guide approached the largest one, rifled through its contents, and brought out a belt.

'Where should we bind this wicked young pup?' asked the Master, casually. He looked around. 'I think we'll tether it to the four-poster bed.'

As the guide pulled and a sorrowful Charlotte barely resisted, the three of them made their way over to one of the huge four-posters in the Pleasure Suite.

'Spreadeagle her,' said the Master, lightly. Soon Charlotte's arms and legs were scissored far apart and tied to the posts of the bed.

'Now, tell me you deserve to be disciplined,' said the Master, stroking the belt lightly over her buttocks. Charlotte said nothing. The Master teased the belt across her arse. 'Tell me you –'

'I won't say it!'

The man gave her a light taste of the belt.

'Please. Can't I retain some dignity?' The words were half enraged, half sobbed.

'*What* dignity? You're naked. We're all staring at you. You came when I spanked you. You got wet when I forced a little plug up your butt.'

Charlotte was slithering around even more at his words. Vernon looked at Suki, who was growing wetter beside him.

'She holds on to her pride,' whispers Suki. 'She doesn't understand.'

'Tell me you deserve to be disciplined.'

A second leathering.

'Tell me . . .'

'All right! All right!'

'Say it. Say the words, my pretty dear.'

'I deserve to be disciplined. Satisfied?'

The words were there, but it was easy to sense that she was still holding back.

'What do you deserve exactly?'

'To . . .' She buried her face into the pillow, and closed her eyes tightly.

A third stroke, firm and fast.

'Oh, you bastard! I deserve to . . . to feel your belt against my arse!'

'Dear, dear. We mustn't call our Master a bastard. I believe it's not the first time, either. Some more indiscretions to be chalked up in the Punishment Book,' he sighed. 'But for now, we've got you to admit that you've been wicked, that you had to be taught.' He fondled her twitching rear. 'It really hurt, didn't it?' he whispered.

'You know it did!'

'Hurts almost as much as the pleasure you receive when you're good. Think about that . . .'

He touched her tits.

'What was our deal, Charlotte?'

'I'm to become a pleasure slave.'

The words were half-defiant, half-whimpering. The guide sighed.

'Exactly. A *pleasure* slave. And one of our friends wants to take pleasure from your sex right now.'

The guide's cock straightened; Vernon's cock straightened. Suki frowned and took both of his hands.

'Please, sir. I am as hot as she is,' the native girl whispered.

The guide grinned at them both, then turned to Vernon: 'Your woman will be ready for you in five minutes, sir.'

Five minutes – he could hardly wait! Vernon settled

101

down to watch the mirror, noting the Master was still teasing Charlotte's fiery posterior.

'Such a sore little butt,' he murmured sorrowfully. 'I do hope we're teaching it to be good.'

'Yes, I'll be good. So good.' Charlotte was writhing, perspiring.

'I hope you'll please our rampant male friend.'

The Master continued to knead Charlotte's buttocks with varying degrees of severity. When she was subservient he released the pressure; when she was arrogant he increased the force of his grip.

'Untie me, and I'll please your friend with my fingers,' murmured Charlotte, beseechingly.

'No, no, dear. We can't trust you yet not to put a consoling hand on that chastened rear.'

'I won't! I promise.'

'More obedient girls than you have promised. But the temptation to protect those tender globes, to put a cool hand on that well-warmed flesh is just too much.'

The Master smiled.

'In fact, my friend likes bad girls to remain tied up. And he likes them blindfolded. So we're going to tie this scarf over your eyes. It helps concentrate the mind.'

So saying, he took a black cotton square from the nearest guide, and tied it round Charlotte's head, knotting it at the back, checking that she couldn't see anything through it.

'Now await your pleasure, slave,' he said, and pressing a button, the Master nodded.

'He's ready for us,' said the guide. Suki made to follow them, but Vernon kissed her lips, then pushed her back gently in her chair.

'Keep the seat warm for me,' he said softly. 'Watch, and you may learn.'

Breathing hard, he followed the youth through two sets of doors till they entered the Pleasure Suite. It looked even larger inside than it did viewing it from behind the glass.

'Here is your first owner,' said the Master to Charlotte, standing back a little. 'Show by your wetness and your words that you are happy to receive him,' he ordered, before taking a seat at her head.

There was a silence. Vernon stared down at Charlotte's helpless, staked out body. Her rear end was red, and he touched it, revelling in the heat.

'Please sir. Please untie me,' whispered the spreadeagled Charlotte.

Vernon looked at the Master and shook his head.

'Ask only for cock, slave!' warned the Master. 'This man does not waste his time in idle words with his inferiors.'

Charlotte said nothing. Vernon returned his palms to her arse. He stroked round and round till she whimpered. He slapped down on one buttock, then again and again.

'Oh! Oh!'

She wriggled until he made both sides symmetrical. Then she pushed her bottom back the little she could in her bonds.

'I think she's begging to be fucked,' the Master murmured. 'Say it, Charlotte. Beg for a fucking.'

'No!'

She spat the word out angrily into the pillow and pulled at her bonds.

'Your cunt wants it. Your guest knows you want it.'

He indicated to Vernon to check how wet she was. Gently Vernon slid his finger between her closed sex lips. They felt dry on the outside but opened to reveal a cup of gelatinous wetness.

'All that heat rushed to your bum, and some of it reached your pussy,' murmured the Master. 'And now the pussy wants a tom cat to make her come.'

Charlotte buried her head deeper in the pillow, though her buttocks tightened. Vernon slid a hand down the cleft, which was slick and hot.

'You're about to be fucked tied down over a bed. Can you imagine?' murmured the Master. Charlotte moaned quietly. Vernon's cock throbbed within his briefs.

It was strange, the Master watching – the guides watching. He thought of Suki watching from behind the mirror, and his balls felt as if they'd explode. It was lucky he'd allowed his little naked native girl to tongue him to full pleasure twenty minutes before. It meant he could hold out longer now, and make Charlotte writhe against his rock hard cock.

He touched the puckered mouth of her anus, noting the slight redness.

'You've displeased our friend by taking your plug out,' the Master said. 'He has the right to punish you for such misdemeanours. Imagine, Charlotte, if he takes off his belt . . .'

'No. Please. I'll give him such a good time. I'm wet for him.'

'How wet?'

'So wet I can't bear it. I need to come!'

'Only if your owner wishes you to come, you realise.'

'Yes, sir.'

'Yes, *Master*.'

Charlotte refused to repeat the word.

'Teach her manners with your masculine accoutrements,' the Master said, lightly.

Unzipping himself, Vernon placed his cock against the entrance to Charlotte's canal. Tethered and wet as she was, she was easy to enter. He slid in fully, and she gasped and tried to push her hips back to enjoy more cock.

'Greedy,' said the Master. 'Our friend may grow annoyed with you. He may not want to fuck some cheap little tart who's so desperate for his tool.'

'Please . . .' Charlotte's voice was a sigh. The covers were wet beneath her. Vernon half pulled out, before thrusting forward again.

This was exquisite – wonderful! The heat of her arse; of her cunt; her snuffling half-cries. He leaned forward, slid his hands to her front, and cupped her mammaries. The nipples felt hard and tumid; unusually hot.

'More!' whimpered Charlotte again, trying to fight her bonds, to take him in deeper. He slid one hand down her flat belly, and brushed it against her bud. She half-screamed with desire, then squirmed even more desperately. Her clit felt swollen to twice its usual size.

Grinning, Vernon moved his cock out by degrees till just the tip was inside her. Then he played with her sex lips and pussy hair, enjoying her urgent cries.

'Maybe we'll leave you tied up all day,' the Master whispered, 'so you can't touch yourself like a dirty little girl.'

'Please – I need to come! I'll do anything!'

'Like keep your anal plug in overnight?'

'Yes, fit it back now! Stick it in hard! Do anything, anyway, but let me come.'

'Wicked,' murmured the Master. Vernon palmed Charlotte's arse and made her writhe some more.

He rammed into her again and she sighed with relief. 'Please sir, do it to me, sir,' she begged throatily.

'Beg for cock, specifically, Charlotte,' reminded the Master, sounding impressively calm.

'Please, sir. Put your cock inside me, right up me, and fuck me hard.'

'How hard?' asked the Master.

'As hard as he can.'

As aroused as he was, that was *very* hard! Vernon gripped her belly and pulled himself deeper into her quim.

'And how deep?'

'So that he shoots his load right up inside me.'

'She's got a filthy mouth on her,' said the Master quietly. 'She's a dirty little bitch.'

Charlotte cried out, obviously approaching nirvana. Vernon continued to thrust, his own ecstasy drawing near. His balls were getting that incredible almost-almost-almost feeling. The rhythm was speeding up in his hips and in his head.

'We're recording this on film, Charlotte,' the Master said, almost conversationally. 'You'll see yourself taking my belt across your arse.'

Charlotte squirmed and sighed and lifted her hips the little she could in her tied-down position.

'You'll see the way it wriggles. You'll see it going from pink to deepest red.'

Vernon thrust and thrust.

'You'll watch yourself beg for a stranger's cock,' added

105

the Master. Orgasmic yells half-muffled by the pillow, Charlotte came.

Jesus! That sound always finished him off! Muffling his cries into her back, Vernon exploded inside her. He licked her shoulders, pleased that they still tasted the same. Her hair was wet, though, her hairline slicked with perspiration. When he pulled out he saw the river of desire between her legs.

'It's amazing what a good talking to can do,' said the Master, smiling. 'We'll just leave her there for a bit to reflect on her sins.'

Dazed, Vernon stood up and put his well-milked manhood back into his trousers. Staring in the direction of the mirror and wishing he could see through it, he winked towards where he thought Suki would be sitting, and gave her the thumbs up. He was about to thank the Master when the man smiled and indicated the tied-up and blindfolded Charlotte, putting his finger to his lips.

'If sir will accompany me to the lounge,' he said, calmly, 'Sir can relax with a drink.'

A double whisky awaited him behind the mirror, though Suki, as a slave girl, had to make do with a soft tangerine-like drink. Vernon lay back in his chair and sipped the malted spirit. He watched covetously as the maid servant anointed Charlotte's arse. The tumult was abating in his emptied balls; in his sensation-stick. Suki crouched on the floor beside him, her lips to his trousered calves, nuzzling. He could sense her large eyes pleading for attention, but he refused to meet her gaze.

Staring into the mirror he felt a perverse sense of enjoyment. Both women wanted him now; both wanted him to pleasure them hard! He gazed out at his girlfriend's well-oiled softness. Already he wanted to touch her fevered flesh again . . .

As he watched, a guide came in and undid the bonds which held Charlotte's arms and legs to the bed's corners. After a moment of flexing each limb, she crawled into a kneeling position on the bed.

'You've done well,' said the Master, striding through the hall towards her.

The watchers noted her flush of pleasure.

'Thank you, sir.'

'You can go back to your cell and rest till after lunch. I'll send a maid to wash your hair – another bath awaits you.' He paused and winked. 'A *cool* bath, of course!'

Charlotte blushed.

Sighing, Suki curled her hands round Vernon's ankles. Then she tugged off his sandals and licked his soles. Her tongue slid insistently between each toe, and he sighed with satisfaction as her wetness teased each cavity. Then her teeth nipped gently at his lower legs.

She traced her kisses behind his knees, slipping her tongue into each hollow. Her lips moved closer and closer to his hirsute thighs. He was vaguely aware of her hands beginning to ride upwards as he watched the Charlotte he'd just fucked to orgasm being led from the room.

8

'Today you will meet your Mistress.'

Waking up from a lengthy sleep, Charlotte blinked the confusion from her eyes.

'My *Mistress?*' She stared blankly at the girl who'd brought her food yesterday. As her gaze settled on the tray, she realised she'd brought her breakfast again.

'Meet your Mistress. Yes.' Smiling, the girl took up her post kneeling at the foot of the chaise longue. Slowly Charlotte reached for a plate of yoghurt and apricots.

'You mean the Master is married?' she asked, feeling vaguely disappointed.

'No. The Master belongs to no one except himself.' The girl paused. 'Nor does the Mistress.'

'Then they're not related at all?'

Again the other girl hesitated.

'Some say that they are brother and sister. They have a similar dignity. And they can both punish equally hard.'

'Great!' muttered Charlotte. She finished the creamy fruit compote and picked up the coffee pot, pouring herself a generous cup. Then she reached for the buttery croissant and wedge of crumbly yellow cheese. 'My compliments to the cook,' she said, finishing the remains of the repast. 'Obviously well trained!'

'The cookery training is rigorous. Very painful.'

Charlotte winced and moved her small bottom against the floor. 'Remind me never to enrol for classes, then.'

'They're compulsory. We have to learn everything in time.' The slave crouched closer to the ground and her gaze became downcast. 'Girls have been here for years and are still getting things wrong.'

Charlotte swallowed, then reminded herself that her training here was of two months' duration.

'Should I have my bath now?' she asked.

'Yes. It is ready.'

'That makes two of us, then!'

Sticky in the early morning warmth, Charlotte walked self-consciously up to the painting and pressed the flower. The picture moved back, revealing her bubble-rich bath. She felt ridiculously pleased. Eagerly she soaped herself, being gentle with her hindquarters. Despite yesterday's extra bath and a night spent sleeping on her tummy, her buttocks were still pink today. She'd have to be extra careful not to earn another lambasting. She couldn't bear new heat on this already tanned skin . . .

'Mistress will see you now.' The girl's voice quavered. 'Be good,' she added. 'Don't displease.'

Charlotte wrapped herself in the towel, and then gave it up reluctantly.

'How can I please her?'

As if afraid to answer, the slave shook her head.

Wordlessly, they walked from the golden building, through the vast empty Training Grounds.

'Where are the other workers?' asked Charlotte.

'Still sleeping. Mistress likes to make an early start.'

'Just my luck to meet her while I'm still tired!' Charlotte murmured.

The girl looked alarmed. 'Be alert.'

They walked to a one storey block painted a glossy black colour. The girl pressed a buzzer, and a guide opened and ushered them indoors. As she led the way, Charlotte could see the guide's buttocks were crisscrossed. She walked gingerly; her hips were obviously still stiff.

'Mistress, may I beg your indulgence? You have visitors.' So saying, the guide bowed and ushered Charlotte and the slave girl in.

'Mistress, I have brought you the newcomer you asked for,' said the slave girl. She bowed almost to the ground.

'Good. Now get out,' the Mistress said.

The girl fled.

Confused by all the bowing and scraping in the doorway, Charlotte hadn't had a chance to get a proper look at the seated Mistress. Now she bowed low herself, anxious to earn the woman's favour from the start. She was learning fast how to be obedient. She was determined to protect her arse.

Finishing her bow, she looked up.

'We meet again,' said the woman.

Karo! Karo was her Mistress! Karo whom she'd met the day after her inauguration; whom she'd dismissed as a maid servant, refusing her oral sex . . .

'Mistress. I didn't know who you were when I was rude to you,' Charlotte said, her voice quavering.

'Exactly. What if I'd been an honoured guest your Master wanted you to please?'

Charlotte felt the panic start in her breast; she felt the vulnerability of her bottom.

'I . . . I didn't think!'

'You're not supposed to think. Why are you here, Charlotte? To learn. To obey.'

'Yes, I'll obey.'

'To the letter?'

'Yes.'

'Yes, *Mistress.*'

'Yes, Mistress,' Charlotte repeated, reluctantly. She admitted to herself that saying servile things to a woman wasn't as difficult as saying them to a man.

'Then do what I asked you to do before.'

Charlotte's mind went blank. She swallowed.

'What . . .?'

Lying back on the vast couch, the woman spread her legs.

Oh God, not that! She'd never fully . . . But everyone said the Mistress could be cruel if you failed to please her. Her legs trembled as she walked towards the woman's opened labia. She knelt down, put her tentative mouth to the fleshy lips, and kissed the salty flesh, licking experimentally. She spat out a hair, and licked again.

'Oh, dear. We really aren't trying ...'

She felt strong hands under the armpits. They felt too muscular and too angry to belong to a woman like this – unless that woman had spent years lifting weights and working out; working out how to manipulate a trembling slave.

As Charlotte mused, the hands propelled her upwards and forward. Within seconds she was lying across the length of the settee.

'Shall I punish you for your earlier rudeness?' Karo stood, looking down at her. 'I could use a table tennis bat ...'

'Please, don't – I'll tongue you for hours! I'll stick my tongue right up you.'

'That bat has served me well in the past,' said the woman, taking one out of a concealed drawer under the settee. 'I've given many a work-shy slave twenty strokes.'

Cringing, Charlotte buried her head in the settee cover, and felt her globes hoisted further in the air. The woman had one hand across her back in an ungiving grip, whilst the other held the bat.

'Remember the rule – obedience at all times,' said the woman, raising the implement. 'Repeat that phrase every time the bat comes down.'

'Obedience at all times! Obedience at all times,' gasped Charlotte immediately before the bat had a chance to fall. Each word slurred into the next; a wail of despair. There was a long pause – but no pain. Her Mistress snorted.

'I'll accept your apologies for now. We'll be testing your devotion in a little while.'

She gave Charlotte one warning stroke with the bat, then pushed her from her lap so that she fell prostrate on the floor. 'Keep lying like that on your belly.' She picked up something from across the room. 'Now twist your head round, looking back at me. There.'

To Charlotte's shame, she took a photograph of her nervously clutching her posterior.

'I'll be recording you at various stages of your training,' she said.

Sitting on the edge of the settee, she touched Charlotte's bottom. 'Were you very afraid of a beating?'

'Yes, Mistress.' She still couldn't believe that she'd been given a reprieve.

'In that case, you'll especially want to please.'

Again the woman leaned back and spread her legs. After a second's hesitation, Charlotte slid out from behind the woman and pushed her robes away. Kneeling, she put her right hand over her Mistress's *mons*. She placed her mouth against her labia and stuck her tongue up her wet canal. For a while she licked hard, flicking her tongue in and out, then sliding it around the perimeters. Her Mistress sighed quietly, and tightened her fingers in her hair.

'Kiss my clit, slave,' she whispered. 'Not too hard or I'll have to punish you.'

Noting when the woman sighed with rapture and when she pulled back, Charlotte pleasured her with her full, wet mouth. She grazed the tips of her teeth against the pubic path, and used the end of her tongue to flick hard, then find a softer rhythm.

'Just on the clit, now,' the woman gasped, obviously nearing the summit.

Charlotte did what she could, although her tongue was tiring.

'Don't fail me,' warned the woman, tightening her hands against Charlotte's bottom. The pain in her butt created new energy; Charlotte tongued and tongued.

'Oh!'

The woman didn't cry out unrestrainedly the way Charlotte did when she orgasmed. Only her wildly pulsing *mons*, the sudden flexing of her buttocks and thighs revealed the true extent of her ecstatic release. Dutifully, Charlotte licked up the excess fluid.

'Say "thank you, Mistress",' the woman whispered, pushing her head away.

'Thank you, Mistress,' Charlotte mumbled, feeling sleepy. She daren't lean back on her bottom; she daren't get up from her knees.

'Sleep,' said the woman, indicating the couch. 'I've some

112

other girls to attend to. When we come back we'll continue our little chat.'

Charlotte slept. When she woke up, there was a tray of food beside her. 'Lunchtime,' said her usual guide. 'You're to have it here.'

'And then . . .?'

'Then our Mistress will finish dealing with you.'

'I pleased her with my tongue,' said Charlotte, feeling happier.

The girl looked away.

'Has she ever used the bat on you?' Charlotte added, as the girl waited for her to finish with the lunch plates.

The girl nodded, grimacing.

Charlotte looked at her own rump: 'She gave me one hard stroke with it. I cried out with the pain.'

The girl nodded her head: 'Our Mistress is skilful. She knows how far to take a girl. Do exactly as she says.'

'I intend to!' said Charlotte, with feeling. She tucked into tender noodles and fish that tasted faintly like salmon and was garnished with strips of green vegetables and herbs.

'Coffee?' asked the girl. 'It'll wake you properly, help you to do what's requested next.' She smiled at Charlotte nervously before taking the tray and scurrying away.

For a while Charlotte half-dozed, then she heard the door open. Seconds later, her Mistress came in. Charlotte got clumsily to her knees.

'Thank you for lunch, Mistress. Thank you for allowing me to sleep, Mistress.' She remained hunkered down, unsure what to do next.

Unsmilingly the woman walked round her, inspecting her. 'Come and lie across my lap,' she said.

Charlotte gulped, hating the prospect, but did so. Anything to avoid angering the woman and earning another bat stroke like the one she'd already had . . .

'Does this little bottom still hurt?' asked her Mistress, running an exploratory palm across its surface.

'Yes, Mistress!' Charlotte gasped, fighting the urge to cringe away. She must lie here calmly, and suffer the ministrations. Soon she'd be allowed to go back to her cell and relax.

'Why did I punish you this morning, Charlotte?'

'For . . . for not licking you well enough the first time.'

'And what other ways have you failed me?'

'I . . . I don't know.'

'You failed by being rude to me in your cell. You refused to do my bidding.'

'I'm sorry, Mistress. I beg for mercy.'

'I'm not feeling merciful today.'

Charlotte began to whimper. 'Please, not my arse.' She put her hands round to cover it, but the woman gripped her wrists and pulled her fingers from her punished flesh.

'Yes, it's a wicked little bottom, Charlotte. We must teach it manners.'

'But I'll be so good . . .'

'My palm will *make* you good, Charlotte. But first of all, we're going to play the anti-wriggling game.'

She stood up abruptly, pushing Charlotte to the floor, and pressed a button on the nearest wall. A guide came hurrying in. 'Put a collar and lead on this creature and take it to the Self Control Centre,' the woman said. 'Time for lesson number one.'

Beyond fighting now, Charlotte got down on all fours and lifted her head up slightly to receive the closely fitting collar. Then, as the guide held her leash, she crawled like a dog out of the black building through the grassy fields to a high silver dome.

'We keep the best restraint tables in here,' said the Mistress, walking slightly behind Charlotte and occasionally tapping her bum with her walking stick. 'I often use it to bring the newer girls to heel.'

'I'll come to heel. Just ask me,' whimpered Charlotte, looking up at her.

'You think you will, my dear, but the palm or the rod gives you that extra incentive every time.'

They walked along corridors, and up a flight of stairs. Charlotte tried to rise to her feet to climb them, but the request was denied. Humiliated, she crawled all the way, and was led into a long sunlit room with tables. Each table

114

had leather loops for the slave's wrists, ankles and neck, and another which fastened securely across his or her back.

Charlotte realised what each loop was for as the guide lifted her onto the nearest table, and fastened her down on it. The leather restraint across her lower back made her buttocks feel even more exposed. As ever, her legs were tied apart, and her sex was apparent. The strap round her neck prevented her from turning round to see what would happen next.

But she *felt* what happened next – felt it exquisitely! Her Mistress ran a teasing finger down the cleft of Charlotte's bum. Charlotte whimpered with lust and wriggled her posterior desperately.

'You liked that,' the woman said, 'but it was almost too much.' It was a statement, not a question.

'Yes, Mistress,' Charlotte murmured, regardless. She wanted to do the right thing.

'Next time I do it I don't want you to wriggle,' added her Mistress.

Long long moments ticked by. Was she still there? Had she gone? Had she taken the guide with her? Were they filming her again, perhaps? Charlotte lay there, eyes open, straining to hear a sound, wishing her neck hadn't been immobilised. All she could think about was the vulnerable crack in her buttocks. Any second now a finger could slide down that incredibly sensitive path.

She wouldn't move this time – she wouldn't! The finger slid down sensuously, and she writhed.

'Bad girl. That's your first slap guaranteed,' said the Mistress.

Again Charlotte suffered a long wait in which she promised herself she'd pass her test this time.

She didn't. The touch was just too exciting, too tormenting. Her buttocks wriggled of their own accord; her loins swelled and throbbed. She didn't want the touch again! She wanted it to go on forever! She wanted them to leave her alone! She wanted to come! She couldn't think. She could only feel that hellish hand doing amazing things to her nerve ends. Who'd have thought that a few inches of flesh could be this aroused? She wanted to touch her clit. She knew she would come in seconds. 'Please,' she whispered as the finger stroked down. 'Please.'

'Please more? Please less? Be articulate, girl!'

The finger played with her bottom cleft again as if to make sure her words came out choked and urgent.

'Mistress, I beg you. I need to come!'

'Only after you've been soundly spanked,' the woman said.

'No!'

'She's not ready to ask for a spanking yet,' her Mistress said. She fingered the girl's crack again. Charlotte wriggled and whimpered. 'We're up to fifteen slaps now,' said the woman. 'Fifteen hard spanks.'

The seconds ticked by.

'Make that sixteen – no, seventeen,' she added, doing a doubly tantalising stroke by running her fingers first down the cleft and then back up.

'I'll do anything!' Charlotte whispered.

'Ask for a spanking,' the woman said.

Charlotte closed her eyes against the guide's smirk. She felt the finger start on its relentless track again. 'Please, Mistress, give me a spanking,' she begged.

'Tell me you've got a randy little backside and a greedy cunt,' added her Mistress.

'I've got a randy little backside and a greedy cunt,' Charlotte whispered, her facial cheeks flaming in contrast to her still-unmarked arse.

'Oh, you need this spanking. You deserve it.'

She felt the woman's hands stroke her rear; she heard her palm cut down; she felt the sudden all-over sting. Charlotte lay there, trussed and helpless, awaiting further whacks.

'Such a sensitive bottom,' murmured the woman, bringing her palm down hard again. She slapped first one buttock then the other in a viciously rhythmical attack. 'And it colours so prettily,' she added. 'There was another slave last year whose bottom took on a lovely glow like yours.'

She spanked relentlessly at Charlotte's aching rear. 'I

have to confess, dear, I especially looked forward to punishing her. She used to get ever so many things wrong. If she wasn't over-cooking the meat in the kitchens she was making the wrong steps in our dance studios. I had her over my lap almost every day.' She sighed. 'She's been assigned to a different camp now, so I rarely see her. But aren't you the fortunate one, getting to take her place?'

Charlotte whimpered, her mouth opening against the restraining table. Her Mistress spanked her more soundly.

'You'll get a thorough training from me, slave. Your bottom won't go without.'

She added a few extra slaps Charlotte was sure she hadn't earned through wriggling. But she wasn't going to question her Mistress. No way!

'Get up. Bend over that chair.'

She felt hands undoing the restraints from her extremities. After a few seconds she felt strong enough to get into a crouching position, and the guide took her weight beneath the arms and guided her to the floor.

Unbidden, Charlotte crawled over to the chair her Mistress was standing beside.

'Grip its back. Spread your legs apart. Lean slightly over it. Look back at the camera. Keep your eyes downcast.' Again the flash exploded as the woman took a photo of Charlotte's flushed face and even more scarlet rear. 'Stay that way,' she ordered.

Charlotte stayed; her legs trembled. She could see that the guide in front of her was dying to touch his pulsing cock.

'We promised you an orgasm,' murmured the woman, touching Charlotte's swollen bottom.

Charlotte moaned. All she wanted now was to go back to her cell.

'Guide. Lick this slave.'

The boy's eyes flickered with distaste and he stepped hesitantly towards her. The Mistress slapped her hand against her robes and glared at him. The boy hurried over to Charlotte and got down on his hands and knees between her scissored legs.

'Lick her well, slave. I have a nice new knout that I haven't used on a male back yet . . .'

The boy shuddered and his tongue found the hood round Charlotte's clitoris and licked rhythmically away.

Charlotte wailed, and took one hand from the chair to put on his head, intending to guide it in exactly the right direction.

'Keep gripping the chair, bitch,' her Mistress said.

Flinching, Charlotte took hold of the chair back again, letting her head hang forward. This was too much – that almost-hit-the-spot-that-time feeling. It was terrible to think that the man pleasuring you didn't want to be there, and awful to know that the woman who'd just thrashed you mercilessly was now watching you writhe under a stranger's lips.

The licking intensified. She felt a hand beneath her chin raising her head and forcing her to look at her Mistress. The woman was staring into her face, crouching on the ground. 'I've got a whip across my knees, Charlotte. Look at it.'

Charlotte looked at the cruel black hide, and groaned.

'If you let go of the chair without permission I'll use this on you.'

She groaned more loudly. The licking reached fever pitch.

'Such a noisy girl!' A pause. 'I could stop him licking, or let him continue and punish you for being noisy. What do you think?'

Her groin was giving her the answer: 'Punish me, please!'

Her voice sounded guttural; breathless. Tongue on clit. Tongue on clit. Tongue on clit. Heat and wet and throbbing, pulsing, nearing . . .

'Put you down for a whipping at a later date. Maybe beat you before an audience in the square?'

'Yes, Mistress. People watching . . . watching my whipping!' She was shameless now. She'd say anything if they'd let her come.

The boy's tongue was working overtime. It was exquisite. No one had ever pleasured her down below with their mouth for this long before.

118

'Orgasm now, or I'll warm your arse again,' said her Mistress, as she closed her eyes with impending ecstasy. Crying out and doubling forward, Charlotte came and came.

The boy kept sucking.

'Please stop,' she whimpered.

Their Mistress repeated the order.

'You've done well,' she told him.

'Can I enjoy her, Mistress, when I take her back to her cell?'

'No,' the woman shook her head, 'she's a special category. Take any of the other girls tonight, though. Tell them I ordered it, that they must please you with special care.'

Charlotte listened, half dazed, to the instructions. She wouldn't have minded fucking the boy: she felt horny as hell. She felt wanton, as if she was capable of anything. She wanted to act like a slut; wanted to suck and lick and open her hole . . .

'How's your bottom, Charlotte?'

She gulped. 'It's very sore, Mistress.'

'How's your anus?'

She gulped harder, and cleared her throat. 'It's . . . it's fine.'

'No anal plug, I see?'

'My breakfast girl took it out before she brought me to you.'

'She did well. These were my instructions. I don't like anything coming between me and my slaves except my hands.'

'Yes, Mistress. I understand Mistress.'

Charlotte stayed gripping the chair in the afterglow of her orgasm. Her bum felt swollen. Her quim felt hot. Her legs felt weak.

'But there's no reason now why your anal plug shouldn't go back in, is there?'

'No, Mistress.' Her heart sank at the thought. And her buttocks tightened. They were always tightening! As the guide led her over to a low punishment bench, Charlotte willed them to relax.

'I'm not even going to tie you down. I trust you to re-strain yourself,' added her Mistress, lightly. 'This isn't a punishment. Just a form of training to help you become a more useful pleasure slave.'

Charlotte bent over the bench. It was awful having her bottom exposed again.

'Open your legs wider,' ordered her Mistress.

Charlotte obeyed.

'Now relax your arse.'

This bit was harder. The plug settled against the rim of her anus, and she flinched away.

'If I have to tie you down it'll be worse.'

'Please don't tie me down, Mistress. I'm sorry, Mistress.'

'Open your arsehole wide.'

She pulled her own cheeks apart, in an attempt to reduce the tightness. She felt oil being slicked down her crack, and massaged into her rectum. She felt the plug being placed at her opening again.

'Ask for it nicely,' whispered the woman.

Charlotte closed her eyes. She couldn't!

'Beg me to ram this plug up your butt, Charlotte, or else . . .'

It was just a small plug – it wouldn't hurt her. It was the shame of it she objected to.

'I'm about to get a much bigger plug, Charlotte. I'm about to hose the grease away and ram it in dry.'

'No, please,' Charlotte whispered, biting her lip, 'I want this one inside my arse.'

'You can ask more descriptively than that!'

'I'm a dirty girl, I want men to fuck me.' She felt the plug pushing back her resistance. 'I want to widen my arse-hole a little so I can please their cocks.'

'You appreciate the men may not *want* your arsehole?' asked her Mistress.

'Yes, Mistress, but in case they do . . .' The plug went in further. She cried out.

'What else might they want, Charlotte?'

Her mind and pulse were racing. 'My mouth. My quim.'

'Or maybe they'll think your holes aren't fit for them.

Maybe they'll just wank themselves all over your big round bottom and tits.'

'Yes, Mistress. Let them wank over me, Mistress.'

As she rubbed her Mount of Venus against the punishment bench, Charlotte's orgasm began to build up again.

'Permission to come, Mistress,' she whispered, raggedly.

'Permission granted, slave.'

Whimpering her gratitude, Charlotte took her right hand from the side of the punishment bench, and moved it down to her wetness. She was drippingly needful, and the room smelt of sex.

She stroked herself, and felt the plug being pushed in further. Stroked. Felt. Stroked. Felt. Moaned.

'Your own fingers on your cunt, and a plug up your arse!' whispered her Mistress in a disapproving voice. Charlotte peaked into pleasure, tightening her thighs against her fingers, crying out against the wooden bench.

'Did you like the slave licking you?'

'Yes, Mistress.'

'Did you like it when I stroked the crack between your arse?'

Charlotte paused. She had and she hadn't. 'Yes, Mistress. Yes!'

'I thought so. You really are shameless, Charlotte. Now get down flat on the floor on your belly and kiss my feet.'

Shuddering, Charlotte got up from the punishment bench, stretched out on the ground, and began licking each toe, and kissing each nail, and the flesh in between. She could sense the woman staring down at her, but she daren't look up.

'You have done well.' The voice sounded measured but quietly pleased at the situation. Charlotte swallowed hard, feeling proud.

'Thank you, Mistress,' she murmured, wondering what her reward would be. An alcoholic drink? A day off? The right to wear clothes?

'I live to please my Mistress,' she murmured obsequiously, deciding she'd learned the rules of the game and that from now on life would be sweet.

'I'm glad to hear that, Charlotte,' Karo murmured cool-ly. 'For as a pleasure slave you've to please both men and women from now on.'

9

'Time to please.'

She woke up to these words from her breakfast maid the following morning. Who did they want her to . . .? It was useless asking the maid, who was forbidden to say. Charlotte thought over her options as she bathed and ate. She'd already pleased Karo, so she decided they were going to make her fuck one of the guides.

She bet that was it – the guides had been eyeing her breasts and buttocks hopefully, looking gloatingly at her anus, for days. Their frank gazes had settled on every sizzling centimetre of her naked quim . . .

Nervously, Charlotte followed the girl to the Entertainments' Hall, where she was reacquainted with the Master. She hadn't called him *her* Master yet . . .

She entered the large hall, wondering who'd soon be entertaining her. She was very wet at the exciting uncertainty, and could show any man a good time. Still the blush rose to her cheeks as she looked around and saw twenty-odd male slaves all staring at her nakedness. Her hands cuffed behind her, she was prodded into the centre of the hall.

Moments later, as she stared at the ground, the door opened again and a guide brought in another girl. This one was about five feet six, with dusky skin and masses of black wavy hair. As she got closer, Charlotte could see that she had almond eyes and white teeth and tits with dark brown nipples. Her pubic hair sprouted out around her like an untrimmed bush.

Her hands were also cuffed behind her. She glared at

Charlotte as they were pushed together, and said: 'This is the pits.'

'You're telling me!' said Charlotte, relieved at last to have found a pal, a possible soul mate. Here was someone who didn't chant that obedience was all or spend half her time talking about the common good.

'I'm Charlotte,' added Charlotte. 'What's your name?'

'Lari.'

'I thought Lari was a man's name?'

'I'm all woman,' said Lari throatily, and grinned.

She certainly was! Any man would find her attractive. But this morning they weren't destined for any man.

'Let the floorshow begin!' the Master said, genially. He walked up to Charlotte. 'The object of the game is for you to make this creature orgasm. Obviously if you fail you'll be chastised extremely hard.'

Charlotte inhaled deeply, and nodded. 'Can you unlock my hands, sir?'

'No. Both of you must retain your restraints.'

'But . . .' Charlotte wondered how to fulfil her task without stroking the slave's clitoris with her thumb.

'Don't disobey, girl. Fulfil your obligations. We have a device or two to speed you on your way.'

So saying, the Master nodded to one of the guides who walked over, carrying a long thick appendage. Looking closer, Charlotte saw it was a seven inch black dildo. The grinning guide fastened it around her waist.

'I'm not having that thing in me,' muttered Lari, backing away from her.

'You are if I'm to escape further whipping!' gasped Charlotte, grabbing her and wrestling her to the ground.

For long moments they rolled about, nipple against nipple. Their soft bellies rubbed against each other; their cuffed hands abraided the other's flesh. Finally Charlotte's superior weight tired the other girl, and she remained, gasping, on her back, her feet drumming feebly. Charlotte pushed a knee between her thighs to drive them apart.

'You're going to come if I have to fuck you all day,' she whispered, lining her body up so that the dildo was roughly next to Lari's sex lips. 'They've already used a belt and a table tennis bat on me. I'm not giving them the excuse to use anything else.'

'I'm no lesbian,' muttered Lari, trying to buck Charlotte off again, 'I won't ...'

'Are you sure?' whispered Charlotte, realising how wet the girl was around her hirsute triangle. She'd intended to kiss her and lick her breasts until arousal was evident, but Lari felt more than ready now.

Smiling, Charlotte pushed forward, and the dildo slid up the other slave to the fullest.

'Jesus!'

The darker girl's face creased into lines of pleasure, and she exhaled hard.

'Pretend it's a man's cock,' gasped Charlotte, starting to thrust back and forward in an increasingly confident rhythm. She didn't have hands free to pleasure Lari's breasts, so put her mouth to them, teasing the sensitive areolae till the girl beneath her moaned.

'Maybe you're a secret lesbian,' whispered Charlotte, shoving the dildo harder into her partner. 'I think you'd really like to suck my tit flesh.'

'Make her suck your tits or we'll take a cane to your backside,' warned the Master, walking around them.

Charlotte pushed her body forward some more. She pushed her nipple against the girl's lips, but the girl threatened to bite it. Charlotte drew back.

'Six strokes for Charlotte entered in the Punishment Book,' the Master said.

'Bitch!' Charlotte whispered, shoving her hips forward so that the dildo rammed further up Lari than ever. Lari groaned and raised her arse.

'You want it really!' whispered Charlotte, bucking faster. Lari's eyes were open but unfocused now; a thin layer of sweat was visible on the unfringed section of her brow. Charlotte increased her speed and the dusky beauty writhed hopelessly. Charlotte thrust and thrust and the girl came.

For long moments they lay there, then the Master

approached them. Dazedly Charlotte looked up. All the guides were hard.

'This is a rehearsal, of course. When trained you'd do this before our clothed guests, and probably be chosen by one of them afterwards as his slave for the day or week,' explained the Master. 'They'd doubtless invent some little games of their own.'

'I tried to get her to suck my tits, but she threatened to bite them,' Charlotte said, plaintively.

'The six strokes are still due. You can have them tomorrow,' continued the Master. 'Think about how you could have tried harder to obey.'

'But *she*'s the one who was difficult! *She*'s the one who deserves the thrashing!'

'We gave the order to you,' the Master said.

'It's not fair,' muttered Charlotte as the guide helped her to her feet and unstrapped the dildo.

'Now go out of that door and shower together,' the Master said.

Wearily, aware of the other girl following close behind her, Charlotte went to the shower room. A guide stood at a distance to make sure that they used the same spray.

'Six strokes because of you,' said Charlotte, pushing the other girl viciously under the hot water.

' 'Cause I haven't got a slave mentality!' the girl said.

'Nor have I,' raged Charlotte, stung. 'I've refused to do lots of things!'

'If it's so awful,' said Lari, 'why don't you run away?'

'How?' Charlotte lowered her voice even further to outwit the guide who was staring at their wet, lathered bodies.

Lari looked thoughtful: 'When we get out of here they'll probably leave you to go back to your cell.' She soaped her breasts, paying particular attention to her still-hard nipples, 'Start off in that direction, then head off towards the forest.'

'And then?'

'Then keep your wits about you. These people know what they're doing! Walk to the clearing where the planes are and hide. Observe the guides, see which planes they prepare for take off. Stow away.'

'You'll come too?'

'In a different plane,' Lari nodded. 'Doubles our chances of success.'

'I guess so,' Charlotte said, slowly. She cleared her throat: 'Has . . . has anyone ever escaped before?'

'No. Fools that they are, they don't seem to want to! They're brainwashed if you ask me. The Master tells them they can leave after three months if he's misunderstood their desires or something.'

'And no one goes?'

Lari shrugged. 'I'm just passing on what my breakfast girl said. She admitted the Master once thought a girl was latently submissive who wasn't. When he realised his mistake she was given a substantial cash payment and flown home.'

'And she didn't tell anyone?'

'Obviously not. The place has never been busted! I think she understood their lust for power in her heart.'

'She's on her own, there, then,' said Charlotte. 'I think they're all animals!'

'Then we'll make a run for it after this.'

Was that what she wanted? It must be! It was madness to suffer further humiliations when she could return to the sanctuary of Vernon's flat. She'd get her revenge on him by selling all his furniture and leaving his phone connected to the speaking clock. She'd go to Jeff and persuade him to be hers all the time. It should be simple given the persuasive techniques she'd been taught during the past few days.

'I'll make a run for it,' she agreed softly. 'Providing they don't drag me back to my cell on that stupid leash after we've had this shower.'

They did. Inside, she fretted. They had forced her hands and knees to cover the grassy ground back to her quarters, while she was wishing she was moving towards the forest instead.

'Loved seeing you licking that girl,' said her guide, his cock jerking enthusiastically. 'Loved seeing that dildo going up her to the hilt.'

Charlotte paused. She obviously had a fan club! Maybe she could use it to her advantage. Perhaps . . .

'What else would you like to see?' she whispered, seductively.

The boy stopped in front of her, trembling. 'We're not allowed . . .'

'Who says?'

'The Master. The Mistress. The law of the island.'

'And if you disobey?'

'The whip. The cane. The knout.'

'But if you're not caught out by your actions?'

'Guilt. Fear. No peace of mind.'

'So much pleasure – only a few pangs of conscience,' whispered Charlotte.

'Why are you doing this?' The boy stared down at her, his brow creased.

'I'm doing it because I want to. Because I haven't had a man for days; I've been teased by women. Because my flesh has needs.'

The boy stood, the leash slack, still uncertain.

Charlotte sat back on her haunches so that her breasts jutted out. 'We could be in my cell now,' she said, 'naked bodies rubbing up against each other. No one would know.'

'I'd know.'

'You'd know what it was like to suck my tits, know how hot and tight it feels inside me.'

The boy let out a long sigh. Charlotte stretched her head forward and nuzzled his balls.

'God, not here! All right, in your cell. Quickly!'

'Undo this lead. If I stand upright we can get there faster,' Charlotte coaxed.

His eyes glinted. 'No, I like you like this. I like leading you. Anyway, we've got all afternoon.'

Charlotte's heart sank. It was true. She'd heard the lunch bell some time ago when she was pleasuring Lari. The meal-bringing girl would have left a salad in her cell. Unless the Master had further plans for either of them within the next few hours they wouldn't be disturbed until tea.

Still, she was sexually excited anyway, and the guide was well formed; handsome in an eager, youthful way. She stared at his small round hips, and the heavy sac between his legs, as he pulled her towards the building where she lived.

'How would you like me to fuck you?' he gasped, pulling more and more eagerly at her collar.

Charlotte licked her lips, looking for a way in which she could keep some control over the situation, and ultimately escape.

'I've always had this fantasy,' she said softly, 'of a man pinning me against the wall with his weight as he pleasures my tits. He takes his prick out and slides it up me, and fucks me standing up until I come.'

It was a hard position for a man to maintain; tiring for the leg muscles. Maybe he'd sleep afterwards, and she could slope off towards the planes.

Her cell door was open as usual; the food was waiting. She ate quickly, hungrily. Fucking Lari must have tired her out! The guide watched impatiently as she swilled down her fruit juice but she ignored him. She needed new energy to have sex with him, energy to help her escape.

'I'm hungry for more than this,' she murmured, licking the last traces of salt from her plate.

The boy tugged at her lead.

'Screw me up against the wall,' said Charlotte, indicating him to let go of the strip of leather. Clumsily he unfastened her collar. Standing up, she put her back to the cell wall, and spread her legs.

'I want you,' she whispered, bending her knees to give him access. She took his cock in her right hand, and guided him in. 'See how ready I am?' she added, aware that she was lusciously wet from rolling about with Lari, and watching the sensations that the dildo had given to the other girl's cunt.

The boy groaned into her shoulder. Her hands were hanging by her sides, perspiring lightly. She realised she was more used to having them tied together or tethered to a post nowadays. She flexed her wrists and brought her palms down to rest on his arse, his cute little arse, pulling him more fully into her throbbing quim.

'I'm the forbidden one,' she taunted. 'The one you weren't supposed to have. The best lay!'

'Everyone wants you,' groaned the boy. 'We're not allowed . . .'

'You've done it anyway! Soon you'll shoot your load inside me. You'll tell the other guys how hot I was, how wet!' Her fingers moved up from his thrusting bum, and found the single key looped on to a plastic rope round his waist. The Master key no doubt – everything here seemed to involve the name of that man!

Charlotte worked carefully at the metal fastening which held key to rope, as he gasped and pushed. An hour or two from now she could be cradled in the back of some plane headed for the civilised world . . .

'Uh,' muttered the boy.

'Do it harder!' she urged him.

She moved her fingers in rhythm with his thrusts, admitting to herself that he had a fine young cock. The risks she was taking made her labia swell and pulse, and her nipples erect. The boy's own nipples stood out against his tanned muscled chest.

Flooded with new wetness, she weighed his scrotum in her palm, enjoying its tender toughness.

'God, I need this!' she added, pushing her belly against his more insistently as he increased his speed. Under cover of the movement she freed the key, brought it round, and inserted it in her anus. Thrilled by the victory, she closed her legs tightly around his shaft.

'Kiss my breasts,' she begged.

The boy bent his head, and tongued them both eagerly.

'They've wanted a man's mouth on them . . . a man like you.'

'Everyone wants you,' said the boy. It seemed to be an obsession with him. 'Everyone wants . . .'

'Their cocks are smaller. They couldn't thrust so good.'

He gasped, blinked.

'You feel so big inside me,' she moaned.

He inhaled again.

'So thick and rampant!'

The boy came.

Now she wanted him to go – but she mustn't make him suspicious.

'Can we lie down together?' she murmured, looking towards the chaise.

'I shouldn't . . . maybe for a little while.'

'Just for ten minutes,' she said pleadingly. 'If you get hard again, I could tongue you. Your cock looks so nice, so clean.'

The boy smiled, kissed her lips, and kissed her shoulders. He pulled out of her and together they walked to the chaise. They lay down, and Charlotte made sure she stretched out on top of him. She stroked the perspiration from his brow, and nuzzled his neck.

Soon he slept – she'd known he'd have to. Scarcely breathing, she rose up from the seat and walked to the cell door. She unlocked it and slipped out, hearing it lock automatically behind her. No one would hear him if he woke up and shouted. Hopefully he wouldn't be missed for hours.

A plane! A plane! Soon she'd be with Jeff; with her own people. Lightly, Charlotte hurried from the building, and started to make her way towards the forest like Lari had said. Had the other girl been as successful, as wilful? Would she be the only one to carry out The Great Escape?

Sunlight. Soft grass. Sweet air. She felt a momentary sadness to be leaving here, and chided herelf for her sentimental streak. Go. Now. She sprinted faster, running at varying speeds for fifteen minutes before reaching the forest's edge. She cursed the fact that she had no clothes or shoes to protect her soft skin. Twigs and leaves crackled before her and beneath.

There was nothing to worry about – just a few scratches; nothing compared to what they'd do to her if she went back now. Her bottom quivered at the thought. There was no returning. Damn that Lari. Damn the girl for putting complicated ideas in her head!

'Hey! Charlotte!'

Her heart almost stopped.

'What a fright!' she said. '*Lari.*'

'They let me keep the dildo,' said Lari. 'I used it on my guide!'

'You what?'

This was a novelty.

'He likes men. I talked him through a gay scene. Really helps that my voice is deep!'

'Where is he now?'

'Asleep, I think. I stole his key and locked him in my cell.'

It was too easy. Much, much too easy. Charlotte felt the first stirring of misgivings, of fear.

'Same here,' she said. 'One guide might have a moment's weakness, forget himself. But two ...'

Rustling sounds came from the bushes. Both girls screamed. A third girl emerged, blinking in the sunlight. She was one of the guides. 'What are you two doing here?' she asked, looking as frightened as they were.

'We're ...'

Charlotte sought a reason, and failed to find one. She didn't understand enough about the rules of this island to give a plausible explanation for her presence in the woods. Again she felt her buttocks tingle; felt her vulnerability. 'Pretend you haven't seen us,' she said.

'You haven't been granted permission to be here?' The girl looked horrified, 'Go back now. Maybe no one will find out ...'

'We're going forward,' Lari said. 'You can't stop us.'

Charlotte hesitated.

'Maybe we should go back.'

'You do what you like,' said Lari. 'This was my idea.'

Charlotte thought of Jeff, and decided to press on. 'We'll have to make sure she can't stop us,' she told Lari, entering into the spirit of the thing. 'Keep her captive for a while.'

They each made a grab for the girl but she stepped smartly backwards, evading them. Her small nipples seemed to harden with fear. Her brown eyes darted wildly about. Then she screamed, a high pitched scream that seemed to carry across the island. And took off at a run.

Charlotte and Lari plunged after her, mindless of the rough ground beneath them. They had to stop her before she told someone they'd broken the rules! Both girls stared hard at the enemy's taut buttocks bounding ahead of them. I'd like to teach her a lesson for eluding us, Charlotte thought.

Faster. Faster. It was amazing how fast you could run when the alternative was a flogging. All three of them, Charlotte acknowledged, probably had the whip on their minds. The girl stumbled, righted herself, and took off again. She dodged round a particularly wide tree trunk, and disappeared.

She'd tripped, and fallen into a little hollow in the ground. She was now trying to stand up again, but Charlotte grabbed her right arm. Hurrying up beside them, Lari grabbed her left. 'We need something to tie her up with,' gasped Charlotte, looking around for a particularly obliging creeper.

'No problem,' said Lari. 'She's got that rope with a key they all wear round their waists.'

And so she did. Wasting precious seconds, Charlotte undid the knot, and used the twine to bind the girl's ankles together.

'Why not tie her to a tree?' Lari asked.

'Because she might not be found in time. It gets hot here. She isn't carrying a water bottle.' Charlotte turned to the girl. 'This should slow your trek back to tell on us.'

The girl screamed.

Again it was a peculiarly shrill effective scream; the type of noise an animal caught in a trap might make. Charlotte gagged the girl temporarily with her hand.

'Have you got anything to gag her with, Lari?'

Lari didn't. That was just one of the problems you encountered when you weren't allowed to wear any clothes.

'We have to go. Even a plane going to the next island won't leave much later than this. There are only a few more hours of daylight,' Lari said.

Agreeing with her new friend, Charlotte let go of the

girl's mouth, and ran off, following Lari into the woods towards the clearing. She winced to herself as the girl screamed and screamed.

What could they do? They couldn't knock her out – they weren't monsters. Charlotte itched to spank the girl's bottom, though, for causing such a fuss. Surely no one would hear her out here? Surely no one would come after them? But someone had.

They burst through the trees; saw the ten male guides; saw the Master. They saw the collars and leads waiting for them; saw the ropes to bind their disobedient ankles and wrists.

'No. Don't!' whimpered Charlotte, backing away to find another grinning guide behind her.

'Yes. Do,' said the Master, indicating to the nearest guide to clip her collar in place.

The collar fitted snugly around her neck, and felt familiar. She'd been bound and led around like this before. There was nothing to worry about, Charlotte told herself, ready to crawl through the woods on her hands and knees. Nothing at all.

'Let them walk,' said the Master. 'This area's not safe to crawl round in.'

Charlotte got stiffly to her feet.

'Take them to the New Offenders Court.' That sounded ominous. The man was tapping that damn stick against his thigh. 'The accused get to stand in the dock, my dear.' The Master smiled crookedly. 'As you can imagine, they often can't sit down after sentence has been carried out.'

'Part of me didn't even want to . . .' Charlotte said weakly.

'We'll be teaching a short sharp lesson to the part that did.'

Led on her lead beside her, Lari was glaring ahead, mouth set ominously.

'Do you know anything about this court thing?' Charlotte whispered. Her anxiety increased as the wilder girl shook her head.

What would they do to them? What would they do to *her*? Legs and belly weak with imagining, Charlotte was marched to a part of the island she hadn't seen before. There she was led to an imposing brick building, and taken into its main mahogany-wood furnished hall.

The girl was already there – the girl they'd tied up and threatened.

'Do you see the accused?' asked a man dressed as a judge.

'Yes, M'Lord.'

The girl pointed to Charlotte and Lari. The male guides were stiff again. That had to be a bad sign. What punishment were they about to see carried out?

'You saw the accused running away?'

'Yes, your Honour.'

'A serious offence,' murmured the man. He fondled the large whip upon his desk. 'And was there a ring leader?'

'The slave Lari said it had been her idea. At one stage her co-conspirator Charlotte considered going back.'

This wasn't so bad! The witness was on her side; she was corroborating the statements she'd already given to the Master. Charlotte relaxed slightly in the high wooden dock.

'Charlotte also stopped the other girl tying me to a tree. She said she didn't want me to remain undiscovered or get dehydrated.'

'Commendable,' said the judge. 'I'm impressed.'

He gazed thoughtfully round the court for long seconds. 'So, you think the slave Charlotte has been led astray?'

The girl hesitated: 'To a certain extent yes, your Honour.'

'I agree,' said the judge. He stared at Lari, his voice becoming softer and more taunting. 'You bad, bad girl.'

Lari glared back, her mouth clamped shut mutinously. Her breasts heaved; her small fists were clenched at her sides.

'I will pronounce sentence on the slave Lari,' the man said. He turned and addressed the guides.

'Note what happens to a slave who spurns our hospitality. Lari is to be taken to the Punishment Chamber tomorrow and kept there for the entire day.'

135

Charlotte bent her head. Now she was to receive her own sentence. Even standing up she was very aware of her bottom. To be bent over and tormented again . . .

'Charlotte?' She looked up. The judge sounded kinder, more understanding. 'This wasn't your idea. You expressed reservations about the trip?'

'That's right, M'Lord,' she whispered. 'I'm sorry I went along with it.'

'I believe you,' said the man. The Master nodded. The guides sighed.

'This girl has led to your undoing,' continued the judge, 'Look at her. Renounce her.'

'I . . . renounce you,' said Charlotte, uncertainly. She'd say whatever she had to to save her arse.

'Tell her she's been a bad girl.'

'You've . . . been a bad girl.' God, this was embarrassing!

'Tell her she deserves to feel the full force of the whip, the cane.'

Charlotte said it. Lari glared. The guides grew stiff again.

'Tell her that her actions have hurt you, that she deserves to be hurt back.'

Again she repeated the words. It got easier.

'You've been wicked,' she repeated after the judge. 'You deserve the thrashing of your life.'

The judge nodded. 'And you're the right person to teach her a lesson, Charlotte. Think of the situation she's put you in by her selfish manipulative ways!'

Charlotte gasped. She hadn't been expecting this. She looked helplessly from one nodding head to another.

'The Punishment Chamber has everything, Charlotte. We'll show you round it now.'

'Thank you, M'Lord.' She looked suitably deferential, respectful.

'Then you can go to your cell for the night,' added the man. He looked at her closely: 'Spend your dreams productively, planning on how you'll treat this wicked slave girl. Think about how to make the lessons you drive into her last a long, long time.'

The judge smiled as Charlotte's gaze travelled from the whip on his desk to Lari's pale buttocks. 'Tomorrow she'll be yours to correct as you see fit.'

10

'You really want me to chastise her?' Charlotte stared at the Master, then at Lari who was being forced to kneel before her with head bowed. The man nodded steadily:

'You heard what the judge decreed.'

Charlotte swallowed awkwardly several times in succession. Last night's court trial seemed distant now, surreal. She'd woken early, half believing it was a dream, half hoping so. Her stomach was heavy and tremulous. Fear and disbelief beat a powerful pulse through her veins.

She had gulped breakfast, and bathed more swiftly than usual, accelerating the morning's rhythms. She had babbled on about all sorts of nonsense to her breakfast guide.

'You know what you must do today,' the guide had said, but even the walk to the Punishment Chamber had had an ethereal quality. She'd feared that she wouldn't be able to go through with it; that she would baulk at the task and thus earn further chastisement for herself.

Then boys were unlocking doors, ushering her through, and closing them again behind her. She blinked once, twice. The vast Chamber stretching out before her eyes seemed like a film set, a fantasy. Then the Master had arrived, making it all too real . . .

'Choose your implement, Charlotte,' the man said evenly now, walking up to her.

'But . . . surely someone like the Mistress who enjoys punishing slaves should do this rather than me?'

The Master smiled: 'Don't stall for time, my dear. Procrastination can be painful.' He looked her up and down consideringly. 'You're the one this wilful little girl led astray.'

'I can't . . .'

She'd never whipped anyone before; never caned anyone; never as much as administered a spanking. Now here she was being told to correct a bad bottom, to choose the first instrument she wished to use on Lari's hips.

Wrist cuffs hung from the walls. Ankle chains were evident at various strategic places. This was no cold dungeon, though – the walls were painted cream and the carpet made of thick, golden fleece. The room was warm, as were all the rooms associated with the Training Grounds. They had to be, Charlotte thought dazedly, with most of the inhabitants spending their lives in the nude.

'We're waiting, Charlotte.'

She turned to the man. 'Will you be overseeing us all day, sir?' It was strangely exciting to have an audience watching her take charge.

'No.' The man paused. 'But a guide will look in periodically to make sure you are teaching our friend a lesson. Make sure you don't break any rules.'

'Rules, sir?' asked Charlotte, warily. She wondered if they'd find some way to turn the day's events against her, against her buttocks. Appear outwardly docile, she reminded herself. Do what they say. One day you'll get revenge, get free!

'The rules of the island, Charlotte. The first one is that you never break a slave's skin. We also suggest that the discipliner warm the recalcitrant flesh gradually, by subtle degrees.'

'And if I break the rules?' asked Charlotte, curiously.

'Let's just say that you'll be heavily chastised yourself.'

No danger, Charlotte thought, trying to smile submissively. If she had her way she was only going to administer a moderate slippering: it would hurt more than enough. It took relatively little to make sensitive female flesh writhe and wriggle. She knew – she had suffered the surprisingly painful slap of an angry male palm on her rump.

'So, Charlotte, hand or slipper – which is it to be for starters?'

'Slipper, sir,' murmured Charlotte, awkwardly, knowing

she couldn't bring herself to slap Lari's bottom with her naked palm.

'And do you want her tied over a trestle table or held over your knee, my dear?'

Again Charlotte swallowed and felt hot. She herself hated going over a knee more than anything else. It felt so undignified and humiliating. And all that wriggling about made you wet ...

'Strap her down over a table, please,' she murmured, deciding against the flesh to flesh intimacy. She'd punish Lari as lightly as she could get away with, and stop whenever the Master and rampant guide left the room.

'Do as she says,' the older man said to the guide conversationally. Wearing her inevitable collar, Lari was pulled over to one of the punishment tables; there she was stretched out and secured in place.

'The slippers await you,' murmured Charlotte's Master, leading the way to a walk-in cupboard. Leather footwear with varyingly large soles was stacked next to photographs showing how fully each one could redden an intractable arse.

'I'm spoiled for choice!' giggled Charlotte nervously. Her pulse was racing. Perspiration pooled beneath her arms. The Master tapped his stick against his leg, and she hurriedly reached for a size six slipper. She weighed it tentatively in her hand.

'If I'd wanted to, could I have used a belt on her for starters, sir?'

'You could, providing you kept the strokes sufficiently light at first. If you start slowly a slave can withstand more punishment. It's much more satisfying for the one who's wielding the lash.' He looked at her calmly. 'Remember the object is to break her spirit, Charlotte – not her skin.'

'The wicked one awaits,' one of the male guides said, his cock springing upright.

Charlotte walked towards where Lari was trussed at the other end of the chamber. As she crossed the room she tried to psyche herself up to slipper the girl medium hard.

The duskier girl had been bad, she told herself; she'd

refused to let Charlotte tongue her nipples for the floor show. She'd earned Charlotte a still-to-be-carried-out six strokes of the whip. She'd taunted Charlotte into running away, and had been ready to tie up that guide and leave her indefinitely. Still it was difficult to imagine punishing the girl; bringing an implement down on her lightly sun-tanned backside.

Maybe not so difficult ... Charlotte reached the trestle table with the spreadeagled Lari and stared down at the girl's incredibly vulnerable bottom. It was tied there, like an offering. She could do anything she liked! Tentatively she stroked her finger down one globe. Heat rushed to her *mons* as the girl's flesh tightened. The Mistress had used a version of this game on Charlotte herself.

'Tell her she's misbehaved,' encouraged their Master, coming to stand at Lari's head and looking down at her. Charlotte remained beside the helpless bottom, fondling it, making the girl writhe.

'You've been a naughty girl, Lari,' she said softly.

Lari muttered something. It sounded like a curse.

'Wicked enough to warrant a whole day's chastisement,' Charlotte added threateningly.

She picked up the slipper and placed the sole against the girl's bottom, lightly gliding it up and down.

'Say sorry,' she whispered, 'and maybe I won't use this on you quite so mercilessly. Say sorry, Lari. Say it now!'

Lari swore again. Charlotte picked up the slipper and brought its sole down on the waiting posterior. Lari yelped. She jerked in her bonds. Charlotte repeated the whack again, using more force this time, bringing the leather down on the unpunished cheek.

'Pig!' Lari gasped.

And earned a third lick of the slipper.

'You cow!' she moaned as it hit the crease where bottom met thigh.

'Don't taunt me. I'm just getting started,' murmured Charlotte. 'Save your insults until I'm really into my stride!' She threw the slipper down and turned to the Master. 'Any suggestions?'

'We have a punishment stool – good for applying the birch or the cane.'

'The cane,' she said, aware that she'd seen a similar chastisement before in the school room. That little scene had given both Vernon and Guy the hardest pricks . . .

Would it excite her now? She watched Lari being untied from the trestle table, and noted her quail slightly as she saw the stool with its leather straps.

'You put your tummy on the seat, not your bottom, Lari,' Charlotte said softly, amazed to find that she was actually enjoying the girl's ignominy. 'Then we fasten your wrists and ankles to the foot of the stool.'

Lari said something rude, but her position made the words indistinguishable.

'You can gag her at any time,' said the Master. 'Some of our guests like a girl kept silent from the start.'

Charlotte thought about that, the pleasure of watching their mute pleading. 'No,' she said consideringly. 'I want to hear her grovel, savour her screams.'

'I won't scream,' muttered Lari. 'You can't make me.'

'I'm going to make you,' said Charlotte. 'Make you beg for release.'

'It took me a long time to make her do that,' their Master said, the bulge in his trousers becoming more evident. 'A very long time indeed.'

How long would it take Charlotte? She had the entire day to make this girl say what she wanted her to. Charlotte walked round the stool and its tied-over victim, and stopped beside her bottom which was still much too pale. It would take longer to colour than a white backside would because the flesh was a light beige tinge. But, providing Lari was wicked, she would get there in the end.

Teasingly Charlotte laid her palm across one cheek, then moved it over to the other. She ran a finger down the crease of Lari's arse and watched her wriggle and exhale. Her labia shone wetly between her taut slim thighs. She was breathing hard.

'The slipper was just to warm you up,' Charlotte said softly. 'I'm going to cane your bottom now. It's going to sting.'

She drew back the rod of wood so that it stayed parallel with Lari's posterior. Brought it forward, and smiled as the girl gasped. It left an admirable pale stripe.

'Are you sorry yet?' she asked quietly, moving round to face the girl.

Lari shook her head; her eyes glared their defiance at her erstwhile friend.

'The caning ends when you genuinely repent,' Charlotte reminded her. She administered another choice stroke.

'Yes, please. I'm sorry!' gasped Lari, half-angrily.

'You don't sound as if you mean it,' commented Charlotte, using the rod with more force.

'I do! I . . . I'm really sorry!'

'Sorry for what?'

A pause. Lari obviously hadn't thought through her story. 'Sorry for everything I did wrong.'

'Words are cheap,' said the Master, impassively. 'Let her show by her actions and voice tone that she's truly apologetic, that she recognises you're in charge.'

'I intend to in due course,' Charlotte said, giving Lari's curves further tuition. 'Believe me.'

Already she felt like the Master must feel – masterful. She felt she wanted to teach this naughty girl a lesson she'd never forget.

A buzzer sounded on the wall. A guide spoke into an intercom, then signalled respectfully to the Master.

'I must go,' he said. 'Have fun, Charlotte – but be fair.'

Nodding, Charlotte squeezed the slave's sore buttocks as she looked round the Chamber, deciding how she should next tame her still wild spirit. She'd called her names; she'd been far from docile. She needed to learn her place.

'I'd like to take her outside soon,' she said thoughtfully to the guide, whose shaft was leaking pearls of desire. 'If you could gather an audience around that clearing I saw the other day . . .'

The guide bowed his head then hurried off to do Charlotte's bidding. Charlotte swiftly untied Lari from the stool and, pushing her to her hands and knees, took hold of her leash. 'You're going to perform tricks for me for the rest of the day, slave. Providing you obey me to the letter, your physical chastisement is over. It's up to you.'

'Thank you, Charlotte,' whispered Lari, and hung her head so that her hair covered her features. Did she look truly cowed?

'Kiss my feet,' ordered Charlotte, feeling the mastery surge through her.

The girl looked up, lips parting in shock and disbelief. 'Why . . . ?'

'Just do it.'

'Charlotte. Please. No! I can't!'

'Call me Mistress,' Charlotte said, coldly.

'Please . . . Mistress.' The girl's eyes were downcast, her mouth petulant. 'Don't make me feel stupid like this.'

'But you have been stupid. You've got us both into trouble. You need to lose some of your stubborn pride.'

'I won't!' said Lari, standing up and jerking the lead from Charlotte's hand. 'I'm not your slave!'

The next few hours will prove otherwise, thought Charlotte grimly. As she mused, Lari's spirit reasserted itself and she raced off towards the Chamber doors, her arse a warm contrast to the rest of her cool flesh.

Charlotte nodded at the watching guides, who sprang into action after the fleeing slave. Charlotte realised she was glad of an excuse to punish that delectable little bottom some more. 'Get this disobedient creature ready for her next lesson,' she said coolly. 'She refuses to kiss my feet.'

The men caught Lari within seconds, dragged her back to Charlotte, and set her down on her lead before her. As Charlotte indicated how she wanted the slave trussed across the table, Lari pulled back like a dog about to be whipped. She kicked and yelped as strong male hands grabbed her and hauled her over the wooden support. In a few moments she'd really have something to cry about, Charlotte thought.

As they were restraining her victim, Charlotte looked out a palm-hardened glove from one of the many cupboards.

'Don't!' Lari was shouting, as they fastened her wrists and ankles in place. 'Don't stretch me out like that again!'

'You should have thought of that before you were disobedient,' murmured Charlotte.

'Please,' Lari was getting closer to sounding as if she meant it. 'I'm really repentant. I'll never disobey you again.'

'If only I could believe that.' Charlotte held the girl's lead and looked down at her impassively. 'See what I've got for you?' she added, showing the other girl the glove.

Lari's eyes widened, she sucked in her breath, and flexed her fingers convulsively. 'Please don't use it on me, Mistress. I'll do what you want, I swear.'

'You've done enough swearing already to earn you a good thrashing. Anyway, it's what the judge wanted,' Charlotte said.

She had a sneaking suspicion that under the rules Lari had showed enough humility to be set free now. But what the hell? The guides wanted to see Lari chastised as much as she, Charlotte, did. And the Master was no longer around ...

'Look at the glove really closely,' she added, tilting Lari's head futher so that the girl's tearful gaze met hers. 'Think of it next time you contemplate calling me names. Repent.'

'I repent,' whispered Lari. 'Charlotte, please ...'

'I said to call me Mistress,' Charlotte said softly, pulling her right arm far back then bringing it down. Lari howled into the table, and writhed like crazy.

'You can have her tied more tightly so that she can't wriggle,' the guide said.

Charlotte shook her head and struck the moving bottom again, and then a third time.

'Anything!' Lari begged. 'I'll do anything you want.'

'You'll take this thrashing till I'm tired of giving it to you,' Charlotte said. 'Then, if I tell you to, you'll beg for more.'

At last she could understand why men liked to do this; why they liked to imagine this. The way the girl moved, the colour of her arse, brought the most incredible sexual charge. This was power and sex and love and cruelty and kindness. Lari would understand that too when she was ultimately given release.

But for now she deserved some re-education, and she was going to get it. Charlotte varied the angle and severity of her palm as she used it on the girl's flaming cheeks. Lari was whimpering openly now, no longer the wilful trouble maker. 'I'll leave you to it,' said the oldest guide. Marching the reluctant younger guides before him, he walked out, locking the door.

'You can stop now!' Lari gasped. 'No one's watching.' Charlotte stayed her arm, but brought her palm over to touch the girl's scarlet rear.

'What makes you think I'll stop because we no longer have an audience?'

Lari twisted her tear-streaked head round: 'But I thought . . .'

'You thought wrong. I'm doing this because you've been a jumped up little madam who's got me into trouble. Because I'm to receive six strokes of the whip because you wouldn't let me suck your nipples the other day.'

'I'm sorry, Charlotte – I mean, Mistress. I'll take the six strokes for you. Please free me! Haven't I suffered enough?'

'You're to suffer all day,' Charlotte warned, her *mons* soaked with pleasure. 'And I'll see you receive more than six.'

'Have mercy,' whimpered Lari. 'I'm so sorry.'

'Your poor little bottom is going to be *very* sorry,' murmured Charlotte, her tummy trembling as she looked at the sore spanked globes.

'I beg . . . It hurts so much.'

'It's supposed to hurt.'

'I'll be such a good girl.'

'I'm going to make you good.'

As Charlotte flexed her arm again the three guides came back. 'We've got the clearing ready,' one said. The others' cocks jerked excitedly in unison as they observed both naked girls.

Charlotte nodded: 'You've done well. She's ready. Take her there on her hands and knees.'

'What . . . what are you going to do to me?' Lari asked Charlotte.

'Let the people see what happens to a slave who gets above herself, that's what.'

They put Lari's collar and lead on again, and she followed them uncomplainingly outdoors into the sunshine. She walked on her leash across the grass until she saw the crowds and clearing ahead.

'Mistress, please don't. I know some of those people. Can't bear for them to see me . . .'

'You'll have to bear it,' said Charlotte. 'It's what I want.'

Lari came mutinously to a halt. One of the guides walked to her rear and raised the stick he was carrying.

'I'll walk!' yelped Lari, setting off across the grass on her hands and knees at a renewed pace. Holding the lead, Charlotte hurried behind her. She stopped when she reached the clearing, and handed the lead to one of the guides.

Naked slaves and guides stood round the grassy perimeter. Gingerly Charlotte put her feet on the wooden board that had been placed there. It felt like a pavement on a hot sumer's day. Even on the rough soles of her feet it was fiery. Lari was going to feel it baking her arse.

Too excited to be nervous, she addressed her audience. 'Some of you will have heard that a slave tried to escape yesterday. I've been given the task of punishing her. I want you all to see.'

She looked back at Lari, who was hanging her head, her face hectic. Her bum, she knew, was equally flushed and red. 'Bad dog. Come to heel,' she said, softly.

Lari looked up. She licked her lips.

'Come to heel, bitch,' murmured Charlotte, slapping her leg threateningly.

The guide raised his stick and tapped it menacingly against Lari's arse. She yelped and flinched, and looked back at him. She took a step towards the concrete square.

'When a dog is bad like this we have to fetch it,' said

Charlotte. She walked with measured steps over to the girl and took hold of the leash. She pulled her slowly into the centre of the square, staring down at her. 'Then we have to teach it to obey,' she said.

'I'll obey,' whimpered Lari.

'Only because you just felt the stick on your rear end.'

'You're my Mistress. I'll do as you say.'

'Good dog,' said Charlotte. 'Then go round the crowd offering everyone a paw.'

Lari moaned and shut her eyes tightly. 'Mistress – no! Please!'

'The animal has been wilful again. We have to correct its behaviour,' Charlotte told her audience sadly. She noted that the nipples of the female audience and the males' pricks were jutting out. She motioned to one of the guides: 'Stretch her out on her belly on the platform. Tie her ankles and wrists together. Hold her down by the neck whilst I give her what for.'

Cocks leaking, the boys obeyed. Lari repented: 'Please, Mistress, I'll give everyone a paw, like a good little pup.' She sighed, some inner struggle obviously over. The fight had almost gone from her eyes, though the fire was obviously increasing in her quivering quim.

'Get into a sitting position. Shuffle over to the edge of the crowd on your bottom. Then kneel and give a paw to everyone who holds out their hand.'

Lari did so, wincing. Hands started to reach out. A few of them used their spare hands to hold onto their dicks and clits.

'Good dog!' said both men and women, laughing. More exploratory hands reached out to pinch her nipples and fondle her breasts. Others sucked her fingers, uncurling them from the shape of a paw. Lari's face was flushed with shame.

'Is the creature doing exactly what it's told, now?'

The crowd moved back as the Master appeared and entered the clearing. He walked up to both girls.

'She's been a bad dog. She's giving the nice people a paw,' Charlotte explained.

The man nodded: 'That's fine for starters. But why not make the bad doggy beg?'

Lari closed her eyes again, blushing hugely. Her fists tightened.

'Does the dog require further training?' their Master said.

'Have mercy,' whispered Lari. 'No further training to-day.'

'Actions speak louder than words,' said the Master. It seemed to be his favourite saying. 'A dog that knows who its owner is sits up on its hind legs to beg.'

Charlotte tugged at the leash. 'You heard the man.'

Lari faced the crowds, an expression of shamed misery and scintillating sexual excitement on her face.

'I was teamed with her in the Pleasure Suite once. She didn't half make things hard for me,' said a long-haired Junoesque woman, looking coldly at Lari. 'I'd like to see her sit up and beg before me like a good puppy should.'

'Approach your betters. Do as they say,' commanded the Master. Lari shuffled over to the female on her sore bum, and put her hands pathetically in the air.

'Good dog,' said the older woman, obviously enjoying having the upper hand. She patted Lari on the head, and squeezed her breasts. 'Can I check her teeth?' she added, with a wicked grin.

'That rule really applies to horses!' smiled their Master, 'but go ahead!'

'Open sesame,' whispered the woman, putting her middle fingers against Lari's lips. Lari opened her mouth wide. 'Do I get to inspect the rest of her?' the woman continued. Her nipples stood out against her chest.

The Master looked at Charlotte, and raised an enquiring eyebrow.

'She's all yours,' Charlotte told the taller woman. 'Enjoy!' The crowd whistled and heckled as Lari knelt before her fellow slave, pleasing her with her lips.

'Lick harder. Faster. Slower.'

The woman obviously liked issuing orders to the temporarily submissive girl. Amazing, Charlotte thought, how exhilarating it was to be in control when you were usually controlled. It almost made your earlier subjugation worthwhile.

'Aaaaaah!'

The woman came, her cry continuing for breathless moments. She was still standing, albeit shakily, her hands in Lari's hair. Some of the boys, Charlotte noticed, had come without touching themselves. She suspected the Master didn't let them wank without permission: they seemed permanently in need. He'd instructed her not to masturbate without being expressly told to do so. If she disobeyed and was caught she'd feel the lash.

Lari was beyond needing the lash now – she was completely biddable.

'Heel,' said Charlotte, and the punished slave came to heel. 'Back to the Punishment Chamber,' Charlotte added, taking the leash again.

Her head hanging, Lari crawled back to the place where her next lesson was about to begin.

'Did you like licking that slave?' Charlotte asked, moments after the pair of them and two guides returned to the chamber.

'No, Mistress.' Her eyes still downcast, Lari knelt.

'Would you like to lick me?'

'If it's what my Mistress wishes.'

'It is.'

Excitement racing to her *mons* and her nipples, Charlotte ordered the disappointed guides to wait outside. Then she walked over to a mattress in the centre of the hall. It looked scrupulously clean but well worn where the buttocks or tummy rubbed. Obviously she wasn't the only one who got hot as hell and demanded servicing whilst punishing a difficult slave!

'Please your Mistress with your tongue,' she instructed, lying down and spreading her legs as far apart as she was able.

'Yes, Mistress. Thank you, Mistress.' Lari was learning fast.

Quickly she dipped her head towards Charlotte's bush,

using her right hand to part and tease the labia. She settled on a place just above her swollen clitoris and licked and licked.

Incredible! Charlotte held back a moan, put her own fingers to her breasts, and began kneading them gently. She wished she had another slave to tongue her tits for her; to make them as hot as her *mons*.

Lari's tongue was so wonderfully light and arousing. It sent ripples right through her; wave upon wave upon wave.

'More,' she begged. 'Harder. Longer!' She wished she had ten tongues on her; a tongue that would cover her labial lips, her clit, the sensitive areas around her arsehole, and the velvety tunnel of her lust. 'Lick!' she commanded. 'Lick, slave, lick hard! Lick fast!'

Her sore bum obviously a reminder of what would happen if she didn't please her temporary Mistress, Lari licked exactly as she was instructed. Charlotte lifted her hips from the mattress and groaned. Almost ... Almost ... That rush of heat once felt that was never forgotten. Going, going ... She went over the top and cried out and moaned and moaned.

Jesus! She'd been horny since she first saw Lari tied over the trestle table awaiting punishment. She'd got hot handling the slipper; she'd positively creamed herself when wearing the glove. God, the feel of that thick leather; the look of Lari's arse as the two came in contact. Excitement had been building in her crotch as the day progressed.

A day which was almost over. As the first intense glow of her orgasm receded, Charlotte opened her eyes and stared up at the ceiling of the Punishment Chamber. Tomorrow things would be back to normal. Today she had but two more hours in which to enjoy her slave.

'Change places with me, Lari,' she said, getting slowly up from the mattress and addressing the still-kneeling girl.

'Yes, Mistress.' Uncertainly Lari crawled onto the quilted pad and lay down on her back.

'Spread your legs apart.'

With an ashamed whimper Lari did so.

'Now touch yourself in your secret place.'

Lari opened her eyes wide, staring at Charlotte. Her mouth opened, then closed again.

'You mean . . . ?'

'I want you to bring yourself off. Masturbate. Dirty little girls like you should have no problem in making themselves come.'

'Not with someone watching! I can't . . .'

'You can at least get reacquainted with your clitoris. If you can't come, I won't be angry but I want you to try.'

'Couldn't I do something else, Mistress? Please you with my mouth again? With my hands this time?'

Shaking her head, Charlotte went to the door and brought in the curious guides: 'Fetch a big belt or a paddle. If she fails to follow my instructions I'll take them to her arse without delay.'

'I won't fail. I'll do it!'

Memory played behind Lari's eyes and she quickly put the fingers of her right hand to her luscious lower lips. She traced the fluid trail inwards, and spread the hot wet excitement around before letting her middle two fingers come to rest at the top of her labial lips. Breathing quickly, she started to stroke round and round. Not a rubbing motion – more a caressing. Not a hurried approach, but a rhythm she could rely on for a long, long time.

Her eyes had closed now. Charlotte knelt next to her face: 'Look at me.'

Lari shuddered and did as she was instructed. She blushed from shame or desire or both.

'I'm watching you wanking yourself off,' said Charlotte cruelly, deliberately. 'And if you stop I'll tan your hide.'

Lari let out her breath in a long drawn out exhalation. Her mouth creased into a moan of embarrassed delight. 'Oh . . . oh . . . oh,' she said.

'I may take photos of you like this, pass them round the island. Everyone will see you playing with your pussy, getting wet.'

The girl stroked herself harder, and began to whimper. She drew up her legs, and ran her free hand over her breasts.

'Like a bitch in heat,' said Charlotte. 'A dog that sits up and begs, then rubs itself against the furniture.'

'Oh!' moaned Lari. 'Oh! Oh!'

And then she came; her head arching back against the pillow, her eyes closed tightly, her mouth stretched open. For excited seconds a mottled sex flush covered her lower belly and thighs.

'You liked that,' said Charlotte. 'I think you needed an audience. Maybe next time I'll make you bring yourself off in front of all the other slaves in the square.'

'What makes you so sure there'll be a next time?' The Master's voice boomed over her shoulder. Charlotte jumped and turned around: there was no one there. 'Don't get presumptuous!' continued the disembodied voice. 'I'll decide who you punish, and when.'

Damn! He must be behind a one-way mirror, using a loudspeaker system: she hadn't realised the Punishment Chamber had either of these things. Perhaps every room did. Perhaps they had other technical toys. There was so much she didn't know about this place. Lari was still lying on her back, looking around apprehensively. Vacating her place at the girl's head, Charlotte got to her feet.

She faced the door, just as their Master walked in. For long, long moments he looked down at the chastened Lari, at her dripping sex.

'You've done well,' he said to Charlotte. 'Turned her into a much more obsequious little girl than the one I lent you.'

'Thank you, sir.'

The man turned to Lari. 'Now, my dear, how was it for you?'

'It hurt terribly, sir.' Lari brushed tears from her eyes, and shifted awkwardly on her punished posterior. 'Even you never chastised me this hard.'

'Didn't I?' asked the Master, looking at both girls curiously. 'Then you'd better not give me a reason to rectify that!'

He looked at Charlotte. 'In a moment you can go back

to your cell for the evening. There's a bath and a meal waiting. A new shelf of books.' Charlotte thanked him again. She was hungry and sweaty. Most of all though, she wanted to be alone for a wank.

'Same goes for you.' The Master looked with something approaching gentleness at the flushed Lari. 'But first we'll take you to one of the Pleasure Lounges for a lukewarm shower. Then we'll have someone put some soothing ointment on that poor bottom, to take away the worst of the pain.'

At a signal from the man, both girls walked towards the door, one jauntily, one carefully.

'Charlotte, you're to come here tomorrow morning after breakfast,' added the Master, conversationally. 'The little Matter of these six strokes of the whip you're still due.'

'Yes, sir.' She'd hoped that he'd forgotten, or had decided not to give them to her. After all, she'd done so well today! Her glow of self satisfaction faded further at his next words, their implication.

'Lari. Report here in three hours for a guided tour, then return tomorrow morning after your meal.'

'Yes, sir,' whispered the girl, submissively.

'Don't you wish to know why, Lari?' continued the man, smiling.

'Only if my Master wishes to tell me, sir.'

'He does.' The man looked as if he was enjoying some special secret. 'It's to give Charlotte her taste of the whip.'

Bastard, Charlotte thought – she'd feared something like this would happen! Why hadn't she just teased Lari all day? Instead she'd really heated the girl's backside; humiliated her in front of half the island. She'd made her cry and give head and crawl around like a dog, and masturbate.

'See you tomorrow, Charlotte,' said Lari, softly. A cruel gleam had come into her eyes and her submissiveness was starting to fade. Charlotte gulped, and nodded. She walked slowly back to her cell, trying not to think of how hard she'd receive the dreaded lash.

After her bath and meal she endured a restless evening's reading, and imagining. She spent the long, long night lying on her bottom, knowing that by tomorrow she probably wouldn't be able to for quite some time.

11

The wild child was about to whip Charlotte! Vernon settled back in his well-cushioned chair and gazed through the one-way mirror as his girlfriend entered the Punishment Chamber trying to look brave.

'Hands and knees, Charlotte, whilst Lari puts your collar and lead on,' said the Master matter-of-factly. Charlotte swallowed and did what she was told.

Vernon watched as the duskier slave fastened a thick studded collar around his girlfriend's neck and tightened it. She clipped on the studded lead, then led her, crawling quickly, over to the furthest wall from which protruded iron hoops.

Standing on tiptoe, Lari tethered Charlotte to one of the fastenings. 'I need restraints for her wrists and ankles,' she told the guides.

'Bring thongs,' added the Master, pointing out to the boys where to find everything. 'They'll stop her getting free but are sufficiently soft that they won't hurt her wrists.'

'Aren't I allowed to hurt her wrists?' Lari asked, curiously.

The Master shook his head. 'Remember she's going home soon with her boyfriend to the outside world. Marks on her wrists would show even when she was fully clothed.'

Her boyfriend, thought Vernon distantly. *He* was her boyfriend! It was hard to imagine leaving this island with Charlotte during the next few days . . .

He stroked Suki's hair, and kissed her gently. 'The whip is very bad,' the native girl whispered. 'Hits hard.'

'You've had it often?'

'Only the once. I work hard to please my Master.'

'That's more than can be said for Charlotte!' Vernon grinned.

He looked back through the one-way mirror to find the object of his conversation tied facing the wall, blindfolded with a thick black cloth. As he watched, one of the guides tied the thongs holding her ankles together to a ring in the floor. Now she'd remain upright whatever happened; she couldn't dodge out of the way.

'Fetch the whip, Lari,' ordered the Master, pointing at a light black implement with a strong ebony handle. Lari brought it over, ran it through her fingers, and flexed it once, twice, thrice. Eight foot in front of her a naked Charlotte remained largely immobile; only her shoulders jerked occasionally as if in anticipation of the punishment she was about to receive.

'Six strokes for failing to carry out a command,' said the Master, staring at the bound and blindfolded victim.

Lari drew the whip back, and brought it forward across Charlotte's waiting bum. Charlotte cried out, her front embracing the wall so that she was hugging it more closely. Lari took aim and delivered the second stripe.

Even from here Vernon could see the tormented twitch of his girlfriend's rounded buttocks. 'When a girl is tied standing up,' explained Suki, 'she feels the stimulus more than if she's lying down.'

As if hearing the words, Lari directed the next stage of her attack to the girl's helpless thigh backs. Hard leather met soft flesh. Charlotte flinched in her bonds.

'Six,' said the Master, as Lari laid on the final stroke of the flogging. Her eyes were bright, her face animated. Regretfully she let her whip hand fall to her side.

'Untie the slave. Bring her over here on her hands and knees,' added the Master to one of the guides.

Excited as ever, the boy did so. Crawling up to Lari, Charlotte stayed in doggy fashion, looking compliantly at the ground.

'Kiss Lari's feet and thank her for thrashing you,' said the Master quietly.

'Thank you, Lari,' whispered Charlotte, licking her lips.

Kneeling down, the Master lightly slapped first one side of her face then the other.

'I'll tell you when you can lick your lips – or can do anything! Don't ever make a gesture without permission when I'm talking to you!'

'Sorry, sir,' muttered Charlotte. Moisture seeped from her tremulous aroused mouth.

Belatedly she kissed the other girl's feet, kissing each toe, before putting her lips to the main part of first one foot then the other.

'Stand up, slave,' said the Master.

Charlotte stood..

Vernon could see the faint memory of the whip on her firm nakedness. He longed to trace each curve with his finger. She no longer felt as if she were his.

'The whip rarely excites the slaves; it's just for the Master and Mistress,' Suki murmured, watching equally avidly. Her small hands played with the hair on Vernon's chest.

'Exciting to watch, but not to feel, huh?' asked Vernon, curiously. He kept one eye on Charlotte who was still standing mutely, waiting for her next command. Smiling, the Master handed the end of the lead to Lari.

'What would you like to do with her next?'

'I . . . I don't understand.' The darker girl looked wide eyed from the man to the girl who had punished her yesterday.

'Charlotte still hasn't been punished for running away that day. I'm handing over the task to you,' their Master explained.

'No!'

To Vernon's surprise, Charlotte swatted Lari's hands away. Her own hands were quickly restrained by the eager guides.

'But she hates me!' she wailed. 'She hates me!'

'I've suggested she retaliate by giving you intense pleasure – in her own good time, of course!'

'Please – can't *you* correct me instead? Don't leave me with her!' muttered Charlotte.

'I'm not leaving for a while. I intend to watch,' said the man.

'Me too,' muttered Vernon, feeling his dick lengthen. He noted Lari's small hard nipples were standing out against her firm tanned breasts.

'The Master often does this, turning us on each other,' whispered Suki, whose own tits stood equally to attention. 'I had to punish a girl once. I spanked her bare bottom and used a very light cane on her arse whilst she touched her toes.'

'And what did she do to you in return?' Vernon whispered.

'Used a paddle on me for ages. Made my bum burn, because the Master was watching. She thought he'd be pleased with her if she was extra strict.'

'And wasn't he?'

Suki shook her head. 'Uh uh. He said the punishment should fit the crime – that she'd been excessive. He had her tied up and used the paddle on her arse until she screamed.'

'You can't fathom out exactly what the management wants here,' said Vernon, thoughtfully.

'You aren't meant to,' Suki said.

Vernon returned his gaze to Charlotte, who was being marched towards two ropes, the far ends of which were attached to the ceiling. As he watched, they tied her wrists to separate corners and tied her legs at the ankles to two far-apart hoops. Now she was spread in the shape of a cross, her pubis some three feet from the floor and bared for their attention. As the audience stared, two of the guides wheeled over a gym horse and positioned it beneath her sex.

'Get ready to mount it,' ordered Lari.

Charlotte looked down, not comprehending. Not yet . . . At the Master's bidding, Lari walked over to the nearest wall and pressed a button. A thick gold phallus moved slowly out of the gym horse until its tip rested between the aroused girl's labial lips. It was broad and tingling, obviously fashioned to tease wanton female flesh.

'Let's give her twenty thrusts for starters,' Lari murmured. One of the guides manipulated the control panel and the dildo penetrated Charlotte's hungry quim with at least six inches. Her face contorted with a pleasure close to anguish, and she wailed.

'If you come too soon we place this in your arse instead. It's up to you.'

'Not my bum, please, Mistress,' Charlotte whimpered, pressing her heated hole down on the vibrating instrument.

'Forty thrusts right up your arse if you don't rise off this now.'

'You mean . . . ?'

'Use your hands to pull your arms up so that your crevice is above the mechanical cock. You haven't earned this yet!'

Charlotte groaned. 'But Mistress, it thrusts so good inside me. I need to come. I want it . . .'

'Now or you'll suffer the consequences – hard!'

Reluctantly, Charlotte pulled her quivering quim away. After a moment she couldn't hold up her weight, and sank down – but Lari had the dildo retract into the gym horse. By kneeling down at the foot of the one-way mirror, Vernon could see up his girlfriend's vagina – it was a dripping, starving, open gape.

After a long frustrated moment, the guides looked to Lari for clarification. She nodded: 'Give her another cock-like taste.'

The horse was lowered a little so that the dildo didn't reach so high up Charlotte's body. She pushed down, pulling at her arm ropes, gave a frustrated little twist and tried to pinion herself onto its bulk. She failed, swung back a little, and tried a second time, achieving an inch of pleasurable promise up her hole.

Sensing his arousal at the spectacle, Suki began to stroke Vernon's balls through his tight jeans. 'Lari's just doing this to humiliate her,' she whispered. 'Making her jump up and down in the nude.'

Charlotte bent her knees and hauled downwards, her quim clutching the top of the shaft a third time. She made a purchase on it, so that she was sitting astride its thrilling expanse.

'Ten thrusts,' allowed Lari, 'then raise off it again.'

Charlotte whimpered, but did as she was told.

'Flex your ankles,' said Lari. 'Spread your legs even further. Let the guides see your pussy.'

Charlotte blushed hugely, her thighs involuntarily tightening. Lari slapped the backs of her legs hard four times in succession: 'Do it now!'

Swallowing hard, Charlotte did so. Vernon saw the pink underhang of her lips, and the lighter pink stains where Lari's palm had just been.

'Prepare her so that she rides the dildo for ten minutes but doesn't quite reach orgasm,' Lari said coldly.

Eagerly the boys rushed forward. Each activated a handle on the lower parts of the gym horse, which heightened it to within brushing distance of Charlotte's base.

'Now put the vibrator on tease,' added Lari gloatingly. She'd obviously been given the guided tour last night, thought Vernon excitedly. She knew exactly how to use the equipment to best torment her slave!

'She deserves this,' he said quietly. 'She didn't treat me right.'

'I'll treat you right,' whispered Suki, putting her lips to his nipples and taking them alternately in her mouth.

Meanwhile, Charlotte looked all set to kiss Lari's arse – if she hadn't been tethered and helpless. 'Count each pleasure giving thrust,' said Lari. 'If you lose count, we consider putting it up your arse again.'

'I'm so hot I can't think!' whispered Charlotte.

'That's the way it should be,' Lari said.

She ordered the thrusting to begin, and Charlotte screamed blue murder.

'You forgot to count,' said Lari softly. 'That means you get it anally at a later date.'

She slowed the thrust speed to especially slow – or so it seemed to the excited watchers.

'One!' yelled Charlotte.

'Say "Thank you, Mistress, for the mechanical cock thrust," ' Lari continued, with a cold little smile. She propelled the super shaft again: it warmed the girl's interiors.

'Two! Thank you, Mistress, for the mechanical cock thrust,' Charlotte cried. She said the same thing for shafts three, four and five. Her arse moved like it was being stung by a thousand nettles. Her crotch was rubbing against the oscillating surface. Her sex gleamed.

'Up more!' she begged after the sixth. The watchers could see her tugging at the bonds which held her wrists and ankles. Her face was near-orgasmic, her eyes downcast.

'You used the slipper and the glove on me,' said Lari softly, 'not to mention carrying out some of your more fiendish delights.'

Every cock and clit in the room was rampant now: they knew Charlotte was for it; knew she deserved it, that this was natural justice at its best.

'You're going to have the hottest clit on the island,' Lari said, coolly.

She arranged the seventh thrust and Charlotte cried out again.

'The horniness increases after a short hiatus,' said the Master, matter-of-factly.

'Oh dear,' said Lari, walking up to Charlotte's swollen clit and starting to caress it, 'we've been negligent again.'

'Please,' whispered Charlotte. 'Thrust seven. Thank you for giving me the mechanical cock, Mistress.'

'Too late,' said Lari, regretfully. 'You said it too late.'

'But I didn't mean . . .'

'What happens to girls who don't do what they're told?' Lari continued, in a soft firm voice. 'Answer me,' she added, 'or you'll feel a nice thick belt across your arse later on.'

'They get punished,' muttered Charlotte, licking her lips, her eyes closed.

'And where do we punish them?'

'On their . . . wherever you want!'

'Name a place, Charlotte, where a bad girl might be punished.'

The observers held their breath.

'She could be caned on the hands – even the feet, Mistress.'

'Where else?'

'On her back, Mistress. On her front. On the soft curve of her tummy.'

'Go on.'

'On . . . on her arms and legs.'

'I think we've forgotten someplace, Charlotte, someplace important.'

Charlotte swallowed hugely; her toes and fingers flexed.

'Where else could a Mistress punish a bad girl, Charlotte?'

There was no reply.

'If you don't answer we'll have to add the tawse to your list of punishments. I've seen bigger girls than you cry out at a taste of the tawse. Seen them suck cock after cock rather than feel its heat again. I think they've got an especially effective tawse in the cupboard here . . .'

'A Mistress could punish a bad girl on her bottom, Mistress,' whispered Charlotte, defeated.

'That's right, she could. On her wicked little arse.' Lari ran both sets of fingers over Charlotte's well-warmed one. 'I could lay numerous strokes on this pretty reddened bum.'

'Please, no! I'll take the thrusts instead, as many as you like. I'll rise up when you tell me!'

'And deprive this bad little bottom?' Lari said. 'I don't know if I can –'

'I'll show you such a good time with my mouth!' Charlotte promised desperately.

Lari smiled: 'Later I may give you that chance.' She shook her head. 'But for now I've got to concentrate on this greedy little hole of yours which keeps begging for a mechanical cock.'

She started in on the quivering quim again; it was clearly begging for satiation. Meanwhile her globes were jerking, writhing, and growing more and more uncontrolled with each push of the phallus. Each time, Charlotte cried out the number of the thrust and thanked Lari for providing it.

'She's learning,' the Master said. 'If her clit is sensible it will never forget.' He looked at Lari. 'She's repented of her ways. Put the dildo on full speed and let down her arms slightly so that she can find her rhythm.' Lari did.

For a moment after the phallus entered her and stayed, Charlotte hardly seemed to move, as if not quite believing it. Then her eyes closed in a gesture of near rhapsody and she centred her body so that it gripped the bucking rod. Her tits seemed to stand out more against her stretched flesh as the machine fucked her.

'We're all watching, Charlotte,' said the Master, and she screamed a name – whose name? – and came and came.

Five minutes later, the temporary Mistress caressed her slave's twitching bum, making her wriggle even further. 'I hope you're going to be good when I free you,' she murmured. 'I hope you're going to be humble and show due respect.'

'I swear,' Charlotte said, writhing. 'I swear!'

'Release the slave,' said Lari, sitting in a chair, and spreading her legs slightly.

The guides freed Charlotte, and laid her on her belly on the ground.

'Permission to crawl over to my Mistress and please her?' Charlotte asked.

'Permission granted, slave,' said Lari. 'You may crawl on your belly,' she added as Charlotte made to get up onto her hands and knees.

Vernon's cock swelled even further as he watched Charlotte wriggling across the floor on her tummy, her overheated *mons* a marked contrast to the rest of her flesh.

'She wants to please now,' murmured Suki, her small fingers giving their own exquisite pleasure to Vernon's testicles. 'She'll lick really hard.'

She did. As they watched, Charlotte reached Lari's feet, asked for permission to raise her head, and put her lips to her Mistress's labia.

'Granted,' said Lari. 'I want an orgasm within five minutes, slave.'

Nodding, Charlotte set her tongue to work, sucking,

licking, and kissing. She tongued around the other girl's clit till she found the site that pleasured her best.

Only a woman could fully understand the exquisite mysteries of the clitoris, thought Vernon enviously. Only another woman could truly know just how such a licking felt.

'Oh God!' Lari moaned, her ankles flexing, her toes straining into rigidity. 'Oh ... oh ...' Pushing her sex more desperately against Charlotte's mouth, she came.

'Permission to lie down, please, Mistress,' whispered Charlotte, clearly exhausted.

Lari looked as if she was about to refuse permission, but the Master stared at her hard.

'Permission granted, slave,' gasped Lari, wiping perspiration from her forehead. Gelatinous strands of wetness were slowly stringing their way out of her sex, and lay slickly on her inner thighs.

For long moments the Master leaned against the wall, watching everyone's reaction. Charlotte lay prostrate on her belly, her moist entrance a testimony to the teasing that had ended moments before. Her breasts, squashed though they were against the ground, looked more passionately puffy than usual. Lari's looked equally juicy; the nipples were pink-tinged.

'I love you,' whispered Suki shyly to Vernon. He turned to her, and kissed her forehead. Her right hand, which had been cupping his testes throughout Charlotte's taunting ordeal, now squeezed rhythmically at his aching balls.

'Can I suck you off, sir?' she whispered. 'Or would you like to rub your cock between my bottom checks?'

Vernon hesitated, enjoying the thought of either option. He looked through the mirror at Charlotte's satisfied sex and realised he felt nothing but lust and rage for her now. No love. No need to remain faithful. Christ, the way she'd just gone down on Lari so enthusiastically she might even have become a dyke!

'I'd like to slide inside you,' he whispered to his little native girl. Her dark eyes widened, and she reached slowly for his zipper and edged it down.

'How would sir like Suki? On her tummy, on her back, bending low?'

'On her tummy,' he said, his cock twitching with anticipation as she laid herself down on the chaise.

Admiringly he stroked her perfect arse, its darker crease. He ran a finger from the top of her spine to where buttock crack met labial slit. She was wet. He was hard. They were horny. With a triumphant sigh he entered his little slave girl for the first time and began to fuck away.

12

Being licked by another female slave was great – she'd had several orgasms that way during the past two days at the Pleasure Suite! Though there had been an audience it had hardly seemed like work at all. And it certainly hadn't humiliated her as much as that awful day spent servicing Lari. Ruefully Charlotte remembered how it had felt to crawl, to beg.

She'd made Lari squeal by licking her sensuously that day, and had subsequently enacted two lesbian floor shows for the entertainment of the other slaves. No matter how much she cringed before doing so, she was becoming quite adept at tonguing a clit.

Being tongued was so much better, though – you felt superior. You felt excited almost before the slave knelt before you; at the thought of what she'd do. *She*. Charlotte wondered when they'd next twin her with a *man*: she was getting withdrawal symptoms. She dreamed about cock every night.

Even wanking was difficult – she suspected that the Master and Mistress could video her when she was in her cell; they could watch her every movement. This demanded more discreet self sessions – but there were no blankets for the chaise on which she slept, and nor had she an excuse to request any, for her cell remained beautifully warm.

In desperation she'd tried bringing herself off in the bath: underwater wanking. But the warm liquid washed away her hot lubricants, and a parched, over-tingly orgasm was the poor result. Nothing like the wonderful wave upon wave of lust you experienced on dry land. Nothing like a really good session with a man.

If only she could find one, fuck one! What a waste it was, spending day after day in the Pleasure Suite acting like a dyke.

'Am I licking labia again?' she asked archly as the guide appeared to take her to the Suite for the morning session.

'No. The Master said that you're to keep that body of yours toned up. He wants you to go for a run across the grounds.'

'With an escort, of course?' And a collar and lead, no doubt.

'No. You've been here a while now, so you're to go on trust.'

Go on trust. She'd heard some of the other slaves speak of this. It meant the Master felt you were beginning to show your true nature. That you'd do what was required for the good of the island and its staff. Charlotte sighed. She would, too – she didn't mind the prospect of a run. In fact it suited her. Back in the old world she'd done aerobics and gone swimming one a week. And riding of course. Ah, riding with Jeffrey! Riding his cock as well as riding her more traditional mount . . .

Her *mons* tingling, she accepted the water bottle with the built-in compass that the guide gave her, and set off across the fields. She skirted around buildings which she recognised, and waved to some girls she knew by sight who were obviously on their way to work.

Charlotte ran on, finding a pace which suited her. She ran past unfamiliar buildings and unfamiliar people. The sun played over her nakedness, her water bottle bounced round her waist on its drawstring. Her tits moved up and down in rhythmic accord. Her bum felt taut, and shapely; her thighs felt strong.

After many miles she slowed to a trot, then a fast walk, then a stroll. She stopped for a rest in a meadow full of flowers and admired the gold and scarlet butterflies which winged lazily by. She drank some water, picked three luscious pink pear-like fruits from one of the many trees skirting the area, and ate them. Then she lay back, closed her eyes and slept for a while.

When she awoke she felt thirsty, and hungry for something more substantial than the pink fruits. She finished the water in her bottle, and wandered on across the fields till she found a fenced-in melon patch that looked as if it had been dug over that very day. The guide had told her to eat what she wished, and to walk as long as she wanted, her only stipulations being that she must not break any of the Master's rules and must be home for tea.

Lunch, then, was going to be melon – if she could find a way over the waist high fence! Standing on tiptoe, Charlotte put her hands on the wood and pulled herself half way up, glad that the fence didn't have spikes. Then she angled her shapely legs over it and let herself down gently on the other side.

Now she needed something with which to break open one of the melons. Something with which to enter it, she thought, and a tingle of pleasure coursed through her loins. Normally by now she'd be coming under some woman's tongue, screaming out her desire to the rooftops. Normally she'd be avidly eyeing the cock of some rampant male guide . . .

No cock till the Master arranges it, she reminded herself dismally. The only appetite she'd be feeding for a while was that of her stomach which was hollow and dry.

En route to a garden shed in the corner of the orchard, her foot kicked against a pile of stones and small boulders. These would do! Abandoning her trek to the hut she hungrily sought out a sharp one, and used it to access the nearest of the large, green-skinned fruits. She cut into the heart of the water melon, working round the sides until she'd severed it in two.

Juice and flesh and colourful tangy sweetness! She buried her face in the moist redness, and gorged and gorged. At last she looked up, her eyes bright with happiness and satisfaction, to see satisfaction of a different kind . . .

He was tall – around five foot eleven. He was African. He wore a white loincloth: nothing else.

'Hi,' Charlotte said, shyly. She felt caught out and silly, realising that his clothing only enhanced her own tender nakedness. 'I was hungry. I hope it's okay . . .?'

The man nodded: 'Eat. Enjoy.'

'I'm full now.'

She wondered what it would be like to be full of his cock.

'Are you new here?' she asked.

He nodded slightly.

'You tend this garden?'

He shook his head.

'Oh, what do you do?'

'Everything. Nothing.'

'I know the feeling!' she grinned. 'They have me licking women till they come whilst the others watch!'

He smiled. He was really beautiful. Really sexy. She looked covetously at his loincloth, at the impressive length beneath. She pushed her shoulders back so that her breasts jutted out more fully, and looked up at him; eyes wide; lips parting; waiting for him to make the first move.

He didn't. She scanned the landscapes. She hadn't seen anyone else for the last three hours or so. They were definitely alone. 'Fancy a game of snap?' she laughed, feeling reckless.

'How do you play that?'

'I'll point to or pick up an object. You score a point if you can find one the same.'

'All right.'

He squatted down beside her, and his loincloth rode up a little. She tried to see under it as she reached for a twig. 'Snap!' he said, finding a similar one in the dusty ground. She found a leaf and he did likewise. Again he said, 'Snap!'

It was now or never. She thought she'd seen desire in his eyes. Now she would prove it. If she was wrong she'd never have to see him again. After all, this was the first time she'd reached his part of the island. It would presumably be the last, given that she was going home in a few short weeks . . .

'Can you find another example of *this*?' she asked sultrily, reaching below his loincloth. She took hold of his already semi-hard cock, feeling it lengthen and widen in her hand. He swallowed, and shook his head. His dark eyes

170

remained fixed on hers. 'Seems a shame to waste it,' she murmured, 'given that it's so rare.'

Her other hand slid below his balls, and weighed them appreciatively. They felt like firm warm apples. Wishing to feast her eyes on them, she edged the loincloth away, and took it off, revealing thick black pubic hair that rose up to his belly. His cock was thrusting upwards in the same direction, already leaking at the tip.

'There's more than this garden that needs cultivating, slave boy,' whispered Charlotte. She dipped her mouth to his hardness and nibbled at the head till he groaned. He tasted of soap and increasing saltiness. She ran her tongue down his shaft till she reached his balls.

'Touch me,' she whispered, moving closer to him so that they knelt, embracing each other. The man let his weight take him backwards, and Charlotte climbed on top. 'Cup my breasts!' she urged. The man did so. She was having to tell him everything: either he was an especially submissive slave or he just feared getting caught.

'No one will see us,' she promised, as his fingers played with her nipples. 'I walked miles to get here. Everyone else is working indoors.'

The man nodded. His eyes betrayed his lust. His cock was rubbing against her belly. He slid his large hands down her arms, pinning them at her sides.

Black fingers on white flesh. Charlotte looked at their entwining bodies, and excitement raced to her clitoris. This was new. This was different. This was going to be great!

'That's nice,' she whispered, as the African beneath her raised his muscular hips, rubbing his maleness against her aroused and sex-salved femaleness. 'But I know how to make it feel even better than this . . .'

Inhaling in anticipation, she raised herself on her knees, then squatted and rose further until she was poised above him. She centred her opening till it was above his engorged dark prick, then lowered herself so that the tight circle of her muscles just rested on the tip of him; her labia against his leaking loins.

'Better than cultivating melons?' she whispered, staring down at him.

The man nodded. His eyes were watching her throughout. His cock told her he liked what he saw. His balls seemed to stand out to increase the applause.

Groaning, Charlotte worked herself on to him till an inch of his cock had disappeared inside her. 'Want more of me?' she teased.

The man nodded, his face twisting in ecstasy. At last he needed her as much as she needed him!

'Say pretty please,' Charlotte continued, moving her hips so that she circled round, still keeping the same length of him inside her. She wanted him in her fully – but she wanted him to beg. After all, he'd had it easy so far, too easy. She'd done all the running. She'd risked being rebuked, and denied.

'I may pull away from you,' she warned. 'Take away my hot wet sweetness. Leave your cock out all alone in the cold.'

The man closed his eyes again. Charlotte made to rise off him, but he grabbed her round the waist, and pulled her down hard so that she was impaled on the full length of his cock.

'Aaah!' Charlotte cried out, half in pleasure, half in pain. He felt too big for her. He felt as if he filled her so fully that she'd never be able to move. 'Too much,' she whispered. 'I can't take it all.'

In answer the African sat up, still keeping inside her up to the hilt. He rocked her backwards till she was lying flat on her back, her legs together, and moved himself on top of her, his elbows supporting his weight. Now he felt even bigger than before in the cock department. Charlotte felt excited, afraid. She had lost control of the situation; she wished he wouldn't stare at her in that unblinking way.

Still, she needed a man – and he was *all* man!

'Move slowly, baby,' she cautioned. 'You're so big.'

Her new partner obliged, pulling leisurely half out of her, then sliding fully back in. He felt as thick as her forearm. He felt so extended she half expected him to come out of her throat.

'Careful,' she continued, as he rammed forward with increasing enthusiasm. In answer he used his large black hands to cup her small white arse and pull her up so that he plunged even more deeply in.

So he wanted to play dirty, did he? She was an expert! 'Like it rough, do you?' she muttered, using her nails to scratch none too gently at his chest. When he failed to react she tried harder, pinching his dark nipples till they felt like overheated bullets in her hands. Still he fucked on, like a mechanical piston; unstoppable. Not that she wanted him to stop. She just wanted him to show proper gratitude – like Vernon used to when he fucked her. Life had been so simple then . . .

She reached her hands back to his arse and slapped it as hard as she was able. He didn't vary his rhythm, but his fingers closed cruelly on her breasts and tightened till she squealed.

'Oh you bastard!' she moaned.

His gaze said that she'd started it. Such ungiving eyes. But such a promising cock.

She shut her eyes, heard a twig snap, and opened them again. The Master was standing over her. He held his inevitable stick. 'I . . .' Charlotte tried to scramble up, but her partner's weight held her to the dusty ground.

'Finish shafting her,' said the Master to the man.

The African nodded grimly, thrusting faster and harder. Charlotte whimpered with pleasure; with the anticipation of pain to come. The guides were watching her, grinning.

'Beg!' they murmured mockingly. 'Beg!'

Charlotte gritted her teeth as nirvana grew nearer and nearer. It was all the sweeter, knowing she probably wouldn't be allowed to come again for a long, long time . . .

How had the Master known she'd run this way? Did he have her wired for sound or something? She must check her water bottle more minutely for electronic devices. She must work harder to stay one step ahead of the game . . .

'Harder,' she implored, as the horny heat flushed through her mucous-leaking mount. 'Faster.'

Her black beauty obliged and she came and came.

'Uh,' the man above her grunted. He must be getting

close to his own orgasm. Seconds later he pulled out of her and she realised he'd already reached it, recovered, and was walking away. She wiped perspiration from her forehead as his seed began to run from between her legs in a warm stream.

'Stand up,' said the Master to Charlotte. 'Hose her down,' he added to one of the guides. The boy fetched a hose from the hut and turned its cool jet on Charlotte's flesh.

'Stand facing the fence. Spread your thighs apart,' instructed the man. Charlotte did so. She felt the water hit with some force at her labia, forcing the lips apart, and rinsing away her own wetness and that of her partner in crime. She turned this way and that as instructed whilst the guide hosed her still swollen breasts, the flesh of her tits, and her belly. He splattered her sweat-streaked back and thighs.

'Now bend over the fence,' continued the Master's voice when her shower was over. Charlotte tensed, and swallowed. She looked back to see the African going into the little hut. At least he wasn't getting to see her humiliation – that was something! She'd felt so in charge a few moments before when she was on top.

'Over the fence, Charlotte,' said the Master again. 'Quickly.'

Charlotte stretched up and let her arms drop carefully over till they reached the ground. The rough top of the fence rubbed cruelly at her belly. She watched resignedly as two of the guides used thin belts to fasten her ankles and wrists in place at the foot of the fence.

'This is for following the rules of your pussy and not the island,' said the man, conversationally. Charlotte blushed with shame. She was glad her face was pointing away from them, that they couldn't see her turn red. Not that they wanted to concentrate on the colour of her face. They had two other scarlet cheeks in mind . . .

She shuddered, and tensed. She could tell her bum made an inviting target and wished she could twist round to see what they were about to do.

The first rap warmed both buttocks roughly in the centre. She cried out and rubbed frantically against the fence top, awaiting the next strike. She was being punished by something long and hard – he must be using a stick, or something similar. He used it again now further down her helpless bottom cheeks. Charlotte shuddered. He was marking her inch by inch in a controlled manner, obviously colouring her bottom a uniform shade.

'It wasn't my fault!' she cried, but the whack of the stick drowned out her words, and she yelled in anguish and frustration. 'I didn't want to!' she added. The stick heated her posterior again. 'I'll do anything,' she whispered, then heard one of the guides mutter something and give a dirty laugh.

But she'd submitted to their will, so they untied her and held her upright. She watched as the Master walked over to one of three tethered horses, and untied the largest beast. Effortlessly he swung onto it; he obviously rode bareback. The Master motioned to the guides: 'Lift her up.'

The guides did so. Charlotte felt herself being swung through the air towards the beast and the man astride it. She tried to work out how to get her leg over its side, and discovered, seconds later to her shame, that they'd laid her across it on her belly. Her head hung down towards the ground on one side, her legs down the other. Her bum was a helpless toy directly under the Master's hands.

'I can ride properly!' she gasped, trying to raise her head. 'A friend owns some stables.'

'I want you to ride like this. I want to stroke your wicked little arse.' His hands did so, bringing fresh pain, fresh desire, and fresh embarrassment. 'I've organised a welcoming committee, Charlotte. They'll enjoy seeing you being ridden home like this.'

'I hate you,' she said.

His thumb traced slowly down the cleft of her spread cheeks and she trembled and shrank against the horse flesh. She wanted to come so badly! She felt so hot!

'I believe I'm not the only one you hate. I heard what you said about our other darker friend.'

175

Her head hanging towards the ground, Charlotte nodded: 'It wasn't how it looked – he made me! I just stopped for a rest.'

'You're tired now,' said the man. 'Tell us this after tea, after you've slept and eaten. That's if you still want to. Otherwise we'll let the matter rest.'

Rest, rest. Charlotte lay for the remainder of the afternoon in her cell on her stomach. The Master had handcuffed her hands in front of her so that she couldn't wank. She tried rubbing herself against the chaise where she lay, but couldn't get close enough to the stimulus. Her rage and turned-on tension grew and grew.

Someone would pay for this somehow. If that guy hadn't played so hard to get, if he had just fucked her a bit sooner, they'd have gotten away with it and she'd be creaming her crevice at the memory by now. She wanted him to be taught a lesson: a sore lesson. Why should she be the only one tied over that bloody fence?

'Tea time.'

Her usual guide came into her cell, set down her meal, and undid the handcuffs. Charlotte ate hungrily, aware that she'd only had fruit for lunch.

'I'm to take you to Court after this,' the girl added awkwardly.

Charlotte nodded. 'I'm a witness, not the accused. I'll be fine.'

The girl looked away and said nothing. Charlotte finished her meal and made desultory conversation for fifteen minutes or so. Then a buzzer sounded in her cell and the guide stood up.

'Be careful,' she said, looking worriedly at Charlotte's striped backside.

'Don't worry,' said Charlotte. 'I'm off the hook – literally! I've already had the stick.'

In silence they walked to the Court and the guide left her in the witness stand. Last time she'd been here she'd stood trial with Lari in the dock . . . She wondered how Lari was. She hadn't been paired with her lately. She'd tell her about the illicit cock she'd had when she saw her; how they'd been caught.

The judged entered, took his place at the head of the Court, and turned to Charlotte.

'Do you still wish to proceed with this complaint?'

'I do, M'Lord.'

'Let it be entered in the records that she does.'

Charlotte shivered. It was all very formal.

'I understand,' said the judge, quirking an eyebrow, 'that there were no witnesses until the very end?'

'Then it's his word against mine, M'Lord,' Charlotte said.

'State your case.'

'I went running to please my Master. I stopped for a rest, for some refreshments. I must have fallen asleep and when I woke up this man was on top of me, his manhood up my feminine parts.'

'What man? Do you see him here?'

Charlotte looked round the Court at the grinning guides and slaves until she saw the solitary black male slave.

'That man,' she said, pointing to him.

Again that inscrutable stare.

'You would never have agreed to have intercourse with him?' the judge clarified.

'Never, M'Lord. I know my Master decrees who I should and shouldn't have sex with at all times.'

'Indeed,' said the judge, looking like he hoped he'd be next on the agenda. Charlotte gave him a winning smile. She wondered if they'd let her thrash the dark-skinned man herself. That would teach him for not being as keen as she was! Maybe she should have done it at the start.

'Bring the evidence on,' said the judge.

Charlotte stared, surprised. He'd said himself that there weren't any witnesses until the final moments of their session. She saw the video camera wheeled in. Then a cinema screen was rolled down, and she began to tremble with shame and fear.

'This was taken from the hut. The camera records automatically,' said the defence. 'We can see and eradicate wildlife that's damaging the crops that way.'

Fuck it! Charlotte stared at the screen, hoping that they were calling her bluff, watching her expression for signs of anxiety. With difficulty she kept her features smooth, her body immobile. In truth her hands wanted to creep protectively to her posterior to hide it from the whip.

'We'll fast forward to the evidence,' continued the defence. The melon fields, occasionally infiltrated by a small foraging animal or bird, sped past the court's watchful eyes. Then a human figure entered the arena, picked up and broke open a melon, and ate some of it. The defence slowed the film to normal. Charlotte watched herself feeding, and watched the man she'd seduced approach.

The entire Court house was watching too; watching her reach out for the man's balls and remove his loincloth; hold his prick; lick it, tongue the sides, push her nipples closer to his hands.

'As you can see,' said the defence, 'this woman made every move towards my client. Then she accused him of forcing himself on her whilst she slept.'

'What have you to say for yourself?' the judge asked Charlotte coldly. She stared at the floor, her mind racing.

'I . . . I'm sorry. I don't know why I said what I did. I was afraid.'

'You should be.' The man looked at her sternly. 'It's not long since you were last here as a runaway. We want head to tail obsequience, not lip service, my dear.'

'Yes, M'Lord,' Charlotte whispered, miserably.

'I sentence that tail to a lesson,' said the judge. 'It's to be chastened till it cries.'

At a sign from the judge a guide stepped forward and handcuffed Charlotte's arms in front of her. He led her out of the dock towards one of the Punishment Chambers where the Master, two guides and a small audience already sat.

'Approach the wronged one and beg for forgiveness,' said the Master from his front ring seat as she knelt before him. For a moment Charlotte stared at him, puzzled. Then he indicated a tall figure sitting in an armless chair at the top end of the hall.

The African! She was going to be corrected by the African!

'Crawl on your belly, Charlotte,' added the Master, matter-of-factly. 'But be quick.'

'Yes, sir.'

Heart and mind in overdrive, wondering if she could find a defence, Charlotte lay flat on her stomach and wriggled towards her tormentor. Hopefully he'd be as slow in punishing her as he had been about having sex!

She reached the man's feet.

'Bend over my knee,' he said. 'Push your arse in the air. Count each spank out loud.'

'Yes, sir.'

'Each time your feet leave the floor you'll get an extra slap on the backs of your thighs or between.' For a slave boy, he suddenly sounded very self-assured. She hoped she'd get the chance to humiliate him back.

Knowing she'd be punished more if she resisted, Charlotte stood up, her hands still cuffed before her, and, wishing they'd at least let her wear panties, stretched herself over his lap.

'Higher,' he said. 'Get this right up where I can reach it.' He tapped the centre of her tender cheeks.

She tautened her calves, pushed her bum up, and let her head hang lower.

'Better. A fitting target. Now count.'

'One!'

The strength of his palm on her flesh, still recovering from the stick, almost took her breath away. The word came out in a half-gasp. Her soles came off the floor.

'You moved your legs – one thrash for further disobedience,' he said, striking the soft crease of flesh at the back of her right thigh. Charlotte gasped again, but this time kept her feet on the ground.

'Three,' she moaned, as he applied the next spank to her other buttock. She could picture his big black hand on her small pinkening bum, and how it must look to the watching crowd.

Though he was bare to the waist, he wore white trousers this time, emphasising her own stripped vulnerability. It was terrible being held like this, writhing against his lap. His cock was hard again – she could feel it.

'I know they're making you do this,' she whispered. 'You could spank me much more lightly, though – they're too far away to see exactly what's going on.'

'Could I?' The man's fingers traced her flesh, bringing fresh heat and desire to Charlotte's wriggling bottom. 'Why would I want to do that?'

'I'd do what you wanted me to do – act out your fantasies!'

The man used his palm to dole out slaps four and five. Charlotte counted them out loud in little gasps. She bucked and groaned.

'Please! It stings! You could stop soon. I'd meet you later . . .'

'What would you do for me?'

'Shag you till I milked you dry!'

'But we're not allowed,' whispered the slave.

'They'd not be expecting us to transgress a second time,' murmured Charlotte, trying to take his attention away from her bottom. 'We'd get away with it, have a really good time.'

'But if we got caught you'd blame me.'

Damn! She'd reminded him of her earlier betrayal! The man hoisted Charlotte's backside further into the air and warmed it some more.

The spanks were so hard that she forgot to count. Her feet left the floor, both offences earning her extra thigh-dealt punishment. They were hard, measured, merciless slaps. Each was quickly followed by a next. It seemed never-ending; a squealing, kicking torment. There was such power in that large arm.

'Let me suck you,' she begged. 'Eat your balls for hour after hour! I'll take your length deep in my throat.'

The man shook his head. He seemed angered by her suggestions. Charlotte's bum glowed. Her belly was sore and chafing against his thighs.

'You could piss in my mouth,' she whimpered, wondering if he wanted to humiliate her totally. 'I'd swallow down every last drop.'

Every aspect of her being became centred on her arse. She wanted to fake tears, but was too shocked to think up sad images. His treatment of her was so flagrant she somehow couldn't cry.

'Please . . .'

She felt as if she'd spent her life across his knee having her poor bottom pummelled. She forgot the watching crowds and thought only of her tormented little rump.

'Have mercy,' she begged. 'Let me lick you, kiss you . . .'

'You forgot to count. I'll have to start all over again,' he said.

She cried then, tears of pain and misery and frustration. Like a parcel he'd grown tired of, he pushed her from his lap. 'Bring this creature to her feet, guides. Put on her collar and lead. Make them tight.'

Charlotte felt strong hands beneath her arms, in her hair, pulling her upright. They held her there. She felt too weak to stand.

'The girl is a disgrace to the Training Grounds,' said the African as her collar was wound round her neck, buckled. 'She needs some long-term correction of a more thought-provoking kind.'

Charlotte looked up at him. Could a slave talk like that to the Master? She heard footsteps behind her, then the Master stood between them both.

'What do you suggest, sir?' he asked, respectfully.

Sir? Realisation dawning, Charlotte closed her eyes.

Oh God! The African was obviously an honoured guest or an overseer! Someone in authority, who now knew that she still wasn't doing what she was told.

'Take her to the largest communal Correction Hall. Chain her up. Leave her there overnight.'

They couldn't. They wouldn't! No matter what her previous misdemeanours were, she'd always been bathed and fed, her punished contours soothed with cream before she was led to her cell for a night's sated sleep. Chaining her sounded barbaric. Especially when communal implied there'd be other people there as well.

'Can't I go tomorrow?' she whimpered. 'I'm tired.'

'You deserve to be tired. Bad girls don't get to rest.'

The African looked at her coldly. Charlotte remembered his face as she pinched his nipples, and slapped his buttocks. How could she ever have mistaken this authoritative man for a slave?

'Take her away,' the Master said. The guides did so. The African followed the three of them down the hall, and across the grounds into a building she hadn't been kept in before. The guides unlocked a padlocked door, and entered. Peering through the gloom Charlotte could make out a long hall where every five feet or so another male or female slave was chained to the wall.

'Stretch your arms up,' said the African, pointing to a hook above her head. Charlotte did so. The chain exerted a slight pressure on her arms so that she had to hold them fully out. 'Sweet dreams,' added the man, walking away from her. He pulled down a blind at the far wall and the remaining lights went out leaving her in total dark.

Had she been there minutes or hours? After a short time Charlotte's arms began to ache and she stood on tiptoe to relieve them. After a few moments this led to a pain in her calves. Meanwhile the agony that was her bum changed to a strong itch which continued unabated. She tried to scratch it by twisting in her chains and rubbing it against the wall, but that made the heat spring up again; it made her wince and jig about on the spot for a moment. The soles of her feet felt cold.

Her cold feet made her bladder want to void. She resisted for a while, but they hadn't said she couldn't piss herself. She let go an unseen stream of water, feeling some of it run down her legs. The rest splashed on the ground: she heard it but couldn't see it. She heard someone else do likewise at the other end of the room.

Then something whistled through the air to the left of her, followed by a startled male cry; then a female scream and a low moan.

'Aaah!' begged a second female voice. 'Please, I'm sorry. Have mercy!'

Footsteps faded away.

'What's going on?' cried Charlotte into the silence which followed.

Someone cleared their throat.

'When you're tethered in the Correction Hall the guides, slaves and guests have the right to punish you. Many come in and whip you when you're least expecting it throughout the night.'

That was all she needed! Her arms and legs already hurt with the strain of keeping upright. She'd never sleep . . .

She slept, or at least dozed, and was woken by a stinging sensation across her upper thighs and buttocks. She turned blindly towards the source, and felt the pain lash across her belly instead. She turned back, pulling at her bonds, seeking a move that would free her from the torment. Turning round and round, she felt the belt or similar implement lash at her vulnerable bottom and its equally tender underside. She cried out, hearing other slaves cry out in similar suffering around the room.

'Stop,' she whispered, unable to see her attacker. 'Please.'

She felt hot breath on her neck, and hands on her breasts, kneading them. She stayed facing the wall, trying to fathom whether they were male or female hands teasing her areolae into taut pink towers.

The mystery hands thumbed her nipples, then moved on to the soft fullness of her breasts. Fingers stroked down to her belly, taking her mind off the punishment that had gone before. Palms moved to her back, the fingers caressing each inch of her shoulders, her waist, her bottom. Charlotte sighed her pleasure, and felt strong fingers pushing her thighs apart.

Immediately the position exerted a strong rack-like pull on her arms and she cried out and tried to straighten. Angry hands slapped her legs and she stiffened, then kept them scissored dutifully in place. The hands began again, insidious fingers tracing the cleft of her cheeks, fondling further down with agonising slowness till they reached her lower lips. Opening them. Opening her. Making her breath leave her body in an excited hiss.

She could feel her wetness slick against her inner thighs, feel the heat coursing through her. An arm came round her belly and held it firmly. A hand parted her labia, and probed its warmth.

Fuck me, she wanted to beg, but daren't in case she offended her unseen lover. With effort, she kept her body as he or she had positioned it, her legs spread wide, arms stretched mercilessly upwards, facing the wall in the ongoing dark.

Something moved against her entrance – a cock or a dildo. It nudged its way in slowly. She sighed. It thrust in some more, causing frissons of penile-like pleasure. Charlotte moaned.

The man moved faster. It was definitely a man. She could feel his pubic hair against her. He squeezed her breasts in his hands as he plunged in and out. She could feel her climax build, her breathing increasing. Her nipples were hardening and lengthening; her *mons* was increasingly wet.

She felt her thighs tense up as she prepared to go over. The man felt it too, and stopped.

'Please,' she begged. 'Keep going! Fuck me. I need it.'

For long moments he held her immobile as sensation faded from between her legs. Why was he doing this? She tried to wriggle back against him, to create her own friction. But he restrained her in a strong grip so that she couldn't move a centimetre of her liquefied female flesh.

At last he started to pleasure her again, slowly, carefully. Charlotte tried to hold back her whimpers; she tried not to betray her rising desire. He obviously didn't want her to come yet – but she had to! If she could keep her excitement very quiet, orgasm silently . . .

Again her legs tensed, betraying her. Again her tormentor stopped, and held her frustrated flesh in place.

'Let me come,' she begged. 'You'll feel my contractions on your cock, so strong, so gripping.'

Still he curbed her mercilessly, refusing to increase her sensations for achingly long moments till her fire ebbed. Then, ever so achingly slowly, the teasing thrusts began again.

It seemed to go on for hours. She was soaking, sweating. Pleading. Writhing. Half mad from the hellish position and equally hellish need. Again and again he stopped just before she climaxed. He made her beg.

After about the seventh time, as her limbs showed that she was almost there, he withdrew completely. She waited for him to re-enter her to start to fuck her again, and listened in disbelief as he moved away from her desperate clit, her desperate tunnel. He was leaving her with her hands chained and the hottest wettest love hole imaginable between her legs.

Snorting with thwarted need, Charlotte walked her feet inwards to relieve the pressure on her stretched arms. She tightened her thighs together in an effort to release the pressure between her legs. Every cell of her body was crying out to come; pleading for it.

'Please,' she whispered into the blackness. 'Please.'

But her taunting lover had gone, and she was left alone with only her thoughts and her unquenched desire; left with swollen labia, swollen tits, an aching arse. They wouldn't get away with this, she told herself: they just wouldn't! She'd have her revenge. She had to hatch a plan.

13

'They did that to me lots of times.'

Charlotte stared in anxious pity at the convent girl. It was three days after her night in the Correction Hall and her arms still hurt. Worse, though, was the memory of that provoking cock, taking her to the limit then denying her. Who had it been attached to? Why had he been so cruel?

'Lots of times?' she repeated dully. 'But why?'

'I was still following the dictates of my upbringing, wasn't being true to my nature. They wanted me to really be myself.'

'Which involved?'

'Well, they kept asking me to say dirty words. I couldn't – wouldn't. I had to be re-educated before I could really let go.'

'And now?'

The girl smiled proudly. 'I organise some of the floor shows.' She touched her tits so lewdly that Charlotte felt uncomfortable and looked away. 'I literally have a ball!'

'How long did it take for you to admit you were sub?' Charlotte was sure they'd made a mistake about herself, and that they just wouldn't admit it.

'I'd had . . . dreams about being made to obey for years,' admitted the girl softly. 'But actually giving in to another's will in real life takes time.'

'How much time?'

'Many months. I don't know exactly how many. The days all seemed to blend together for a while.'

'And what did they do to you?'

Charlotte looked at the small blonde figure with the elfin

186

haircut and admitted to herself that lots of men and women would want to do things to her.

'They tied me up and played with me till I begged them to let me come.'

'Didn't they whip you?'

'No.' The girl shook her head.

'Use a belt on you?'

Again a negative. Charlotte was nonplussed.

'Didn't they punish you at all?'

The girl nodded: 'God, yes! They made me watch nude films and listen to sexual songs.' She swallowed hard, 'They forced me to take my baths with another man and woman who held me down and soaped my nether regions. No one had ever seen me naked before, far less touched me! I used to think that I would die of shame.'

Different strokes for different folks, Charlotte thought amusedly. She'd never been shy when it came to adult films and books; could curse with the best of them when she was twelve; was exploring the boy next door beneath his clothing when she turned thirteen. She'd never been like this uptight miss!

'At first I just had to say the rude words out loud in my cell,' said the girl, who'd been twinned with Charlotte today for a sexual playlet. They'd been handed scripts in which the convent girl acted out the part of a Victorian Mistress and Charlotte played her servant who'd stolen a precious brooch. The Mistress would beat Charlotte with a hairbrush until Charlotte devised some way to make up for the theft.

'You can improvise at this stage,' the Master had said with a knowing smile, leaving them to perfect their erotic lines.

Now, as the two girls waited to take the stage, they spoke of their training.

'And after you learned the rude words?' prompted Charlotte.

'I had to say them to a man. I had to ask him nicely for his cock.'

'Anywhere specific?' continued Charlotte, feeling her nipples stiffen into arousal.

187

'In my mouth. In my quim. Even in my arse.'

'I've never had it fully in the arse,' admitted Charlotte.

'You have to be really lubricated, take things very slowly,' explained the girl. 'Even then it's sometimes not possible. If your partner's too big, it can hurt like hell.'

'Yet you asked for it anyway?'

'Just this one time. They wound a belt round my waist and through a hoop so that it held me to the floor. I was naked of course – as usual! Then they tied my hands together above my head, pushed my knees up to my chest, staked my legs out so that they had full access to my quim.' She closed her eyes, her breathing quickening. 'One of the male guides – I think he must have had a degree in cunnilingus! He put his tongue just below my clit and licked and licked.'

'It's hard to fight that,' admitted Charlotte, remembering the time the Mistress had had a boy suck her.

'I did my best to remain a good girl,' her new friend said.

'But . . . ?' Charlotte prompted with a dirty giggle.

'His tongue felt so good. I started to move against it. My clit felt so hot.'

'And then?'

'Then he stopped.'

' "Beg for his tongue," said my Master. I begged for it. Then seconds before I orgasmed they told me to beg for cock.' She shuddered. 'The boy was going to take his tongue away again – I couldn't bear it! I begged for his cock. "Beg for it up your arse," my Master said.'

'You begged,' Charlotte said flatly. It was a statement, not a question. The girl nodded.

'After I'd come my Master showed the boy how to rub the wetness from my quim around my anus, and use his fingers to transfer some of the wetness within.'

'You were still tied up?' asked Charlotte, curiously.

The girl nodded: 'They kept my hands tied above my head, but freed the rest of my bonds and laid me over a stool.'

'What did it feel like?'

'At first I didn't think it was possible. He was so engorged, so excited. He pushed and pushed. Somehow he got the head in. I felt myself opening a little. Then he slid his hands beneath my belly and held me close.' She sighed. 'His weight was on top of me by then – I felt his length push in more fully. I cried out. He felt enormous. I tried to wriggle away.'

'But you promised,' said Charlotte.

The girl nodded again: 'I promised. So when he told me to stay still I did so. I didn't want my clit to be tormented again!'

'Did he actually come inside you?' asked Charlotte, curiously.

'Eventually! I was so tight it was hard for him to move. I wanted him to climax and pull out.'

Charlotte smiled softly: 'So what did you do, little convent girl?'

The girl grinned. 'Talked so filthily that he came really quick!'

'What did you say?' whispered Charlotte, wishing this was part of the floor show. The guests would love this; they'd come where they stood!

'I said "Shoot your load right up me, big boy. Shove your cock hard up my arsehole till it feels like it's gone into my womb." '

A guide appeared as she spoke, and handed them both their uniforms.

'About time too,' muttered Charlotte, getting to her feet.

'One of the girls went into labour early,' said the guide, 'which is why today's play is behind schedule. We've all been busy helping make it an easy birth.'

'You have children here?'

Charlotte turned back to her new friend in surprise. She'd always seen this land as strictly Adults Only.

The girl nodded. 'We have a nursery on a remote part of the island. The children won't come to the adult part of the Training Grounds until they're eighteen.'

So the Master's scheme would be able to keep going indefinitely ... Thoughtfully, Charlotte put on the frilly maid's outfit she'd been given, not at all surprised to find that it contained tiny crotchless knickers and a mini dress with an apron that stopped at the top of her thighs. The way things were going she could be captive on the island forever, tormented by future generations of mini Masters. She had to reach Vernon, to remind him of how much he loved her and needed her as his girlfriend again!

Suddenly too worried to concentrate on the silly play, she went through the motions, earning both herself and the convent girl ten strokes each with a table tennis bat.

'Enter them in the Punishment Book,' said the Master. 'We're too busy to mete them out today.'

People were still running back and forth bringing gifts for the tired mother and new baby. Someone said the Master had organised a celebratory party in his rooms for the entire island that very night.

'Thought you liked the floor shows?' asked the convent girl, looking at Charlotte sourly as they left the stage.

'I do. I'm just missing my boyfriend.'

'Where is he?'

'Here.'

The girl looked surprised. 'You want to return to him?'

'Of course I do. Like, today!'

'Then tell him to tell the Master that. A girl can only leave if it's discovered that she's not really sub, or . . .'

'I'm not sub!' interrupted Charlotte.

The girl looked at her sceptically, then continued: 'Or if her partner – whoever handed her over or recruited her – says she can leave.'

Eureka! A light went on in Charlotte's head. She'd just thought of a way where she could see Vernon, and sexily convince him that he needed her back full time.

'When does this party start?' she asked, casually.

'7 p.m.'

At six o'clock, Charlotte was served a light tea.

'Save some space for the snacks at the party!' said her serving guide.

Charlotte nodded. 'Just leave my cell door open and I'll make my own way there. It'll save you coming back.'

'But . . .'

'What can I do? I know I can't escape via the planes and that's the only way.'

'I guess so,' said the girl. 'I suppose you deserve a second chance on trust.'

She left. Five minutes later Charlotte sneaked out of the building. She had to get in touch with the Master before Vernon left for the party! She had to succeed!

She knew exactly where she was going. There was a phone booth in the largest of the wheat fields. Its threat kept workers who weren't near a Correction Room from producing shoddy work. Charlotte had once seen it put to use, when a slave fell asleep after his lunch break.

'Sir, please send an overseer down from the Tutor's House with a rawhide whip,' the chief foreman had said into the phone.

He'd set down the receiver, and the slaves had immediately returned to their tasks, their bodies stiff with tension. The foreman had stared at the misbehaving slave: 'You know the drill, boy. Male slaves are punished standing up, whilst female ones are bent over the fence.'

He pointed to a tree at the perimeter of the field, and the unfortunate man walked over and embraced it. His buttock muscles rippled with the fear of what was to come.

En route to a floor show, Charlotte had stopped to witness the scene, and had sidled over to the phone booth afterwards. The phone had a list of extension numbers beside it so that newly appointed staff could contact anyone with encouraging ease ...

Charlotte made for the phone now, squinting through the evening gloom to find the direction of the wheat field. She stopped as she saw the doorway open to Lari's block of cells.

Lari could make things even easier! She sprinted in, and walked along two corridors peering through bars till she found the girl. Her door was unlocked, presumably to let her go to the party. Charlotte stepped in: 'Lari. Could you do me a favour, please?'

The darker girl had a deeper, more masculine voice, and would sound more like Vernon. The Master was more likely to be taken in.

'I can't,' said Lari when Charlotte finished explaining. 'But I can take you to the phone. And I'll take full responsibility if anyone catches us!' Charlotte begged.

'Your plan isn't for the good of the island,' Lari said evenly.

Charlotte winked: 'Yeah, sure!' Then, looking more closely at the girl, she realised she wasn't joking. 'You mean you've fallen for that crap?'

'It's the truth here. It makes sense here,' said Lari, quietly. 'It's not for everyone, but it's right for me.'

'Not for me, though,' said Charlotte. 'Forget it!'

Lari raised an eyebrow: 'Are you sure?'

'I'm absolutely sure! I know my own mind.'

'You fight it.' Lari paused. 'Of course, part of the whole point is fighting it. It makes the ultimate surrender so sexually sweet.'

'Bugger the ultimate surrender!' said Charlotte, sourly. 'Some bastard the other night wouldn't let me come at all.'

'You didn't plead prettily enough. You weren't good enough earlier,' said Lari, unsympathetically.

'And I'm not starting now,' Charlotte replied.

The two girls stared at each other blankly. Was this placid girl now reading a book really yesterday's wild child? Charlotte turned away.

'You . . . you'll not tell on me, will you?'

'Only if I'm asked.'

Lari was unlikely to be asked. Charlotte was safe for now, then. Wearily she left the girl's cell, hurried to the wheat fields, and found the phone. The extension of the Master's private rooms in his mansion was listed. Shaking, Charlotte dialled.

She spoke through her hand, trying to deepen her voice and disguise it. Lari sounded much more masculine, but Lari had become a wimp!

'Hi. This is Vernon. Can you send Charlotte over to my quarters for the evening? I feel like a private party, if you know what I mean!'

There! Just the right blend of confidence and innuendo. She'd dash back to her cell now, and hope they brought her to Vernon as he appeared to wish. Then she'd please him with her tongue. Oh, Christ, how she'd please him! He'd never have been licked and sucked with such ongoing devotion before!

'We'll send her to you in half an hour,' said the voice. Charlotte thanked them using her deepest tone, and put down the receiver with a grin. She ran back to her cell, closed the door, and wiped the sweat from her underarms away with her palms. Soon she'd be making Vernon wonder how he'd ever survived without her! Soon he'd be spurting again and again under the insistence of her fingers and creamy conduit.

She heard her cell door opening and looked up to see a male guide smiling at her. 'You're to come with me,' he said. His shaft bobbed at his belly, thick and hard.

'Oh?' Charlotte tried to look surprised. 'I thought I was going to the party on my own?'

'Oh, you're going to a party, sweetheart. A party you'll never forget!'

A party à deux, thought Charlotte excitedly. Her nipples had begun to throb with anticipation. It was so long since she'd fucked Vernon it would almost be like shagging someone new.

'Do we really need that?' she asked, as the boy fastened on her dog collar and buckled it tightly. He snapped on the lead, and pushed her down on all fours.

'Believe me, we do.'

When she was free – and just before she left the island – she'd ask Vernon to arrange for her to thrash some of these uppity guides and slaves, thought Charlotte angrily. Maybe she'd arrange for *them* to have collars and leads fitted. Maybe she'd drag them round the Training Grounds for the day!

With mounting irritation, she crawled painfully through the grounds, wondering where Vernon was located. Did he have a cell like hers or a suite of rooms? What did he do with himself whilst she performed tricks in the Pleasure Suite? Did he have any idea just how often she'd suffered the lash?

The ground was cold under her palms and knees. Her neck felt hot under the collar. Something wasn't right, here. In fact something was wrong!

'Where am I going?' she asked.

'To the party.'

Not to Vernon's, then, unless he was to meet her there . . .

'I thought I had to make my way there myself,' said Charlotte, casually.

At least she tried to sound casual. Her throat felt dry; her voice an uncertain croak.

'That was before . . . there's been a change of plan,' said the boy, grinning. He tugged sadistically at the lead so that Charlotte was forced to increase her pace.

They reached the Mansion, where other guests were filing in, laughing and joking. Everyone else was standing up, unchained and unleashed. A few of them whistled and slapped playfully at Charlotte's exposed rump as she crawled by.

'Can I get up yet?' she asked the guide as he led her into the main hall, where trestle tables of food were laid out round the sides.

The guide shook his head: 'You'll not be getting up for a long, long time.'

They knew, then. Charlotte felt her belly turn over. She swallowed with difficulty.

'Tonight's entertainment,' said the Master, striding into the middle of the hall, 'centres around a disobedient slave.'

He pulled one of the hellish punishment racks into the centre of the room. 'Come here, Charlotte. Good girl.'

Where could she go? What could she do? Resistance was useless. Her lead trailing as the boy let it go, Charlotte crawled shakily over to the rack. She stared at the ground; hesitated; she stretched her naked body over the padded surface, cringing inside.

'State your crime,' said the man as she was bound, spreadeagled, in place.

'Impersonating another.'

'The reason?'

'To try and break free.'

'Don't you think it's hurtful to us that you want to break free?' said the Master, beginning to fondle her tense, taut bottom.

'Yes, sir.'

'And people who are hurt tend to retaliate, don't they, dear?'

Charlotte closed her eyes. 'How did you know it was me?' she whispered.

'My guests and tutors all have a password. You didn't say it. Then we checked with Vernon . . .'

'Doesn't he want me back?' Charlotte asked, aware of how pathetic she sounded. Yet the pathos hid a simmering rage.

'He'll have you back soon enough. Remember we pre-arranged a time,' said the Master quietly.

Charlotte nodded, her eyes fixed on the rack beneath her. That earlier promise had receded in her memory: she'd been through so much since then.

'What do you think we should do to a girl who pretends to be someone else, who commits deception?'

Firm fingers stroked her arse. Charlotte gritted her teeth. 'You should . . . you should use a hairbrush on them.' She prayed they'd limit her correction to that.

'You're right,' said the Master, slowly. 'We should do so. And what should we do to an employee who is planning to run away?'

'I . . .' Charlotte tried to think of an excuse or a mild punishment. 'I don't know, sir,' she whispered ultimately.

'Then we'll have to surprise you,' the Master said. 'For now, the slave will be chastised with a hairbrush,' he told the applauding crowd.

Sadistic bastards! Charlotte kept her eyes tightly closed, but could hear their laughs. The first slap hit her arse, and she opened her eyes and yelled loudly. The second followed swiftly across the other cheek.

She should be used to this by now – yet you never got used to it! The third spank sent heat radiating through her bum. Her feet drummed in their leather loops until she was

195

told to keep them still for fear of further punishment. Her flesh rubbed against the underbelly bolster as she slithered and jerked.

'Tell me you don't want to leave us,' the Master murmured long moments later.

'But I do,' she sobbed, 'I do!'

'Are you sure, Charlotte. Really? I think that's the old Charlotte talking. I think the new Charlotte could be very happy here if she let go just a little of that stubborn pride.'

You would think that, wouldn't you? Charlotte thought viciously. You'd like me to become just another of your mindless devotees, hanging on to your every word. Aloud she said: 'I want to leave and I will – when Vernon collects me.'

'We're hoping that you'll change your mind by then,' the Master said.

He used the hellish warning of the brush's back to skim her warmed bottom, gliding over its vulnerable contours. Charlotte closed her eyes against the sudden hot rush of lust.

'We'd really like you to stay with us, my precious. We'd like you to beg . . .'

She begged as he put his trousered cock to her quim, still leaving her tethered. 'Fuck me,' she whispered.

'Not yet.'

'When?' She wanted him now, shamelessly.

'When you automatically bow and beg,' he replied playing a considering hand over her haunches. 'For now, taste a promise of the pleasure that could be yours . . .'

He put his silk-clad hardness against her entrance so that it pushed in about an inch of the way.

Jesus! Charlotte moved her sex back as best she could, beyond caring about the pull on her stretched sore arms. She pushed and pushed, and was gratified when he did the same. He was just touching her, just giving her a little of his exquisite penile power inside her. Within moments she cried out into the silence and climaxed again and again.

She wanted to kiss his hands, lick his feet. In a moment she'd beg to . . .

'We didn't finish punishing you, my dear,' came his coolly appraising voice.

'You did!' Charlotte gasped, adding belatedly, 'Sir.' She was amazed that their partially merged flesh hadn't changed anything at all.

'No. We merely disciplined your bum for impersonating another. You've yet to be corrected for the more heinous crime of plotting to run away.'

'But I didn't get as far as leaving my cell!'

'It's intent we're punishing you for, dearest.'

There'd be nothing dear about what he was planning to do next . . . 'Not my bottom again,' said Charlotte, wishing she could snake her hands round to cover it.

'That depends on our guest overseer,' said the Master, signalling to one of the guides to approach his chair.

14

Who was this guest overseer the Master had just mentioned? Why had he beckoned to this youthful guide? Charlotte flinched away as the boy approached her. She felt vulnerable and stupid. He freed her ankles and wrists.

'Fetch a blindfold for this slave,' the Master said evenly as she got onto her hands and knees on the Punishment Rack. The boy left the room and soon returned with a thick black cloth. 'Our guest is shy. He doesn't want you to see him,' murmured the Master amusedly, using the material to cover Charlotte's eyes.

Could the guest be that little bastard Guy? She'd never liked him! Given that he'd visited the island before, his tastes obviously ran to witnessing pain. And he'd evidently enjoyed spanking that grown up schoolgirl on one of their first days at the Training Grounds, making her squeal . . .

Tensing, she heard a door open, and footsteps approaching. There were some scuffling sounds, and a murmured conversation. Both voices sounded male. Guy gloating over her nakedness would be terrible. Guy thrashing her soundly – or fucking her – would be infinitely worse!

'Don't I get a say in this?' she asked, still kneeling, with a trace of her old defiance.

'You lost your say when you misbehaved,' the Master replied.

'Says who?'

There was a long, cold pause.

'It's my island. You've been treated well here and only punished when you failed to obey the rules.'

'Your rules,' muttered Charlotte angrily.

'On my land. It's always been that way.'

It was true. Kings had always ruled their kingdoms, landowners their property. This didn't make it right or remotely fair! Still what could she do? She felt a hand behind her head, and saw the blindfold. The guide knotted it, and now she could see nothing except the black heavy mystery created by the cloth.

'Our guest has outlined his plans for your correction,' continued the Master's voice evenly.

That must have been what all the murmuring was about.

'He wants you bent over a stool ...'

Charlotte wriggled.

'... And tied to it securely whilst he teaches you to obey.'

'No!'

Even as she cried out, Charlotte felt the Master grab her wrists, and pull her hands away from their protective stance over her already-chastened young bottom.

'Not my arse,' she begged. 'Not again!'

'It's what he desires,' continued the Master. 'And you want to do what our important guests desire, don't you, Charlotte? That's what we've been training you for. That's why you're here.'

'Yes,' whispered Charlotte, trying to think of ways to delay or curtail her punishment. 'But I could please him with my body, take him deep inside me and tense my muscles so his shaft is squeezed really tight.'

'And maybe we'll let you show off such prowess later. But for now ...'

She felt strong hands beneath her armpits, lifting her up, half carrying and half pulling her towards what felt like the centre of the room.

'Be gentle with me, why don't you?' she muttered sarcastically under her breath. It was scary not being able to see: her awareness of her nudity somehow intensified. All she could think about was her flailing limbs, the expanses of differently coloured flesh.

One bit wouldn't be pale for long: she'd lay bets on it. It was already pink from the strength of the Master's brush. What would this guest do now? And for how long would he do it? Would she ever get to know who he was?

Did she want to? What if it was Vern? She bit back the possibility. He wouldn't! He loved her! He'd never as much as spanked her during the time they'd lived together; far less chastised her over a stool. He simply wasn't the type. Or was he? Some of those young guides looked like choirboys yet their pricks swelled and jerked at the sight of a girl tasting the belt.

And she was about to taste it now, no doubt. Sure calm fingers took her shoulders from the front and bent them forward. As her blindfolded body dipped over, her arse stuck out. She felt her soft belly scrape against polished wood. This must be the stool, then. They had just bent her over it. She held her breath as they rearranged her limbs, listening for any identifiable sounds.

No sounds. The room was eerily silent. Was this part of the plan to break her or had everyone else quietly filed out? She felt a hand on her right wrist, then the cool touch and tightening of leather. Seconds later her left wrist was strapped to the stool legs as well.

Long moments passed. Don't ever start, her body cried. Get it over with, her brain contradicted. She wanted the lash. She feared the lash. She feared what they'd make her say. After endless moments, more footsteps approached. She felt her right ankle being encircled. Then first it and its partner received the strong leather restraints. Again moments trickled slowly by and nothing happened. Now she'd been reduced to the status of a waiting arse.

Waiting for what? For whom?

'I'm sorry I planned to run away,' she said into the silence.

'Speak only when you're spoken to,' said the Master's voice from somewhere to the left of her; he sounded remote.

'You're to be spanked with a palm-hardened glove for your crimes,' added a younger male voice, which sounded like that belonging to one of the guides. 'These are the instructions of our guest overseer who will carry out the task.'

'Please, sir, how many?' asked Charlotte, swallowing noisily. She wasn't supposed to be speaking, but she had to know!

You could bear it more if you were given a finite number: could count them in your head, and know when you were on the home stretch.

'Until our guest decides you've repented of your ways,' the guide replied.

'I've repented already – I swear!' gasped Charlotte, wishing she could wriggle about more and make herself feel less vulnerable. Every time she was held down waiting to have her bottom warmed she genuinely wished she hadn't transgressed.

'I'll be so good,' she promised.

'Later,' the guide said coolly. His words were obviously being whispered to him by the man who was about to thrash her arse!

'If you'd just give me a chance to explain ...' added Charlotte, desperately.

'Any more explaining and we'll have to apply the gag.'

Not the gag! She'd been gagged before: hated it. She fell silent. She heard something scrape, like leather on wood. Seconds later sensation seared across one tied cheek.

She bit back a cry. Footsteps approached from behind her. A cooling hand felt her rump. The guide's voice, again acting as translator, said: 'You must learn to do what you're told immediately. You must mend your ways.'

'Yes, I'll mend them. Give me one more chance, only don't punish me ...'

'Then tell the crowds that you're a wicked young madam who deserves to be thrashed.'

Charlotte flinched, but opened her mouth to obey. Then she shut it again. She'd submit verbally to the Master, but she refused to say such things to that jumped up little know-it-all Guy! Guy whose eyes had always said that she was just Vern's live in piece of rubbish; his bit of flesh.

The man had made it clear that he thought his mate Vernon could do so much better. I'll not give him the satisfaction of hearing me beg for mercy, Charlotte promised herself. She gritted her teeth together and marshalled her remaining resources. She would take that glove on her arse till Kingdom come rather than demean herself in this way!

'I'm not hearing you,' said the guide. 'My gloved hand is getting twitchy.'

'See a physiotherapist then,' muttered Charlotte, who then howled as his palm lashed down. It lashed down again – well, more sideways, really, as though the person was varying the spanks so that they warmed each inch of her arse.

Fuck off, Guy, Fuck off, Guy, she said to herself again and again, concentrating on her long-term dislike of the man. It was a dislike she'd always managed to keep under the surface, though she'd told Vern a few times that he saw too much of his cocky young mate.

Cocky! That was unfortunately the key word in this hellish situation. Would he have the right to fuck her after all this? Position was everything: she knew her quim made an inviting target. He could just slide in. She was so wet . . .

She was wet because the Master had fondled her clit, not because of his less welcome ministrations. If only they'd accept that, and stop trying to make out she was some submissive little bint! Fuck off, Guy, Fuck off, Guy, she said inside her head again to keep her resolve going. Under the direction of the glove it was fading fast.

But her punishment had to stop soon, for hadn't the Master said you must never hit hard enough or long enough to make the slave bleed? Didn't he keep the canes and bats light, and didn't he say you shouldn't dole out any punishment you couldn't bear yourself? Charlotte felt a growing disdain. She doubted if Guy could bear this relentless hot ache – the cowardly little bastard! She wondered if they'd ever have a day where slaves got to thrash the guests!

She closed her eyes as the hard gloved hand whistled down again. Not that she'd be there by then: she had to hold onto that. Hold onto the fact that soon she'd be back in the real world and this place would be like a surreal dream.

'Say you've been a wicked little madam,' repeated the guide's voice evenly.

'Fuck off and die,' Charlotte said.

She felt a momentary satisfaction, followed by a jolt of teaching torment. He'd put his full strength into that one. She cried aloud, her eyes opening wide but unseeing behind the covering scarf. Tears blurred over her face. Her nose felt liquid.

'She's had enough,' the Master said. 'Untie her. Take her back to her cell and give her bottom and her female parts relief.'

Privacy. An end to humiliation and pain. For a moment she wanted to kiss him, and crawl on her belly as he wanted. Then hands were unbuckling her bonds and helping her up and the moment passed. Still blindfolded, she was led from the hall. She heard people murmuring to each other as she was helped onwards. She kept her head up, determined to look proud and strong before the hateful Guy. She was sure it was him now – he'd wanted to break her; wanted to make her squeal and sob and beg.

He'd wanted to make her squeal and sob and beg. Vern stood, dazed, still clutching the glove as the guides untied Charlotte. Had she really had enough? He'd felt he was just getting started when the Master told him to cease. He looked more closely at her bottom as it was led past him. It was a fiery red.

How many times had he struck it? He could remember his excitement at watching her take the brush. He'd wished he was overseeing the rack that she was spreadeagled over. He'd wished the man would bring the brush down harder, faster, more!

Then it had been his turn. He'd almost come as they strapped her down over the tall wooden stool that made her arse stick out. It was so simple yet so perfect. Her bottom looked so accessible that way. He'd spent a long time planning how she should be held down, set out, and teased into talking dirty; teased into begging for his cock.

He bit back the thought. Maybe that wasn't going to

happen now. They'd taken her away from him. They'd told him to stay here, alone. Then the audience had filed out, leaving him with this glove and no one to use it on. They'd left him with a prick the size of the Eiffel Tower.

He'd banked on fucking Charlotte whilst she remained tied over the stool; whilst he could see the glistening leaves of her sex from where he stood smacking her. A good thrashing, a glass of wine and thou: a perfect night. Instead here he stood in this empty hall with his leaking manhood, remembering the scene just past.

His prick was still stiff, still tense with wanting. It had been so for ages; the need had intensified as soon as he had picked up the glove. Giving her the first stroke had been almost as exciting as entering her. Judging by the stiff cocks and nipples around him, the audience felt the same!

The second slap had also given him some satisfaction. He'd liked the way she gasped – as if she wasn't expecting it at all. But you've really been expecting it for hours haven't you baby, he'd thought gleefully, adding a third stroke, then a fourth. They'd told her she was to be punished for both impersonating him and planning to do a runner. Her little rump had been nervously anticipating this warming-up from the moment she'd been led into the hall.

Such a silly girl. Such a wilful girl. So . . . unfaithful. Well, he didn't know that for sure, of course, but the signs weren't looking good. He and Guy had gone to the nearest mainland for three days to stock up on film and other photographic developing aids. There he'd made some important work-related long distance calls. He'd also phoned his answering machine to check on his messages, using the remote control code to access the tape.

In six weeks there'd been a lot of messages, all for him – except for three of them. They'd been for Charlotte from someone called Jeff at the Riding School. Hearing the first one, he hadn't been too worried: something about her not turning up for a pre-paid lesson and would she arrange another ride as soon as possible? Charlotte wasn't normally so forgetful, but what the hell? Maybe she'd gotten confused about the dates or something.

Then the second call, obviously made a few days later: please contact Jeff about future bookings. There was an emphasis on the *please*. Then the third, which said he'd collected that riding crop she'd ordered and would she come down and receive it as soon as she could?

It was then that the alarm bells had definitely begun to ring, for he knew his Charlotte. She loved animals and would never use a crop on one. God, she wouldn't even let him use a knock-down spray to kill household wasps and flies! Granted, she could be a real bitch in other ways – *was* a real bitch in other ways. But not where her furry friends were concerned.

Which meant the call about the horse whip was a ruse. So why did Jeff really want to see Charlotte? Presumably because he was fucking her – or getting close. Been riding someone else perhaps sweetheart? Vernon had mused viciously, and brought his hand down harder at the thought.

He'd planned to shag her till she squealed: now she was in her cell squealing with gratitude as they put some soothing balm on her sore bottom and fucked or frigged her till she convulsed with ecstatic release. 'I'd have made her squeal all the harder,' he muttered, pacing the hall.

He stopped as the Master walked in.

'I'm sorry if I went too far, sir. She'd received these phone calls from another man . . .'

'Come with me to the big house and discuss it,' the Master said. 'There's nothing we can't sort out.'

Vernon did as he was told. It seemed right to do so. He sat back on one of the velvet sofas and accepted a twenty-year-old whisky, and a plate of savoury crackers from a splendidly naked blonde-pubed female guide. Gradually he relaxed and told the whole story. The Master looked interested throughout.

'I can't prove she's got a lover yet,' he finished, 'but it's looking likely. I was so good to her when we were living together, yet it's looking like she betrayed me. I just wanted to take my revenge on her arse . . .'

'Of course you did,' said the Master, soothingly, 'but we should never hit out in anger, Vernon. That's for fools. Pain should be a thought-about, carefully delivered thing that the recipient knows they deserve.'

'She deserves it all right,' muttered Vernon.

'But she thought she was still being thrashed for planning to run away,' the Master said.

'How could I tell her this was about Jeff without revealing myself?'

'If you're not ready to reveal yourself maybe you're not ready to punish her constructively,' the other man murmured with a smile.

The Master had all the answers. Vern suddenly wished that he himself even understood the questions! Once he'd known that he loved Charlotte and that she didn't love him as much back. But now ...? He felt he'd sold himself cheap, that love should be based on communication; a real understanding. He'd never understood Charlotte, and she'd never cared enough to even try to understand him ...

'I suspect you're tired,' said the Master. 'I suspect you need to go back to your quarters.'

'That would be nice.'

The Master pressed a button on the wall and a guide appeared. She bowed deeply. 'Bring our guest six pleasure slaves. Have them parade their charms!'

As Vernon stared, nonplussed, the naked girl bowed again and left the room. A few moments later she was back, leading the girls.

A small Chinese girl with long labial lips that looked endlessly inviting entered the room, followed by a second who was obviously native to the island; tall and slim, with spun-silk black pubic hair and forever legs.

Vernon turned his attention to the third girl who was chunkily built with the biggest bosom he had ever seen outside a magazine centrefold. It looked like she could suckle triplets on each weighty, brown-tipped breast. The fourth pleasure slave was almost boyishly trim; small hips sloping downwards from a twenty-three inch waist, leading to toned-up athletic thighs. The fifth had blonde cropped hair and pale flesh.

But it was the sixth that captivated him. She seemed to combine the mysterious sultry beauty of the Orient with the haughty challenge of the spoilt Westerner. He immediately wanted to hold her, to talk her down and make her writhe under his lips. He'd make her say things she never thought shc'd say. He'd make her come.

'You can choose one for the evening,' said the Master. 'Or even take them all, if you like!'

Quality not quantity, Vernon told himself, surreptitiously adjusting his trousers to hide the growing iron. Anyway, there was no contest.

'I'll take number six.'

'A commendable choice,' the Master said, appraisingly. The girl glared at him then looked belatedly away. As if prompted by some unseen voice she adopted the act of the submissive; head bowing, eyes to the floor.

'As you can see, she needs discipline,' said the Master, 'So far I've been short of time.'

'What would you suggest?' asked Vernon, trying to keep the excitement out of his voice.

The Master sent a guide to the nearest cupboard. 'Why not try this plump little cane?'

The girl flinched, but kept looking at the ground. 'Don't spare her,' said the Master.

'Where should I take her?' Vernon said, tapping the rod against his leg.

'Back to your rooms, of course.'

'But Suki's there!'

The man stared at him. 'So?'

'So . . .' Vernon began. He thought some more. Of course, Suki wasn't really his girlfriend. She was his pleasure slave, even if he already cared for her lots. This new girl was also his pleasure slave, albeit temporarily. He had nothing to hide! 'Shall I bring her back in the morning?' he asked feverishly.

'She'll be collected. After the night you're going to have you'll probably want breakfast in bed!'

For now he wanted the girl in bed – and then some! The guide fastened a collar and lead to the girl's neck and she grumpily got down on her hands and knees. Trembling with anticipation he led her out into the Training Grounds towards the quarters he thought of as home.

When he got back he tied her lead to the inside door-handle, got the handcuffs he'd once used on Suki from the cupboard and cuffed the girl's hands in front of her. 'Suki!' he called. 'Come and see this.'

Obviously waking from sleep, the smaller girl came drowsily through the bedroom doorway. The smiling sleepiness left her face when she saw the newcomer. Uncertainty flickered across her brow.

'My present for the evening from your Master,' Vernon said. 'What do you think?'

He ran his middle fingers down the girl's neck, across her breasts, weighing their fullness. He felt the nipples elongating lustily against his hands.

Suki's eyes widened. Her mouth narrowed. The rosy flush of sleep was replaced by the dull flush of embarrassment and shame.

'She's . . . quite pretty, sir,' she said, gravely.

'She's beautiful, Suki,' Vernon corrected, with a gentle frown.

'Shall I go? Make tea?' Suki added, obviously trying to recover her composure.

'No. I want you to see,' Vernon said. He turned to the other girl. 'Name?'

'Ensya.'

'Your Master wants you to learn humility, Ensya. You're to follow me to the bedroom now for a thrashing with this cane.'

The girl looked away, the convulsive movement of her Adam's apple the only sign that she was affected by his orders. 'I'll untie you,' said Vernon, 'but you're to keep your hands cuffed in front of you throughout.'

He ordered Suki to precede them into the bedroom, and sit on a chair at the foot of the giant four-poster. Suki walked proudly in. As he unknotted her lead from the door handle, Ensya kept her head down, and stared at the floor. Her earlier agility gone, she crawled awkwardly to the bedroom, and lay down at his bidding on the bed.

'That's it. On your tummy,' said Vernon. He looked with admiration at the girl's lightly tanned skin and curving posterior. He didn't intend to cane it much. He wanted to enter her as soon as possible instead. Still, she had looked very spoilt earlier on, and had glared at him and the Master in the mansion for no reason at all.

'You're to be punished for a disrespectful attitude, for not showing suitable humility,' he said.

The girl kept her face in the pillows and didn't answer.

'I don't think that bottom's high enough,' added Vernon, getting angry, and took two of the pillows, pushing them under her belly so that her arse was raised. The action seemed to make it real to the girl.

'Please sir, don't hurt me. Don't use your cane!'

'I'll only hurt you till you see the error of your ways. I'll not cane you hard.'

He studied her flesh more closely. It was totally unblemished. 'Have you ever been caned before?' he asked.

'No, sir.'

'Whipped? Paddled? Belted? Birched? Knouted?'

'No, sir,' said the girl. 'No. No.'

'Then what have they done to you?'

'On my first day the Master spanked me because I tried to run away – I missed my boyfriend. Then I found out that he was the one who brought me here and I took to hating him instead.'

'Why did he bring you here?'

'Because he said I was haughty.' The girl gave an impatient little shrug of her shoulders which showed just that.

'I think you're haughty, too,' murmured Vernon, beginning to palm her almost virgin bottom. 'I think this arse needs taking down a peg or two.' He paused and said more loudly: 'I wonder why the Master hasn't dealt with you more fully?'

'He said I'd be a perfect present for the guests,' Ensya whispered, blushing. 'Please, sir. Don't use your cane.'

'I have to, just a little. Just to know for sure that you're truly sorry. Then you can show your thanks by pleasing me with your mouth.'

'I could please you now, sir,' Ensya murmured, and Vernon was sorely tempted. But he was equally tempted by the prospect of making her rump a little sore!

'Four strokes,' said Vernon out loud. He placed the cane against her primed young bottom for a second, raised it, and brought it down with medium force. Ensya yelped.

'Oh! It hurts! It hurts!' She drew her knees up and twisted round to face him.

'Get back into position now,' Vernon said.

The girl shook her head. 'Let me suck you instead – please. I want to!'

After your three other strokes,' said Vernon. 'I could have made it more.'

The girl shook her head. 'It stings so. I feel silly like that.'

'You're supposed to feel silly.'

Mutinously the girl refused to budge. She was his present from the Master. Now Suki would have a present! Vernon called to her. She walked up the carpet alongside of the bed slowly, eyes sad.

'You wanted me, sir?'

'Yes, to provide a little holding power. Sit on this disobedient slave's back.'

Ensya howled as Suki approached, but she was no match for the two of them. Quickly they turned her over, pillow under her belly again, hands still cuffed to the front. Then Suki sat astride her upper back, facing Vernon. Both looked with anticipation at the girl's now helplessly raised young arse.

One pink stripe testified to the stroke already given. 'Two,' said Vernon, picking up the rod again. 'I'm applying it over the first one,' he added conversationally, 'because you've been bad.'

'No!' Ensya wailed, but it was a hopeless wail. She knew when she was outsmarted; she knew she'd done wrong.

Vernon lined up the cane, and applied it smartly. The girl cried out into the pillow. Her bottom cheeks jerked.

'Three.'

Vernon applied the third stroke. Suki's eyes gleamed

with joy and pleasure. A trail of moisture started from her labia and wet the imprisoned girl's back.

'Master, I beg to suck you,' the girl whispered. 'I beg for permission to take your balls in my mouth.'

Vernon stopped, surprised. Girls usually took much more punishment than this before the sub side of their nature revealed itself. Assuming they had a sub side, that is . . .

He looked at Suki in confusion.

'Ignore her. Beat her!' whispered the smaller girl.

Vernon remembered the Master's more thoughtful words.

'No, she genuinely repents. A person must only be chastised if they deserve it. She's mended her ways.'

He studied Suki more closely.

'I'll punish you later, girl, for giving advice when it wasn't asked for. For giving bad advice. For putting your own jealousy before the island's needs.'

'I'm sorry, sir. I'll do better, sir.'

'For now you can watch Ensya and I enjoying ourselves.'

He watched poor Suki blush again. She hated this! He adored this! He would have his way. Gently he lifted her from her position of straddling the Western girl, and deposited her back on the bedside chair to observe.

Then he started to uncuff Ensya. Her expression, however, persuaded him not to. She likes it like this, he realised, looking at her flushed face. She wants to be fucked in bondage, lying on her punished arse!

Gently he brought her cuffed wrists up till they were lying above her head. He put his right knee between her thighs and nudged lightly. She spread them eagerly, swallowed twice, and closed her eyes.

'Look at me,' he said.

The eyes opened again reluctantly.

'Tell me how you like to be fucked.'

'I . . . on my stomach.'

Vernon smiled and ran an exploratory palm down her warm flat belly.

'Do you come that way, Ensya?'

'Only . . . only once.'

A sudden erotic vision seared Vernon's brain.

'Was it after your Master spanked you?'

A long drawn out exhalation: 'Yes.'

'Yes, sir,' he corrected, and pushed one hand below her nearest buttock, squeezing it painfully.

'Yes, sir,' repeated Ensya, pushing her already spread thighs further apart.

The room was beginning to smell of sex – her sex. Soon the heavy muskiness of his own come would be added to the scent! —

He bent his lips to the girl's right breast, and licked round the areolae. She tasted clean and wholesome. Her left tit was equally sweet.

'If you're on your tummy I can't pleasure these beauties,' he murmured regretfully.

'You could slip your hands round from the back and feel their weight.'

He could. He might. He continued to stroke her breasts whilst he debated how to have her. He wanted it to be good for both of them. He wanted the mortified Suki to be envious and impressed! He wished for a second that Charlotte was here – tied, watching. He wished that the Master had given her to him for the long, long night.

His thoughts returned to the present. Ensya was looking at him quizzically through her thick dark lashes. 'Turn over,' he said authoritatively. 'Keep your legs wide apart.'

She did, though the handcuffs made the movement slightly awkward. Next time, he thought, I'll tie her wrists to each topmost corner of the bed.

But would there be a next time? He, Guy and Charlotte were supposed to be going home soon. He'd spoken to Guy the other day for the few moments he'd managed to persuade him to stop correcting some very wilful twins.

'I'm already saving up to come back here next year!' Guy had said, aiming the rawhide whip again.

'Maybe they'll offer us timeshare!' Vernon had said.

Time, now, to share his penile prowess with the shapely young Ensya.

'Do you think your bottom's been punished enough?' he whispered, stroking each pink-striped arch.

'Yes, sir. I'll be good, sir,' Ensya whispered.

'How good?'

The girl shrugged. Vernon spanked her hard across both buttocks.

'Speak when you're spoken to!'

'I . . . I don't know! As good as you want, sir.'

'In that case you'd better be very good indeed.'

He touched her *mons* and she jumped. She was soaking. He positioned himself between her sex lips and sank blissfully in. He wanted to touch both breasts and her clit. He wished he had three hands. He had an idea.

'Suki. Get over here.'

Dragging footsteps told him the native girl had complied.

'Kneel on Ensya's left side. No, down a bit. Beside her thighs. Now slide your palm under so it presses against her pussy. That's it. Stay exactly like that.'

Ensya moaned. Suki gave a little snort of disgust. Vernon groaned his pleasure. The girl beneath him began to writhe and buck. Vernon increased his speed. The girl increased her excited wriggling. He fondled Ensya's large tits and stared at Suki's firmer, darker ones as he prepared to come.

'What would your boyfriend say, Ensya, to know you've got another little girl touching you?' he whispered.

A moan followed from below, and in answer from Suki, above.

'Would he punish you for being dirty? Would he spank you?'

Another moan. He palpated her breasts harder. She gasped her lust.

'Tell me or I'll stop fucking you.'

He prayed she'd say something – he couldn't bear to withdraw from her without coming now.

'I . . . he'd be shocked. He'd be angry – very angry. He brought me here because he thought I was seeing someone else.'

'And were you?'

He thrust in with one word, out with the next: his balls felt loaded.

'Yes, but not . . . not fucking them.'

He sensed that fucking had been a hard word for her to say out loud, that lust had broken down her inhibitions.

'But you'd have like to have fucked them,' he said.

'Well . . . yes!'

'And that's wicked, isn't it?'

She wriggled in anguish.

'And what happens to girls who are bad?'

She sighed.

'Come on, say it, Ensya.'

'They get taught a lesson, sir.'

'As you're about to be taught a lesson?'

'Yes.'

He drove into her hard. She pushed back. He could feel her thighs tensing in on him. 'You'll have to be spanked again after this,' he said, conversationally.

'Yes!'

'Maybe we'll get your boyfriend back, let him watch. Maybe we'll also find your almost-lover!'

Ensya writhed like crazy and beat her handcuffed arms upon the bed.

'I think we'll let the whole island watch you taking a proper thrashing,' gasped Vernon. 'I'll lay more than my palm on that disobedient little arse!'

Ensya cried out. She pushed forward against Suki's hand then backwards against Vernon's cock. As she drove backwards his balls went into spasms and he screamed his release. Suki glared, then looked away. She wasn't supposed to glare. It took him a moment to think what to do.

'Suki. Lick Ensya's juices from my cock.'

The native girl pulled her hand free from under the other slave. Her mouth petulant, she clambered over the girl towards Vernon, putting her sharp ankles and elbows where they would.

'Ouch!' Ensya murmured, flinching away from the contact.

'Turn over, Ensya. Watch how a professional sucks,' Vernon said.

Suki squatted between his parted knees and put her lips to his shrinking phallus. She drew it into her mouth by centimetres, before pulling her lips away. Holding his cock upright, she ran the tip of her tongue from root to tip, then down again. She repeated the motion all the way round till he was clean.

'Good girl,' said Vernon, patting her on the head. Suki still looked mutinous.

'Now lick out Ensya,' added Vernon, with a little smile. Suki flinched as if she'd been struck.

'Lick her? That garbage?'

'That garbage,' said Vernon. 'Now.' He reached for his belt.

'I'll do it!' said Suki.

She crawled to the foot of the bed, and worked her way up again until she was between the girl's spread thighs.

'You're getting the belt later anyway,' said Vernon, 'for having the wrong attitude. You're getting it hard.'

His prick revived as he watched the smaller girl put her right hand over the other slave's pubic patch, and bend her head to the slippery pink slit. Dutifully she began to mouth away the moisture, licking both sexual scent and semen with her saliva-coated tongue.

'Thank Ensya for allowing you to tongue her,' Vernon murmured sadistically.

'Thank you,' Suki muttered to the writhing girl.

'Now change places,' Vernon said. He watched Ensya's eyes open wide. Suki laughed out loud. 'Suck me good, bitch,' she whispered, 'or your Master will belt you for hours.'

'As I've said,' warned Vernon, 'you'll both need the belt.'

'I've never sucked another woman before,' whispered Ensya.

'Neither had you felt the cane before today,' Vernon replied.

He reached for the heavy strap and wound it lovingly

between his fingers before laying it experimentally across Ensya's tanned backside. As he stroked her pink contours and told her what he was going to do to her, she moaned, and got wet. Warning her of how the first stroke would feel, he wished that Charlotte was the recipient. He wanted so much to warm that wilful little rump.

15

Charlotte stretched out on the chaise, enjoying the feel of the soft material against her bottom. She hadn't been thrashed for a few days, so was making the most of being able to lie on her bum. 'What's on the agenda today?' she murmured to her breakfast guide as she savoured the delicate fish in the scallop-shell serving dish.

'You're to have a visitor,' the girl replied.

Charlotte's heart leapt. It must be Vernon! She hadn't been given a calendar or watch, but most days after lunch she'd remembered to tear a corner from the page of the book she was reading – one page for every day. She'd torn off fifty-two such corners, which meant the two month sabbatical was virtually up.

Some sabbatical! She wished she'd told Jeff where she was going; that she was going. She'd thought that by not saying anything about this trip she'd make him miss her, and make him worry about her. He was such an arrogant man!

She sighed. Still, the making up would be great fun, and didn't she have a story to tell! Sipping her breakfast tea, she thought about the matter further. Perhaps not. She couldn't bear to describe what it was like to be held down, stripped, and spanked by a veritable stranger; made to beg for a come . . .

He'd want her to go to the police but she didn't have a shred of evidence. She didn't have a map reference for the island, and had no idea where it was. Guy would doubtless pretend she'd made the whole thing up, and had some kind of breakdown. Would Vernon go along with the lie?

She sighed. She couldn't be sure any more. One thing was certain: when he came to fetch her she'd give him the time of his life, both in bed and out of it. Later, when they were safely back home at the flat there would be time for recriminations – and how! For now she'd be incredibly sweet to him; she'd make him believe she'd changed into the type of loving girlfriend he obviously craved.

'Your bath,' said the guide, as the wall panel opened. 'In a moment!' muttered Charlotte, pushing away her empty plate and settling back. She felt out of sorts, and restless. She wanted to strike out, and to shout.

'Please,' whispered the girl. 'Don't keep our Mistress waiting.'

'Karo?' Charlotte said in surprise. 'Karo's coming here?'

The girl nodded nervously and her full bottom trembled. Charlotte's almost did likewise till she reminded herself that she had little left to fear. She was leaving soon, moving on, moving back to all that was familiar. All that was tranquil and safe . . .

'Your bath,' said the girl again. 'Mistress likes the girls to be bathed.'

'You take it then,' muttered Charlotte. 'I'm going back to sleep.'

When she next opened her eyes Karo was in the chair across from the chaise, watching her. Charlotte suddenly felt exposed and vulnerable. She wished she'd had her bath. The woman's black tunic and trousers simply emphasised her own fragile nakedness; her helplessness before the whip.

'You'll be leaving us soon,' said the Mistress. Charlotte nodded dumbly. She'd planned to say something sarcastic, but the words had fled. 'You don't have to leave,' added Karo. She looked less imposing than usual. Biorhythms must be having a good day, Charlotte thought maliciously. She wanted to cry.

'Watch this,' said Karo easily. 'Consider it carefully. It's a year in the life of a new slave.'

Becoming more fully awake, Charlotte noticed the projector equipment and screen someone had obviously set up whilst she slumbered. The word BEFORE appeared on the screen in bold black type.

'Before what?' muttered Charlotte.

'Before she came to accept her true nature,' Karo replied.

As they watched, the screen filled with a school room, where a grown up schoolgirl sat at a desk, sucking a pencil. For a while she wrote something on a long sheet of paper, then obviously tired of the task.

'She's been given lines for previous disobedience,' explained Karo. 'This is her first week at the Training Grounds; her third day in school.'

'Obviously doesn't know about the overhead cameras,' said Charlotte, sourly.

'Obviously not.'

Compelled by the scene, Charlotte watched on. The girl stood up, smoothed down her impossibly short skirt, and sidled over to the walk-in cupboard. She listened at the school-room door for a second, presumably afraid that the teacher might come back. Then she shrugged to herself, and went into the cupboard. She rummaged around curiously for long moments, then brought out three large boxes of chalk.

For a while she amused herself by sketching caricatures and cartoons on the wall-sized blackboard. Then she sighed with boredom and kicked the nearest desk. What was she doing now? Why was she doing it? Charlotte leaned forward and watched more intently as the girl opened the school-room window and threw each box of chalk into the grounds beneath. Then she sat down again and started to draw little ink faces in the margin of the paper where she'd been writing her lines.

'Hardly the behaviour of someone who wants to keep out of trouble, is it?' asked Karo, drily.

Charlotte shrugged.

The schoolmaster entered the school-room. He carried a long switch, which he held sideways across his body, tapping it into his right hand as he spoke.

'You have completed your lines, Anna?'

219

'Not quite.'

'Not quite, *sir*,' corrected the man. The taps of his switch handle on his palm intensified. 'Well, bring your pathetic endeavours out to the front. Let me see!'

'Yes, sir.'

The girl looked slightly cowed, but still self-willed and potentially wilful. Walking with her head held high, she marched over to him, and held out the page.

'I asked for a hundred. You've done around twenty.'

'It was cold in here, sir. I couldn't concentrate.'

'Oh, we're soon going to warm you up,' said the man. 'Soon going to re-educate you.'

The girl swallowed and dipped her head.

'Bend over the desk now,' continued the schoolmaster. 'Then lift your skirt up slowly. You can keep your pants on for now.'

'What if I don't?'

Charlotte gasped in surprise. She'd gone long beyond this point, and had forgotten her own earlier stubbornness. Karo smiled grimly.

'As I said, she's new.'

'And does she finally . . . ?' Charlotte began. But she knew the answer. She watched further as the man talked the girl down.

'If you don't, I'll have to call in the guides to undress you. Some of the male ones can get excited; can be quite rough.' He paused. 'I've heard it can take them ten whole minutes to pull down a bad girl's panties. And all the time they're stroking her disobedient little bum cheeks and looking forward to watching what happens to them next.'

'I'll raise my skirt, sir,' Anna whispered. Her face had flushed heavily. Her eyes were glassy.

'Edge it up slowly, centimetre by centimetre,' the schoolmaster said.

Charlotte swallowed hard as the girl did so. The unveiling exposed her taut knickers in regulation navy cotton which covered every inch of her perfectly rounded bum. They revealed the shape of her globe-like buttocks, and the deep crease between. Her arse jutted temptingly out as she did the schoolmaster's bidding, and bent more fully over the waist-high desk.

'Three strokes for failing to finish your lines on time,' said the man easily.

Anna's bottom tensed, relaxed, and tensed again as the first stroke cut down.

'Keep gripping the desk or you'll get double,' the man added.

The girl complied.

'She's obviously been given permission to cry out,' Karo said as the girl moaned into the desk top. 'Sometimes I don't give permission. Did I forbid you to scream, Charlotte, when you were my slave for the day?'

Charlotte shrugged. It was humiliating being reminded of these times, especially today when they both seemed almost equal. That is, she wasn't over the more powerful woman's knee!

'Perhaps I'll get to try it on you sometime,' said Karo thoughtfully. 'Perhaps . . .'

She broke off, her attention diverted by what was happening on the screen. Anna had had three tastes of the switch and had moved to nurse her punished bottom with her cooler palms.

'Put your hands on top of your head,' snapped the schoolmaster. 'And keep them there!'

Walking over to her still-bent frame, he did something to her skirt band. Peering more closely, Charlotte could see that he'd pinned the hem to the waist, keeping the garment up above her arse.

'Now sit down, keeping your hands on your head as instructed,' said the schoolmaster firmly. Smiling, he pulled her knickers to her ankles, explaining, 'You'll just have to shuffle to your seat.'

'Yes, sir. Thank you, sir.' Without looking at him, Anna did as she was bid.

Charlotte felt herself flush with sympathy. At the same time a flush snaked to her nether regions at the thought of the girl's sore bottom coming into contact with the hard wood of the chair. With her hands kept as they were she couldn't touch herself. She could only wait . . .

But not for long.

'I'll just get the chalk,' said the schoolmaster almost to himself, 'and start writing up today's lesson. Your schoolmates will be here in a moment. They're eager to learn.'

The hidden camera cut to Anna's face; to her look of dismay and nervousness.

'Someone's stolen the chalk!' came the schoolmaster's surprised voice from the cupboard. 'The little thief.' He looked at Anna and shook his head. 'It wasn't you, was it Anna?'

'No, sir. I haven't left the room since you brought me here, sir.'

'Good girl. In that case, I'm off to try and find the culprit. Spend the time thinking of how we can punish the thief when we find him – or her.'

'Yes, sir,' muttered Anna, miserably. The man left the room.

All she'll be able to think about now is her arse, Charlotte thought in slave-like sympathy. Yet part of her wanted to see the girl punished further; to see her writhe.

'Note how she keeps shifting on her seat. That uneasiness isn't just on account of her whipped young bottom,' said Karo, amicably. 'As you'll soon see, she's getting wet.'

Not that old argument again, thought Charlotte wearily. Did they really expect her to believe that getting wet whilst being thrashed proved that you were truly sub? Being stripped naked before others could be exciting. So could the sheer mechanical warmth the raised palm or belt produced in the area near your loins.

'Big deal,' she muttered, then sat more firmly on her bottom as Karo reached for the whip she always carried. She must protect her poor arse during her remaining island days!

The schoolmaster returned. He had a male guide with him. The guide's cock leapt into instant arousal when it saw Anna sitting with her hands on top of her head. Her raised arms made her breasts stick out through her blouse, and showed the full pink nipples. Her thighs were splayed against the wood.

'This young man has a story to tell us, Anna,' said the schoolmaster, sounding reasonable.

'I was passing the school half an hour ago,' confirmed the boy, 'when three packets of chalk narrowly missed my head. I looked up of course, to see a girl closing the window of this room – the window with the blind pulled up. I gave the chalk to the janitor downstairs.'

Anna's lips parted slightly. Her fingers drummed against her hair. Her eyes were staring. They darted sideways as other grown-up pupils began to file in.

'Take your seats, girls. There's to be a lesson before the lesson!' So saying, the schoolmaster dismissed the boy.

'Anna has already been whipped privately today,' he told the class, 'for failing to hand in written work on time. Now I find that she's damaged school property as well. She must pay.' The other girls looked at Anna. Some were embarrassed, others were smiling. A couple of the older ones wore evil grins. 'In the circumstances, I have no option but to use the tawse,' continued the schoolmaster. 'Girl. Come out to the front.'

Anna stood up slowly. One of her contemporaries whistled as they saw her bare bottom. Another giggled. Anna flushed bright red.

'Stand with your arse facing the class. Touch your toes,' the man ordered.

Anna blushed some more. But obeyed, obviously glad to flex her arms and change their overhead position. Now her fingertips trailed the floor, her thighs were taut, and her bottom awaited its next assault. The knickers, still bunched round her ankles, testified to her earlier period of correction. So did her bum.

Shaking his head sorrowfully, the man went to his desk drawer, and drew out the implement. He fondled the stiffened leather before holding it before Anna's nervous face.

'How many strokes of the tawse for a girl who's damaged school property then lied about it?'

Anna hesitated. 'Three?'

'Make it six!' cried a voice from the back.

'We'll make it eight for you, later, Claire,' said the schoolmaster, looking menacing.

Claire gulped and looked away.

'Three it is, then – though it'll feel more like thirteen after that whipping,' said the schoolmaster. 'Now keep your finger tips on the floor and don't move your legs.'

Charlotte and Karo watched as Anna took her punishment. Her pert young bottom was hot at its conclusion. Her sex lips gleamed.

'See how aroused she is, how excited?' murmured Karo. 'Watch what happens next!'

Charlotte watched. It made compulsive viewing.

'Stand out in the corridor,' the schoolmaster said when the third lick of the tawse had been administered. 'Keep your hands above your head.'

Knickers at her feet, skirt pinned up, bottom scarlet, Anna shuffled out of the watchful classroom. She closed the class door, and stood staring along the corridor with a wild gaze. Even to the casual observer it was obvious that she was trying to push her thighs together to create pressure on her *mons*.

Seconds later a male guide came along carrying a parcel. He stopped and whistled low and long when he saw Anna.

'What's that?' she whispered.

'Replacement chalk.'

'They're doing mental arithmetic in there – they don't need it,' Anna continued. Her voice was low and husky. 'Stay here and keep me company instead.'

'It's against the rules . . .'

'Bugger the rules!' Anna reached for his thick hard penis.

'No, my way,' said the guide, obviously coming to a decision. 'Face the wall.'

Anna obeyed him. Now her breasts were pressed into the wooden panels of the corridor, facing the classroom where she'd just been thrashed.

'Spread your legs,' whispered the boy.

Anna did so. She moaned as he grabbed her soft belly and slid in to the hilt, his balls banging against her bum.

'See how turned on she is, how desperate?' murmured Karo. 'See how she thrusts herself back against his cock?'

The scene faded to be replaced by the word AFTER. 'After what?' muttered Charlotte, sourly.

'After she's come to obey the dictates of her nature,' Karo said.

The two watched as Anna skipped past the growing audience at one of the Training Grounds' Relaxation Centres. Curtseying low, she took to the empty dance floor, and pirouetted almost on her tiptoes round its perimeters in her flimsy ballet dress. She wore only a black silk crotch thong underneath; the lower section of her arse was plainly visible. Craning forward, Charlotte could see the flesh was virtually unmarked.

'Note that the audience carries small sticks for tapping a recalcitrant posterior,' Karo pointed out, 'but she's so good that such corrective measures are rarely used.'

Good for her, Charlotte thought, shifting restlessly on her chair again. She didn't feel right in her body; she wished she hadn't refused that earlier bath.

Talking of baths . . . She watched on as scene after scene showed Anna in the tub, soaping her large breasts with creamy bubbles. Anna splashing about in the jacuzzi. Anna riding bareback along the beach, the gentle wind in her hair.

'A nice picture?' asked Karo, gently.

'Nice for simpletons.'

'What would you like for yourself, then, Charlotte, if you were to stay?'

Charlotte thought. To orgasm, she realised, with my Mast . . . She bit back the image.

'I don't want to stay.'

'There's no shame in changing your mind, my dear.'

'I tell you, I don't want to! I don't.'

'Because you won't accept you're sub,' said Karo.

It was a statement, not a question.

'Did you think Anna was sub?' she continued.

'Not necessarily,' Charlotte said.

'Then why did she get wet?'

Charlotte dredged up her explanations about physiology and enjoying being looked at.

'Let me show you something else,' Karo said.

She put a new film into the projector and started it. 'We're not proud of this one,' she murmured, 'but we keep it to remind ourselves that we're not infallible, that we sometimes get things wrong.'

The scene switched to a smallish girl of around five foot three.

'This is Ryaka,' said Karo. Ryaka was around eighteen and looked half Western, half Oriental. Her eyes were large and brown but ever so slightly slanted. Her mouth was full and red.

'Here she is being handed over to us by her father,' Karo explained. The girl was kicking, screaming and biting. 'Turned out she wanted to marry someone he disapproved of,' Karo added. 'That's why he brought her here. But he gave us the impression she was always this difficult, that she was genuinely out of control.'

'What if she had been?' asked Charlotte.

'And been sub too? Then her behaviour would have been a way of eliciting punishment. Literally asking for it! A few sound spankings and she'd have seen the error of her ways.'

'I take it she wasn't sub,' said Charlotte.

'Watch. Compare. Learn,' answered Karo.

Charlotte returned her curious gaze to the screen.

The camera had turned its gaze on Ryaka's inauguration; a prolonged spanking doled out by the Master. She yelled throughout it, beat her feet upon the ground and swung them vigorously off the deck. When told to keep still, she continued to flail her legs and tried to get her bound arms free. For this she was told she'd just earned five further slaps with the enforced-palm glove.

The two women watched as she was lifted up from her Master's lap, and dragged on her collar and lead to the nearest punishment bench. She fought her guides all the way, pulling at the leather restraints, and kicking them with her bare feet in the shins.

'Isn't it obvious she hates all this?' asked Charlotte.

'Not at this stage, no. Remember that you – and Anna who we saw a moment ago – also fight to evade punishment.'

'Because it hurts so. Because we hate it,' said Charlotte.

'Oh, your arse hates it, your brain hates it. But your cunt needs it. It makes you wet.'

'Bullshit,' muttered Charlotte uncomfortably.

'Darling, a few slaps on that pretty arse and I could almost talk you into a come! I'd tell you what you deserved, what I was going to do to you. Watch you cream . . .'

Charlotte gritted her teeth, trying to block out the older woman's clit-tormenting words.

Ryaka was being fastened down over the punishment bench on the screen. The Master approached, wearing the glove. He stroked her bottom. He spent a long time doing so, telling her how wicked she'd been.

'Let me go!' Ryaka was screaming. 'Let me go! You can't do this!'

'We've already done it,' whispered the Master. 'Or rather you've done it to yourself.'

'What do you mean?' Ryaka cried.

'You kicked, you swore. Were disobedient.'

'But I'm an independent woman – a career woman! You can't treat me like a slave!'

More teasing strokes of her backside followed. Charlotte wriggled on her chair and surreptitiously pressed her own thighs together.

'You have a slave's mentality deep down,' murmured the Master. 'Your pussy thinks like a slave.' He smiled, 'Daddy knows best and Daddy brought you here.'

'Daddy's a fucking megalomaniac!' spat the girl.

She took the first blow on her nearest buttock, and shrieked in pain and anger. The second made the cheeks parallel. The third seared across both. After the forth, she seemed to stop fighting, and simply lay there moaning into the surface of the bench, her eyes closed, her eyelids alternately relaxing and tightening. Two hectic purple patches stood out on her otherwise pale face.

'I'll say what you want. I'll do what you want,' she whispered. 'Please stop.'

The Master took off the anguish-giving glove. His eyes were triumphant. 'In a moment I'll let you prove your devotion,' he murmured. The crowd smirked. 'Tell me if you want it in your cunt, in your arse, or between your lips, my dear,' he added conversationally, walking over to her still spread legs.

He slid his hand down the crack in her arse, down to her labia. He frowned, and parted her sex lips. He frowned some more, and knelt at her face: 'Did none of that excite you?'

The girl shook her head, exhausted. The man's watchful face became clouded with pity and a confused atypical bleakness.

'Untie her now. Take her to the recovery suite,' he said softly. 'See to it that she has everything she needs.'

The film sped on: brief glimpses of Ryaka being bathed in cool water; a gentle balm applied to her arse with butterfly-light caresses; body oil being massaged into her relaxing limbs. She was shown tucked up in a huge warm bed; being brought breakfast; being encouraged to stroll – now fully dressed – in the sunlit grounds.

Later still she was seen talking to the Master, listening carefully to his explanations.

'. . . pain meant as a prelude to overwhelming pleasure,' he was saying. 'The right stimulus for some.'

Ryaka was shown nodding, signing a disclaimer, and accepting a generous payment in sterling. She was seen waving as she got into the plane that would take her back home.

'One of the few times we got it wrong,' said Karo, sorrowfully.

'You got it wrong with me, too,' muttered Charlotte.

'No. We simply thought it would take less time to re-educate you than it has.' She sighed. 'Now Vernon will collect you and you'll go home and a part of your heart will still be here with us. And you'll be restless and miserable and you'll create hell back in the so-called civilised world.'

228

'I'll risk it,' muttered Charlotte. 'Do I get a large payment?'

'No. Tell who you will. But the real shame is yours so I guarantee you won't.'

Why did they always know what she was going to do, Charlotte thought angrily. Aloud she said: 'Film show over, is it?'

'Not quite,' Karo replied. She paused. 'You've seen how horny Anna got by being humiliated and thrashed – and how it did nothing for a non-submissive like Ryaka. Let's watch you now, Charlotte. Let's see how you fare.'

'Do I have to?'

Charlotte's body felt suddenly still, cold, and wary.

'It's an order,' said Karo, with a grin. Charlotte looked away. 'Watch, Charlotte,' added her Mistress, 'or I'll have you tied facing the screen and I'll thrash your inner thighs till you keep your eyes wide open.'

Charlotte focused her embarrassed gaze on the screen.

The film began on a day she'd already been spanked for turning up late to work.

'Crawl round the room showing the guides your punished bottom,' ordered the Master, still fondling her over his lap.

Charlotte suggested he do something with his own cock and arse that was physically impossible.

'You'll receive a further thrashing for your comments later,' warned the man.

'Leave me alone, you pig! I'm not an animal!'

'Oh, your pussy's like an animal, Charlotte. It knows what it wants . . .'

The man fondled her pink sore cheeks, and the crease where thigh met bottom. Charlotte writhed against his erection, which was clearly visible through his clothes.

'Have mercy,' she whispered. 'Don't shame me like this again.'

'Public shame before private pleasure, my dear,' the man murmured. 'Crawl round now and show the audience your hot little posterior or I'll heat it some more . . .'

'No! Don't! Can't we . . .'

'Orders aren't open to negotiation,' said the Master. 'You've been taught that already.'

He signalled for a ping pong bat to be brought.

Charlotte watched herself wriggling about on screen; her hands going back to protect her already-punished young derrière. She watched the Master pull her hands away again, and order them to be fastened behind her back.

'You never take the line of least resistance, do you, dear? So proud . . .'

Pride comes before a fall.

Charlotte's mouth fell open as she saw the guide approach with the thick black ping pong bat. It was a small but unyielding bat. A bat that would hurt.

'Don't do this,' she whispered, trying to flick her buttocks over, away from the forthcoming torment.

'It's for your own good,' replied her tormentor, holding her firmly in place.

He raised the bat and brought it down on one full pink cheek. Charlotte squealed, and writhed crazily. She felt the second buttock take its punishment, and squealed some more.

'Tell me that you'll crawl round, parading your bottom,' murmured the Master, using the bat with measured force.

'I'll . . .' Charlotte bucked and wailed. 'All right! I'll do it!'

'Beg to do it.'

'I beg. Oh, you bastard! Oh!'

'Spread your legs,' whispered the man. The camera focused in as he helped tease them apart further and further. 'Oh baby, you shouldn't call your Master a bastard. Oh no.'

'I . . .'

Charlotte's eyes were closed, her mouth open. She moaned as the man touched her labia, and pushed down hard against his hand.

'Say sorry,' murmured her Master.

'Sorry.'

'You want to come, don't you, babe?'

'Yes . . . need . . .'

Saliva was making her parted lips glisten. Down below, her sex lips were also glistening as she bore down upon his hand. 'We could take a walk,' continued the man. 'Give you a chance to show off your reddened assets.'

Charlotte parted her thighs further and groaned. She saw her punisher unfasten her wrists, and push her arms in front of her.

'Guides. Come here,' said the Master, indicating two of the strongest boys. They rushed forward, and waited eagerly for further instruction. Making sure Charlotte's palms were flat against the floor, the Master stood up holding her ankles, and pushed away his chair.

Now he was holding Charlotte up on her hands, her weight mainly supported by his body.

'Grab an ankle each,' he told the boys. 'Then walk her over to greet our watchful friends.'

The boys complied, parading her round the circle of grinning slaves, whilst she remained on her hands.

'Lick which part of them you can reach, Charlotte,' said the Master.

'You must be ...!'

'Oh, I never joke, little slave girl.' He placed his hand between her scissored legs, and fondled her quim till she complied. 'Now turn her round, boys. Let the audience see her sore bottom.'

Whimpering in shame, Charlotte was walked round till her back was towards the crowd.

Unseen hands stroked her crimson flesh, and moved to the duskier pink of her labia. Female palms slapped at her quivering hindquarters; male fingers massaged her trembling clit.

'Beg to go back to the spanking stool and be brought off,' said the Master conversationally.

Charlotte inhaled deeply: 'I beg.'

She was his now. At least for now. She had to come. She'd do or say anything to achieve that; she could only think of the shameful spectacle of her exposed sore arse, and her engorged *mons*.

'Beg to go walkies.'

'I beg, Master. Like a dog. Like a pup, on its belly.'

The words were there. It took the right amount of pain to make them come out.

'Good dog, even if you are in heat!'

He walked her – still on her hands – back to his seat, the guides pulling her thighs apart further than was necessary and staring at her slit. Reluctantly they let her down at her Master's bidding till she was once again positioned naked across his lap.

'She begs to come,' he murmured, teasing round the outer circle of her swollen clitoris.

'Yes, sir. I beg!'

'Yet you called me a bastard,' said the man. 'And not for the first time.'

'I . . . I'll make it up to you!'

'Oh little slave, you will.' Coolly he kept up the rhythm as she gasped in increasing ecstasy, 'or you'll feel my birch against your bottom,' he said.

'Yes. Hard! Anything. But let me come,' whimpered Charlotte.

'Maybe after a thrashing! A studded belt? A cat o' nine tails? What will I use?'

'I don't . . .'

'Which do you think would mark your arse more, Charlotte? Make you beg for mercy?'

'The . . . the studs!'

She pushed against his fingers, almost coming.

'The audience would like that,' continued the Master.

'Oh please. Please!'

'Yes, it would please them, seeing you tied to a trestle table, your bad bottom raised.' He paused. 'You'd keep your arse high for me even without a support under your belly, wouldn't you Charlotte? Push it out?'

'Anything! I . . .'

Charlotte came, her orgasmic wails echoing round the Punishment Chamber. Cocks and clefts belonging to the watchers thickened and leaked.

'Look at yourself, Charlotte,' said Karo softly as the film froze on its final frame. 'Really look.'

Despite herself, Charlotte looked, and saw the scorching sex flush cover her on-screen body. She saw the rush of blood to her heated *mons*, and the overwhelming grimace of pleasure on her face.

'Is that the demeanor of a woman who hates everything about this island?'

Charlotte hesitated, torn between the truth she knew and the truth she wanted. Then: 'You think you're gods 'cause you can press a few buttons?' she said.

16

Vern was leaving! Suki stared at him, then at the Master.

'Can I come too?'

She knelt at Vern's feet, and licked them tearfully. He kissed her upturned face, and shook his head.

'That means *she's* coming with you. You're taking her back! You're . . .'

The Master interrupted: 'If by *she* you mean Charlotte, she's about to be corrected for being impertinent to her Mistress. Perhaps you'd like to watch her being taught?'

Suki shivered, feeling unfamiliar rage invade her small cocoa-coloured body. 'Suki would like to teach her some manners personally,' she said.

There was a long pause. She stared down at her lover's and her Master's shod feet, then at her own bare ones. Had she been too forward? Grief had made her bold. This woman had been cruel to Vernon; she had possibly even cheated on Vernon. Yet he was taking her back with him to their world . . .

'How would you like her?' the Master asked.

Suki glowed. She had fantasised about this moment.

'Blindfolded.' She paused. 'Arms tied before her, her legs cuffed loosely to allow some movement, but not loose enough that she can escape.'

'You want to brief a guide to help punish her?'

Suki considered, then said yes.

'And two to restrain her whenever necessary, please,' she added. 'And a guard outside.'

'Take Charlotte to Punishment Hall Six,' the Master said to one of the guides, 'and get her ready. Lead Suki through when her victim has been blindfolded and tied, and the guides are standing in place.'

'Would you like any equipment readied, madam?' the guide said respectfully to Suki.

'No, we'll just start with a whacking using the heavy glove.'

'My arms are strong, madam,' murmured the guide hopefully, before backing out of the room. Suki stood up, suddenly restless. She figured she'd need his strong arms – and his fingers – to bring the recalcitrant Charlotte into line. She took her time walking to Punishment Hall Six. Let Charlotte sweat a little. Let her imagine how the coming hours would feel.

She entered the Hall to find the girl blindfolded and tethered as she'd commanded. Suki sat down silently on one of the many chairs. Coldly she contemplated her floor-crouched victim, who was lying on her side with her knees up to her chest. Thick black scarves bound her slender ankles together. Her hands, tied firmly at the wrists, were clasped in front of her, her full mouth a half-stimulated, half-mutinous line.

Still noiseless, Suki signalled for one of the guides to get her a pen and paper. He complied immediately. Then, for twenty minutes, she wrote down what the guide should do and say. Don't spare her, she wrote at the end, she's a wicked lady. Lacks respect. She settled back in her chair.

Now her body was rested, but her mind was active. She wanted to watch Charlotte wriggle. She wanted to watch Charlotte beg. Later, she'd chastise her personally, but for now she had to work out a plan . . .

For as long as Suki had been writing, Charlotte had been turning her head this way and that, trying to decide where her enslaver would come from. Now she seemed to be drifting, almost asleep.

Suki signalled to the man to take his seat in one of the specially-constructed spanker's chairs. He did so.

'Approach me on your belly, Charlotte. Follow my voice,' he said coldly. The other guides grinned their

235

assent. At the sudden booming sound Charlotte flinched, quickly recovering her composure. She began to wriggle on her soft stomach towards the guide.

It took a long time for her to reach the chair leg, but the sight was pleasing. Her firm young bottom moved up and down as she used her thigh muscles and belly to push her body along. 'Yes, sir?' she asked, raising her blindfolded head in the vague direction of his torso.

'Put this badly behaved creature over my knee, guides,' the voice said.

Suki's eyes narrowed as Charlotte's nipples hardened. She didn't want the bitch to enjoy this. She didn't want her to have any pleasure at all! She'll get a nasty shock when she finds the glove being used on her arse rather than the palm, she thought gladly. That glove could really sting.

It obviously did. She sat forward in her seat, watching intently as the guides picked Charlotte up and stretched her over the waiting lap. Immediately, her tormentor gave her exposed bum two carefully-aimed slaps. Charlotte's mouth opened wide with surprise or dismay. She flattened herself against his ungiving knees at the first slap, but she'd received two spanks on each buttock before she yelled.

'Not so hard! Don't . . .!'

'It's not for you to dictate your sentence,' said the guide calmly. Then he administered six other measured whacks.

'That's just a taster,' he said, as the last spank echoed round the narrow hall. 'Now we're going to have a little chat about your behaviour. Why are you here?'

'I don't know,' Charlotte sniffed.

'You don't know? Would an hour's worth of hard slaps remind you?'

'It . . . it might be because I was rude to the Mistress when she made me watch a film.'

'You shouldn't be rude to your Mistress, should you, Charlotte?'

'No, sir,' whispered Charlotte, blushing slightly.

'Good girl.'

The guide stroked her bottom, teasing it mercilessly.

236

Suki could see the paler girl trembling. Was it with shame or desire or fear?

'How should you treat your Mistress, Charlotte?'

'I should be deferential, respectful.'

'Or else?'

She wriggled again. She was obviously searching for the least embarrassing words to extricate herself from this position. Suki nodded to the hopeful guide.

'Bad girl,' he said. 'Not answering a question. I'll have to thrash it out of you after all.'

'No! I'll tell you . . .'

But the gloved hand was already raised and fast falling down. Suki smirked with satisfaction as finger prints spread out over Charlotte's pretty cream-coloured backside.

Light pink then deeper pink. When the guide raised his eyebrows queryingly she indicated that he should keep going. She watched as Charlotte increased her frantic movements and her cries.

Eventually the guide stopped. 'I'm only resting my arm,' he murmured. 'A slave that is rude to her Mistress doesn't get off this lightly.'

'Please!' said Charlotte. 'Please!'

'I'm not the one you should plead to. I'm just following instructions.'

'Then bring the Mistress here! Let her hear my apology for herself.'

'Dear me – you expect the Mistress to come running when you call?' The guide stroked her sore bum more intently. 'That's bad. That's very bad. You're not thinking straight are you, Charlotte? Not thinking straight at all.'

'No, sir. Sorry, sir.'

'And when a girl isn't thinking straight, we have to wake her up a little. Which usually means a short sharp lesson to her arse.' He fondled her on, and on, and on. 'Only, when a girl's been especially difficult, we don't make the lesson such a short one. In fact, we make it last as long as possible so that she never forgets.'

'I won't forget,' muttered Charlotte.

'You won't forget, *sir*. See – you're forgetting your manners already. A nice warm reminder will soon reach your memory cells.'

Suki raised her hand silently to attract the guide's attention.

'Lie there and await further instruction,' he told Charlotte, letting her slide to the floor. Her audience noted how quickly she rolled off her sore bum, got onto her knees, then stretched out on her belly instead.

Suki smiled grimly as the guide walked towards her, still wearing the glove. 'I want her on the trestle table,' she whispered. 'I'll take over her correction from now on.'

She'd thought of a way to make that lying, disrespectful girl tell the truth about her lifestyle: a way to ensure she suffered much, much more.

She wouldn't have to suffer much more, Charlotte told herself as she stretched onto her tummy, protecting her posterior and knees from the hard floorboards. This would be one of her last ever punishments. Soon she'd be going home. She heard light footsteps approach, then heavier ones. She turned towards whoever was about to torment her now.

'Approach the trestle table on your belly, then wait for the guides to lift you into it,' said the same male that had administered her previous thrashing. 'You get double each time you fail to complete a command.'

Double? No way! Charlotte pushed out her tied wrists before her. The guides had just bound her legs lightly so she was able to wriggle forward, making good time. She sensed her unseen opponent was disappointed at her fast progress; that he'd have liked an excuse to thrash Charlotte some more.

'Ten teasing thrusts with the anal dildo for not answering me quickly enough whilst I was spanking you,' said the guide, announcing her punishment. Charlotte felt strong hands grip her arms and legs. She shivered as they lifted her, and shivered more as she felt herself being placed over the table. The thick cloth round her eyes obscured absolutely everything, but she recognised the feel of the wood under her belly: she'd been chastised over this before!

Even as her senses sharpened she felt the bonds that held her wrists and ankles together being cut free. They left her to flex them for a moment, then pulled gently at each limb before tying them to the four corners of the table, so that she was securely trussed.

'Use the handles to push that block up under her belly,' continued the man softly. 'Get her arse as high as it will go.'

Charlotte gulped. Something about the instructions made this punishment and pleasure seem almost personal. Had she met her assailant before? Could it be Vern?

She stiffened and the guides pushed her arse further into the air, increasing its vulnerability. It *must* be Vernon! It explained why he wanted the other person in the room to issue the talking part of each instruction, and why she'd been blindfolded so that she couldn't see.

She could talk, though. She could promise him things: the type of things he'd only dreamt about hotly and wetly.

'Vern . . .' she started.

'No talking!' snapped the guide.

Charlotte bit her lip. They'd defeated her! But damn it, she'd disobey them on this one. It was vital that she win Vern back!

'Vern, I want you so much. Want to suck you till you're hard, then get down on my hands and knees before you. Want to hold my arsehole open and feel you drive in . . .'

'Gag her,' said a female voice. Was it Karo? Or even Lari! She'd thrashed various women as part of her work as a pleasure slave. She'd also punished others because opportunity allowed for it, or because the Master demanded she should. If they decided to enact revenge, it could be very painful. Very painful indeed . . .

She felt fingers gripping her head, pulling it firmly backwards. She felt the soft gag press against her mouth. They didn't tie it on hard. It was more of a warning than anything. She realised she'd get worse if she spoke again.

Now she'd lost access to her tongue and lips, she

couldn't lick a cock even if its owner stood before her. Vernon had always loved being sucked. He'd have untied her after that.

'Ten thrusts of the anal dildo up the arse,' repeated the man softly. Charlotte heard lighter footsteps come closer. She sensed two people behind her, then the heavier tread backed away.

Something hard nudged against her opening, and pushed firmly. She moaned into the gag, and moved her bum as best she could: somehow she had to indicate to Vern how much she wanted him. Him – not this artificial heat! She wriggled her buttocks provocatively then cried out again as the implement was pushed in a little of the way.

Her flesh was all she had left to tantalise him. No eager mouth. No words. No knowing looks. She concentrated on pushing her hips lewdly backwards. Realised her mistake as the dildo fucked her exposed puckered entrance again.

Damn it! The move had simply made her backside a better target. She pressed her belly against the block that held her up, and flailed hopelessly as the pleasure-tool worked its way into her bum hole. If Vern was wielding it, he was clearly seriously enraged. If, however, he'd merely given the instructions, was he to know how tauntingly she was being chastised?

'Vern,' she moaned through the gag.

The outburst seemed to provoke the enslaver. He or she thrust the dildo in another half inch, making her arse gape open, a second thrust adding to the invaded sensation caused by the first.

'Please stop. I'll do anything!' she shouted through the gag, writhing. There was a pause, then she felt the first knot at the back of her head being untied. The gag was peeled free.

'I'll do what you want,' she muttered again more slowly, 'and I'm sorry that I spoke without permission, sir.'

'You'll be punished for that later,' said the guide.

New footsteps approached. Charlotte heard a muttered conversation. 'Keep an eye on things. See that none of the younger guides have their way with her,' said the voice of the man who'd spanked her earlier. His footsteps, and presumably those of the messenger, faded away.

Charlotte lay there, bound and listening, wondering how long she'd been given a reprieve for.

'Can I do anything to help you?' whispered a female voice.

'Who's there? Who are you?'

Charlotte had thought she was alone in the room.

'Call me Suki,' said the girl. 'I suggested the gag a moment ago to save you further punishment. They were going to birch you outside in the Training Grounds if you spoke again.'

Suki. The name and voice weren't familiar. She didn't think they'd met before.

'Can you untie me?' murmured Charlotte, wriggling the little she could in her spreadeagled position to try and relieve her fiery, dildo-stroked rump.

'It's more than my life's worth,' whispered Suki. 'Sorry – no!' The girl sounded regretful. 'Does your bum hurt a lot?' she added sympathetically.

Charlotte nodded: 'That glove seems to lash over every inch . . .'

'I know I've had it too – I only wish I had some healing ointment. However . . .' She sounded bashful. 'There is a way I could take you mind off it.'

'Don't fight it!' Charlotte said, hearing the sensuous tone enter the girl's voice. 'I'll return the compliment when we can spend time alone,' she continued, licking her lips. She knew how horny watching a thrashing could make you. She knew how you wanted to touch and be touched.

'This'll be our secret,' murmured Suki.

Charlotte felt experienced fingers gently caressing then parting her lushly swelling labia. Beneath the blindfold she shut her eyes.

'Oh, that feels good,' she whispered to her unseen pleasurer.

'Does anyone else stroke you like this, Charlotte?'

She thought. 'Mmm. In the Training Grounds basement

241

once – I was chained there. But he didn't satisfy me. He kept bringing me to the edge and leaving me there.'

'Anyone else?' the voice asked curiously, seductively. The small fingers increased their fondling. The girl was obviously a voyeur. Charlotte squirmed beneath each stroke. 'God! Yes – in the land that I came from. There was this man . . .'

'Your lover?' the girlish voice asked.

Charlotte felt uneasy. What if Vernon was in the room listening to this?

'Suki, please. Take the blindfold off. Let me see you! Let me look at your face!'

'But the guide will be angry.'

'He'll never know – I swear it! You can put it on again when you hear him coming back.'

'I suppose . . .' said Suki. 'I, too, hate being blindfolded.'

Charlotte relaxed. It was great to have a new friend. Lari had been her mate until Lari went all sub on her. Maybe this Suki could take her place?

Then she mentally shook her head. What was she saying? She was leaving any day now. She just had to get through this last ordeal. She felt sure fingers on her hair, and felt the knot lose its tension. Suddenly the scarf was whisked away.

The room seemed bright. She twisted her head round. 'Let me see you.'

Her new helper obliged, coming to stand at her head. She was a pretty little thing: dusky, doe-eyed, undaunting.

'Untie me so that I can see there aren't other people behind us,' Charlotte said.

The native girl shook her head regretfully. 'The guide would lash me . . .' She brightened. 'But I can fetch a mirror, and hold it before you. You can see for yourself.'

She did. As Suki held up the glass, Charlotte surveyed the large room, noting with dread the whips that were displayed from every wall hook. How many of these would they use on her? Breathing fast, she wriggled her helpless hips.

'Where were we?' murmured Suki. 'Oh, you were telling me about this lover who touches you here.'

Charlotte heard the native girl walk round, and felt her fingers sliding close to her clitoris again. Exquisitely stroking. She whimpered and pushed down hard.

She thought of Jeff pulling her jodhpurs down and bending her over the saddle he'd placed on a low table. She pictured him nudging her thighs apart with a strong, sure knee.

'Want to ride, baby?' he'd whisper, licking his hand then starting to play with her pussy lips.

Her increasing wetness would signal a desperate 'yes please'.

'What does he do to you?' muttered Suki, teasing her glistening folds with the lightness of a pinkie.

'He . . . takes me in unusual places.'

Like the stables, or in the fields beyond where anyone could appear!

'Where?' Suki persisted sexily, rubbing gently but firmly.

'Standing up against a stable door,' Charlotte said.

Her voice sounded thick. Her vaginal leaves felt swollen even thicker. She closed her eyes, and imagined Jeff putting his lips to her clit, slicking saliva round and round.

So delicate, so exquisite, so incredibly arousing! Herself panting, begging, a slave to that glorious knowing tongue. The sensation was spreading: first a tensing of the thighs, then a heating of the pubes, then that incredible stillness before the pleasure flowed.

'Jeff!' she screamed, as the native girl took her over the rapids. 'Christ! Jeff!'

Suki laughed, a low laugh that sounded oddly triumphant. Was this the first time she'd succeeded in bringing another woman off? Even as Charlotte mused on the subject, she heard a buzzer sound, and the other girl's footsteps crossing the room.

She opened her eyes: 'Suki – wait! That was brilliant. I could . . .'

'The buzzer sounded – my Master wants me,' Suki said

hurriedly. The door slammed shut and she was left alone for what felt like hours.

Charlotte was still reflecting on her new lover's departure when the Master entered the room with two guides. Both held leads and collars. He carried the inevitable stick. Charlotte's neck felt suddenly naked without its leather covering, and her buttocks gave an involuntary twitch.

'Untie her,' the Master said. 'Set her down on the ground.'

The guides obeyed quickly. Gratefully Charlotte massaged her freed limbs and invaded arse.

'Kneel,' the man said.

Charlotte got down on her knees before him. She stretched her lips towards his trousered groin, but he pushed her back.

'No. I am merely here to pronounce sentence.'

'Sentence?'

'Yes. To describe the way in which you're to spend the next few months . . .'

'I'm to spend them with Vern, back home!' Charlotte said, looking up quickly. She was aware that her voice had risen several octaves, and she sounded out of breath.

'No. He's found out from his answering machine that you were cheating on him with your lover. He doesn't want you back just yet.'

'Yet?' Charlotte asked, her hopes fading rapidly.

'He's going home for a year to assess the situation, to see how he feels.'

'A *year*?' This couldn't be happening. She wouldn't let this happen! 'If I could just see him, please . . .'

'Sorry, my dear. He said he's seen enough of you as it is.' The Master stared down at her lewdly. 'Even if I wanted to oblige, it isn't possible. He and Guy have already loaded their plane with provisions. Five minutes ago they left.'

'I don't deserve this!' Charlotte cried.

The man stared: 'You deserve much more, my sweet. You've been adulterous, tried to run away, have been rude to your betters time after time.'

'But . . .'

244

'... You've seduced celibate guides, impersonated your former boyfriend. You chased an innocent girl through the woods.'

Charlotte swallowed, and looked down. He was so right about everything. He knew how to make her cry, make her come, and make her beg.

'Please don't do this,' she said. 'Please, really. I'll do *anything*.'

'Yes,' the Master said, coolly. 'You probably will. You see, you've done so badly here that we're moving you to Camp Two, across the river. I'm told it's much more ... challenging for wicked bums.'

'You mean rigorous,' Charlotte cried weakly.

'Let's just say that a lot of the girls wish they'd got their lessons right whilst they were here.'

'I can't bear it!' wailed Charlotte.

The Master smiled mirthlessly.

'Karo will doubtlessly bare it for you. She's to be in charge of Camp Two for the next twelve months. Indeed, she'll be taking you there.'

'Karo? But ...'

She bit back the thought: Karo still owed her some punishment.

'I believe Karo has some unfinished business with your hot little bum,' the Master said.

He smiled, and it was a smile that told of all she had done and all she would do; all she would do with her voice, her tongue, hands, and quim.

'Yes, my dear, I'm sure she'll soon take your mind off your homesickness with her sensuous delights.'

They came for her then. They used a silk scarf to cover her eyes and ears, though she was beyond looking and hearing. They tied her hands before her with strips of black velvet, led her to a small motor boat, and lowered her in. The hard seat hurt her bum, and she tried to turn on the side of her hip a little.

'Sit still or it will be worse for you!' Karo's unmistakable tones said.

'I'll take your mind off things later,' whispered another

voice. Suki's voice! Suki who knew how to exquisitely pleasure a girl's hungry clit. Tingling at the thought of the pain and pleasure which awaited her, Charlotte felt herself being carried towards Camp Two.

NEW BOOKS

Coming up from Nexus and Black Lace

Grooming Lucy by Yvonne Marshall
September 2000   Price £5.99   ISBN 0 352 33529 7
Lucy's known about her husband's kinks for a few years, but now she wants to accommodate them herself. She knows it won't be easy – she has heard how extreme his tastes are – and she's asked some special friends to arrange a unique training course for her. But her husband's not the only man with extreme tastes, and some of his friends have their own ideas about how to train Lucy.

The Torture Chamber by Lisette Ashton
September 2000   Price £5.99   ISBN 0 352 33530 0
Catering for every perverse taste imaginable, The Torture Chamber is an SM club with a legendary reputation. Inside its exclusive walls, no fetish is too extreme, and the patrons know how to make the most of every situation. When Sue visits in disguise, she realises that she cannot visit again – the intensity of her reactions frightens her. But others at the club will stop at nothing to share in her special education.

Different Strokes by Sarah Veitch
September 2000   Price £5.99   ISBN 0 352 33531 9
These stories celebrate all aspects of the pains and pleasures of corporal punishment. Disobedient secretaries, recalcitrant slimmers, cheeky maids – dozens of young women, and a few young men too, whose behaviour can be improved only by the strict application of a hand, a slipper or a cane. A Nexus Classic.

NEXUS BACKLIST

All books are priced £5.99 unless another price is given. If a date is supplied, the book in question will not be available until that month in 2000.

CONTEMPORARY EROTICA

THE BLACK MASQUE	Lisette Ashton	
THE BLACK WIDOW	Lisette Ashton	
THE BOND	Lindsay Gordon	
BRAT	Penny Birch	
BROUGHT TO HEEL	Arabella Knight	July
DANCE OF SUBMISSION	Lisette Ashton	
DISCIPLES OF SHAME	Stephanie Calvin	
DISCIPLINE OF THE PRIVATE HOUSE	Esme Ombreux	
DISCIPLINED SKIN	Wendy Swanscombe	Nov
DISPLAYS OF EXPERIENCE	Lucy Golden	
AN EDUCATION IN THE PRIVATE HOUSE	Esme Ombreux	Aug
EMMA'S SECRET DOMINATION	Hilary James	
GISELLE	Jean Aveline	
GROOMING LUCY	Yvonne Marshall	Sept
HEART OF DESIRE	Maria del Rey	
HOUSE RULES	G.C. Scott	
IN FOR A PENNY	Penny Birch	
LESSONS OF OBEDIENCE	Lucy Golden	Dec
ONE WEEK IN THE PRIVATE HOUSE	Esme Ombreux	
THE ORDER	Nadine Somers	
THE PALACE OF EROS	Delver Maddingley	
PEEPING AT PAMELA	Yolanda Celbridge	Oct
PLAYTHING	Penny Birch	

ANCIENT & FANTASY SETTINGS

EDWARDIAN, VICTORIAN & OLDER EROTICA

SAMPLERS & COLLECTIONS

NEW EROTICA 3		
NEW EROTICA 5		Nov
A DOZEN STROKES	Various	

NEXUS CLASSICS
A new imprint dedicated to putting the finest works of erotic fiction back in print

AGONY AUNT	G. C. Scott	
THE HANDMAIDENS	Aran Ashe	
OBSESSION	Maria del Rey	
HIS MISTRESS'S VOICE	G.C. Scott	
CITADEL OF SERVITUDE	Aran Ashe	
BOUND TO SERVE	Amanda Ware	
SISTERHOOD OF THE INSTITUTE	Maria del Rey	
A MATTER OF POSSESSION	G.C. Scott	
THE PLEASURE PRINCIPLE	Maria del Rey	
CONDUCT UNBECOMING	Arabella Knight	
CANDY IN CAPTIVITY	Arabella Knight	
THE SLAVE OF LIDIR	Aran Ashe	
THE DUNGEONS OF LIDIR	Aran Ashe	
SERVING TIME	Sarah Veitch	July
THE TRAINING GROUNDS	Sarah Veitch	Aug
DIFFERENT STROKES	Sarah Veitch	Sept
LINGERING LESSONS	Sarah Veitch	Oct
EDEN UNVEILED	Maria del Rey	Nov
UNDERWORLD	Maria del Rey	Dec

Please send me the books I have ticked above.

Name ....

Address ....

....

....

.... Post code........................

Send to: **Cash Sales, Nexus Books, Thames Wharf Studios, Rainville Road, London W6 9HT**

US customers: for prices and details of how to order books for delivery by mail, call 1-800-805-1083.

Please enclose a cheque or postal order, made payable to **Nexus Books**, to the value of the books you have ordered plus postage and packing costs as follows:

UK and BFPO – £1.00 for the first book, 50p for the second book and 30p for each subsequent book to a maximum of £3.00;

Overseas (including Republic of Ireland) – £2.00 for the first book, £1.00 for the second book and 50p for each subsequent book.

We accept all major credit cards, including VISA, ACCESS/ MASTERCARD, AMEX, DINERS CLUB, SWITCH, SOLO, and DELTA. Please write your card number and expiry date here:

....

Please allow up to 28 days for delivery.

Signature ....